~*PRECARI

All rights reserved. This eBook is licensed for your personal enjoyment only. This eBook is copyright material and must not be copied, reproduced, transferred, distributed, leased, licensed or publicly performed or used in any form without prior written permission of the publisher, as allowed under the terms and conditions under which it was purchased or as strictly permitted by applicable copyright law. Any unauthorized distribution, circulation or use of this text may be a direct infringement of the author's rights, and those responsible may be liable in law accordingly. Thank you for respecting the work of this author.

PRECARIOUS

Copyright © 2014 Bella Jewel

Precarious is a work of fiction. All names, characters, places and events portrayed in this book either are from the author's imagination or are used fictitiously. Any similarity to real persons, living or dead, establishments, events, or location is purely coincidental and not intended by the author. Please do not take offence to the content, as it is FICTION.

ACKNOWLEDGMENTS

A massive thanks to all the blogs on my tours. You're amazing for taking the time to share and review for me; you'll never know how much that means to me.

A special thanks to Love Between The Sheets for always having time to organize my Release Day Blitz and Cover Reveals. You ladies are super amazing and I'll always appreciate the effort you've given me.

Thanks to Lisa from Three Chicks and Their Books for always reading an ARC before releasing and helping me out. Thanks to Kylie from Give Me Books for always sharing and reading for me, too. You girls are amazing. I adore you.

A massive thanks to Ari from Cover it Designs for this gorgeous cover. You never disappoint.

To Lauren, my crazy, awesome editor. You do such a great job. I couldn't do it without you. I adore you, lovely.

To my girls, Belle Aurora and Sali. For always reading and helping me create the best work I can. For always talking to me and making me smile. I love you two, my besties.

And of course, to my admin MJ for ALWAYS keeping my page running beautifully. I couldn't do it without you, girly.

A massive thank you to Kris Scharr. For coming up with the amazing name of Jokers' Wrath MC. As well as picking the name of a character to show throughout the series. You're a gorgeous girl and an amazing fan. Thank you.

And, last but certainly not least. To my loyal readers. You make this real for me; never stop giving such love and passion. You make our journey so amazing.

DEDICATION

This book is dedicated to my very own biker, my husband. Thank you for the countless hours you have put in to helping me out with my work, or just keeping the kids busy while I write.

You know I'll love you forever, my big man.

PROLOGUE

It is in darkness that we find true nature. We fight over the battle of good and evil. One will take us on a path we can live with, the other will take us on a path we can't. There is no in-between. There is no right, or wrong. In that moment when our world is closing in on us, there is only ever really one way out.

Evil will always prevail.

In evil we find power. To escape the black pit of nothingness, it is a quality we need the most. To seek revenge, we will need all of it. It intertwines in a twisted spiral that can't be backed away from—a spiral that will change our worlds, a spiral that will re-create who we are, a spiral that will leave us hanging on the edge of insanity.

These things combined will lead me to do the one thing that will direct my path forever. When my choice is made, I'm ready. What I'm not ready for is *her*. I've gone a long time without feeling, but she'll be the one to change that. In fact, she'll change everything I ever believed in with one simple smile.

CHAPTER ONE

Ahead of the darkness is where I'll find him.

ASH

My boots thud on the stark, tiled floor as I make my way down the long, narrow halls. This place is familiar to me; I've spent the last five years of my life working here. I'm a prison guard. It's not always the nicest job; I'm faced daily with scenes that would send a normal person over the edge.

But to give up, to back down, has never been something I was good at. I'm as stubborn as I am headstrong, and that's exactly *why* I'm good at my job. I'm thorough, I'm professional and I give the prisoners something that no one else can—I give them *thought*. I am always sure to leave them with something that will change a part of them permanently.

They call me Wildcard, for more reasons than one: the first reason being they find it utterly hilarious that I'm a woman in a world that is so heavily dominated by men. The second reason is because I can take a man double my size down on a good day. I'm fierce, I'm wild, and that's why they keep me here.

I'm here for one reason and one reason only: to do my job. I paint my face with a mask that is rarely broken, making sure my eyes show no fear, making sure my expression doesn't give away emotion. After all, it isn't about me—it's about them. They're the ones in the cold, lonely cells for crimes they chose to commit. I'm just here to make sure they stay in line.

I round the corner to the security gates, and smile when I see the Control Officer, Tristan. He's a friend, both inside and outside of work. His job, basically, is to make sure the guards are always doing their jobs correctly. He's fantastic at what he does, and he's a great person to work with.

"Good morning, Ash." He smiles as I approach.

"Morning, Tris. How are things this morning?"

He shrugs. "Same as they were yesterday; hectic."

I laugh, reaching up to tuck a strand of chocolate-brown hair behind my ear. "It's what we thrive on. Anything I need to know about this morning?"

He runs a scanner over a fellow guard who is starting his shift for the day. It doesn't matter if you're a guard or a visitor; you go through intensive security every visit. They can't risk allowing weapons, or any items that can be used as weapons, inside the prison.

"You're on Ward D." He winks. "They're behaving so far."

I let out a snort, before stepping forward and putting my purse down. I lift my arms above my head and he runs the scanner over me.

"Henry is on that ward," I say. "How has he been behaving?"

He shakes his head, running the scanner down over my legs. "How does he always behave? Nice shoes."

I grin down at my boots. I'm not the kind of girl to go for heels. I live in boots—knee-highs, ankle boots, Doc Martens, you name it. The ones I'm wearing today are black ankle boots that match my skinny jeans. Of course I don't get to wear them long. As soon as I'm inside I have to get into uniform, but I don't leave the house without looking sassy. "Thanks, they were a bargain."

"You're good," he says, waving me through. "Have a good day. Meet me for lunch?"

I nod. "Absolutely."

I go through quite a long process just to get into Ward D. Even though we're not a maximum-security prison, this is still where our worst inmates are kept. I am never without another two guards by my side when I'm working in that section, purely for safety reasons, and they're usually male. There are only four female guards in the entire prison.

The prisoners up here are problematic. They spend a great deal of time with our prison psychologist because of the crimes they're in here for. It's her job to decide if they need further treatment in a mental facility. There have been countless suicides. They're criminals, and in most cases their minds are challenged in some way, shape, or form. It's why they choose to do the sick and deranged things they do. In a majority of cases, there is pain that stems from childhood that leads to such activities.

"Morning, Ash," Luke, the guard standing outside the ward, says when I approach.

Luke is only slightly older than me, with wavy brown hair and blue eyes. He seems nice enough, but he doesn't usually say a great deal. It's probably perfect with this job, because he's always straight to the point and doesn't get caught up in any drama.

"How are things this morning?"

He shrugs, staring down the hall. "Fine. You ready to do your rounds?"

I nod. Usually rounds are what I do first. I go around, check out the cells and the prisoners, and then I'm usually sectioned in a certain area where I'll spend the day. Sometimes it's in the break room, other times it's in the yard, and there are also times when I do paperwork in the office. It just depends on the behavior of the prisoners that day.

I head in to get changed, gather my weapons, and then join Luke back at the gates, ready for our rounds.

Our uniform is quite simple. We wear a dark green pair of pants, a light green button-up, long-sleeved shirt, and a pair of solid boots. Our hair—in a female's case—needs to be either short or tied up tightly. No jewelry.

"We'll check Maximus first, and move down from there."

I nod, following him down.

Maximus is one of our more difficult prisoners. He's been behind bars for only about a year after murdering his wife in a rage. He's an angry, bitter man who barely makes progress, spending most of his time cramped in his cell.

Maximus is serving life in prison. He's in his early thirties, and has a history of violence. His first crime was at the tender age of fifteen, when he held up a gas station with a gun. He beat the woman behind the counter so badly she had to have reconstructive surgery to her face. That was just that start of his spiral into a violent life.

Maximus is tall, bulky and bald. He's got a range of tattoos on his body, running down his arms, and even over his fingers. He has got stark blue eyes, and a cold smile. His inner thoughts are quite disturbing, and I feel it has a lot to do with his life as a boy. His father was sent to prison when Maximus was only four for sexual assault. His mother was a drug-using whore, and spent most of her time high and in the arms of other men.

We stop at his cell and look in. As always he's staring at the wall, fists balled tightly.

We are guards, but we are also sent here to be role models for the prisoners. They notice how we behave and how well we interact; we can hold our own, but we also show them a certain level of respect that is said to help them cope.

"Good morning, Maximus," I say.

He turns and locks eyes with me, narrowing them just slightly.

"Did you get any sleep last night?" I ask him, returning his stare, holding his gaze.

He glares at me. "I don't fuckin' sleep."

"Any reason why?"

He growls. "Because I don't trust any fucker in this place. They're all out for blood."

Did I mention Maximus has a bad case of paranoia? He's probably not entirely wrong. There is a certain ranking within the inmates; certain groups that stick together, and certain people who tend to be targeted. Anyone who murders or rapes children barely ever make it through their sentence alive. It's like a secret code. The next in that line are men who hurt women. There are a lot of those, but they too seem to be a target.

"Has something happened we need to know about?" Luke asks, his voice firm but kind.

Maximus shifts, his big body extremely daunting.

"I see them lookin' at me. They're just waitin' for the right time to wrap their hands around my throat and squeeze the fuckin' life out of me."

"Why would you think they want to do that?" I ask. "Has something happened? You know you should report anything that happens."

His eyes narrow and his whole body rattles. "I killed my fuckin' wife. I put my hands around her throat and took her life. They're just gettin' back what she lost."

"Perhaps you need to speak to Mandy again," I say, referring to our Prison Psychologist. "It would seem you're still struggling to deal with—"

"Listen to me, bitch," he hisses, cutting me off. "Hows about you go back to your hoity-toity little palace and leave us here to live with what we've created. I don't regret killing her; I don't regret watching the life fade from her eyes as I held her to the floor. Nothing your little psychologist will say can change that, so give it up."

I get this a lot, too. The name-calling, the 'give it up, you can't help me'. I guess, in a sense, they're right. I can't truly help them if they don't want to be helped. After all, they're in prison because of the crimes they committed; I'm just here to make sure it all runs smoothly, however I do try to make it as comfortable as possible for them. I make a note to tell Mandy about his comments, though.

"Fine," I say, keeping my voice calm. "Are you eating? Joining in the other activities?"

His eyes flash. "No."

"Why not?"

"Because I don't fuckin' want to. Because I want to get out of here alive."

"Why do you want to get out of here alive?"

He clenches his fists. "Because I have unfinished business."

I raise my brows and he snorts. "Don't look at me like that, Wildcard. I know what you're thinkin'."

Oh yeah, did I mention the nickname has spread? The prisoners learned it very quickly the day I put one of the inmates on his ass for lunging at me. It was in the yard, and he decided he'd had enough and tried to take me out. It lasted a matter of seconds before he was on his back. I don't like to go down easily.

"What is it you *think* I'm thinking?" I ask, leaning my hip against the cell.

"That I'm goin' to do something bad and get back in here. Well, you're wrong. I will never come back in here."

"I hope that's true," I say, pushing back. "Good to see you again, Maximus."

Luke gives me a half-smirk and we move down the hall to the next cell. This one holds Jimmy. He's only twenty-eight years old. Jimmy suffers from schizophrenia, and so far is dealing with prison life, however Mandy is working on getting him moved to a better-equipped mental facility. We like to check on him, make sure he's doing okay, but he rarely comes out.

He's serving fifteen years for pulling off an armed robbery at a bank. He shot three people, killing one. He got away with a whole lot of cash, and was caught only weeks later. To look at him you'd think Jimmy was just a normal man, with his sandy-blond hair and green eyes, but there's so much going on behind that exterior.

"Good morning, Jimmy," I say, staring into his cell where he's sitting on his bed, staring at the wall. He does this most days.

He looks up at me, his eyes empty.

"It's good to see you," I say, my voice strong.

I am tough when it comes down to needing to control one, but otherwise I speak to prisoners in a calm, respectful tone. There is no need to make matters worse.

Jimmy begins murmuring to himself, answering questions and making out like he's speaking to another person.

"Do you know what Bill told me?" he asks, finally focusing on me.

Bill is one of the voices that haunt Jimmy.

"What did he tell you, Jimmy?"

"He told me how to escape. He showed me how to kill the guards and get out."

Slightly concerning, but mostly talk. It would be extremely difficult to escape. In fact, I'd go as far as saying it's impossible.

"But you know what would happen if you escaped, Jimmy. Don't you?"

He shakes his head from side to side. "Bill will keep me safe."

"Have you talked to Mandy this week?" I ask.

He presses his cuffed hands to his chest, suddenly changing the subject. "It hurts right here, like I can't breathe."

Jimmy also suffers from severe nightmares. Jimmy's mother tried to drown him in the bath when he was five. He remembers it clearly and tells me often, repeating her exact words.

"My momma tried to drown me," he says, his eyes going vacant as he repeats the same words she told him, words he's told me so many times over. "Jimmy, you're a bad child, and bad children go to hell. I can't look after a bad child anymore. You make me angry because you're such a bad, fat, ugly child. I am doing you a favor. This is where you're meant to be."

The words still give me the chills, and it breaks my heart to know that a child of only five could be treated so badly.

"I'll talk to Mandy, okay, Jimmy?"

He nods. "I like Mandy."

"She likes you, too. Have a good day," I say, staring at him for a second longer before leaving.

We continue down the halls. We finish up with the last six prisoners in the ward. By the time I'm done, it's already lunchtime. I make my way into the break-room and see Tristan right away, coffee cup under the machine. My stomach grumbles as I walk up and stop beside him.

"Do me one while you're there," I say.

"Ash," he murmurs, turning to look down at me. He looks edgy about something; his jaw is tight and his eyes fly past me a few times before he focuses. "How's it going?"

I shrug. "The usual day. How are you? You look stressed."

He shakes his head. "Just a stressful day."

"Hey," one of the newer guards says, turning up the television. "Check it out."

I turn and watch the screen. There are police cars and crying people standing outside a building. I squint and see it's a local café, just down the road from my house. My heartbeat picks up as I listen.

"This afternoon, tragedy broke out in a local café. A gunman, believed to be from the Jokers' Wrath Motorcycle Club, killed four innocent people who were enjoying their lunch out. Witnesses say it was a bloody massacre. Security cameras were down, so information at this point is still sketchy. It is said the victims were a family, the father being multi-billionaire businessman, Johan Reed."

My throat tightens as the reporter goes on.

"Nobody else was hurt and investigations are underway."

"Shit," the guard at the table says. "What the hell would cause someone to go in and kill an innocent family?"

I shake my head, still staring at the screen. "The question is, why only the one family? It's as if he knew them."

I turn to Tristan, who is still staring at the screen, his jaw tight. Luke enters the room and the two give each other what seems to come across as a secretive look – their eyes are stern and their mouths are tight. Tristan even gives a sharp little nod. I narrow my eyes and step closer to Tristan. "Is everything okay?"

He jerks and turns to me. "Fine. I just hate fuckers like that."

My eyes widen. "Ah, yeah, it's never nice."

"No," he mutters. "I gotta run."

That was weird, but I shake it off and turn to the other guards. I don't feel hungry anymore. "Well, back to work, then."

"Later, Ash," Jock, one of the other guards says as I exit the room.

Just another hectic day.

~*~*~*~

I spend the remainder of my afternoon in the dining hall with the prisoners. It's fairly quiet and my shift ends on a good note after the disturbing news earlier.

After I've packed my things, I make my way out. Commotion catches me at the exit, and I turn to see guards bringing in a new prisoner. I step to the side, making sure I'm not in anyone's way. Tristan approaches me as six guards lead a handcuffed man down the hall.

"That's the shooter," he growls, glaring at the man.

As they approach, I catch a glimpse of the man head on, and my breathing stops. I've spent a lot of years in this prison, but I've never witnessed a man as beautiful as he is. Criminal or not, it jumps out and screams at you to look at him. He's tall, at least six feet, and is a hard wall of muscle. Thick shoulders, a lean narrow waist . . . he's all male, strong and sturdy.

That's not where his beauty lies, though. His beauty is in his face: a pair of stark grey eyes, a slightly crooked nose, big, full lips, and a square, masculine jaw. He's got a rugged face, yet it's so incredibly handsome. His hair is dark brown, maybe even black, and it's a few inches long and messy, strands of it fall over his forehead. He's got a tattoo running up his neck, and piercing in his lower lip.

I've no doubt this man is a bad, *bad* boy. It's written all over him. He's powerful, he's scary and he's utterly mesmerizing. I quickly drop my eyes to his attire. He's wearing black boots, black jeans with chains dipping off the sides, and a heavy leather jacket that has numerous patches on the front. The one that stands out is one that says 1%.

As the guards pass Tristan and I, the man's eyes meet mine and I forget how to breathe. He's got a few days' growth on his jaw, and fierceness in his eyes that tugs at me. How can someone that looks like him go into a café and kill an innocent family? He holds my eyes as he passes, sharing something with me, only I can't quite decipher what it is.

"Piece of shit shouldn't even live for what he's done," Tristan mutters as he gets closer to me.

I turn to him. "You're not usually so vocal. Is everything okay?"

He shakes his head, as if righting himself. "Fine, just a long day. You can leave now."

I nod quickly and turn to rush off, staring down the hall again before I go. I see the back of the man, and I can read his jacket from here. He's got a massive patch with a picture of a scary-looking joker skull. In bold, white letters are the words *Jokers' Wrath MC*. I stare at it for a long moment before turning and rushing out.

He'll be the first biker I've ever had to work with.

I won't say I'm not curious.

CHAPTER TWO

Unlocking my front door, I step into my large apartment. I have two housemates, so I got myself a bigger place. I enjoy the company, and could never seem to accept a small, one-bedroom home that I could only share with . . . well . . . maybe a goldfish. If I were lucky.

We managed to get ourselves a fully furnished apartment for a little extra per month. The furniture is nice and fairly modern, so it seemed like a better deal. I occupy the main bedroom, and my housemates, Leo and Claire, occupy the other rooms.

I get along with both of them exceptionally well. Claire is a gorgeous, fun-loving blonde who is somewhat like my light after a dark day. She's bubbly and carefree, and extremely refreshing.

Leo is broody, sexy as hell, and runs his own tattoo parlor up town through the day, and is a fighter at night. He's a bad boy, but he keeps to himself, and having him around is like having a guard dog.

"I got milk duds!" Claire squeals, skipping into the kitchen just as I place my purse down.

"You and your addictions." I grin at her.

"I can't help it. I'm so damned in love with them. Can you tell?" she asks, twirling around, and twisting to stare at her ass. "Is it fat?"

I roll my eyes. Claire has the kind of ass most men would drop to their knees for.

"Why don't you ask Leo?" I chuckle.

She slaps my arm as she passes me, heading towards the fridge. "Quit teasing me about Leo. So what he walked in on me showering? He's got a bevvy of babes, and I'm sure seeing me naked was the equivalent to a gynecologist seeing a vagina—an every-day occurrence that is barely worth batting an eyelid at."

I snort and laugh softly. "God, you give the most . . . interesting descriptions."

She slides her backside up onto the counter and crosses her legs, popping a milk dud into her mouth. "Did you see the news?"

"About the shooting?" I ask, pouring myself an orange juice.

"Yeah, it's so sad."

I can't give Claire any information from my job, but I do tell her, "I saw him being brought into the prison as I was leaving."

Her eyes widen. "Really?"

I nod, stealing a milk dud for myself. "Yep."

"What was he like?"

My cheeks heat as I think about the gorgeous, rugged biker. "He was, ah, just a normal criminal."

"I just can't believe he killed that family. So cold and twisted."

I nod. "You're right about that."

The front door slams and we both turn to see Leo charging in. Damn, he's good looking. Even Claire's eyes move over his body. He's built; I mean, mega built. He's all muscle. His shoulders are broad and he's got abs that go far and beyond a six-pack. His messy brown hair often falls over his face, sometimes getting too long and covering those stunning hazel eyes.

He's covered in tattoos. They run up his arms and over his shoulders. He's got one down his belly that snakes around to his back. He's even got a few on his thighs. The man is an ink machine. His hazel eyes, which are more yellow than green, swing to us and narrow. Claire looks to me, then back to him.

"Problem, Leo?"

He grunts, and walks past us.

"Good to see you, too," I yell out after him.

We hear him throw his bag down with another grunt, and we both turn back to each other and giggle softly.

"He's such a stiff sometimes. He needs a good woman to get him out of his shell. Maybe you can work your magic on him?"

I shake my head. "No thank you; been there, done that, Leo isn't the man for me."

"Ah, the drunken night between Leo and Ash."

"Shut up." I smile. "Don't remind me."

She jumps off the counter and wiggles her hips. "Oh, la la."

I roll my eyes. I used to have a major crush on Leo; something to do with the silent, angry type. My crush only lasted for about six months. The reason for that is because one night we both got drunk, really,

really drunk, and ended up in bed. I was in a low place and it wasn't the best choice I've ever made.

It's not that Leo wasn't great in bed, because he was. Even drunk, he blew my mind. It was just that things got awkward—like, super awkward. We have nothing in common, and it just made things weird between us. It took a few months for us to be able to look each other in the eye again, but we've managed to get there.

"I'm going to shower before you spontaneously combust," I chide her, disappearing down the hall.

"Ohhhh, all nakie and wet," she sings.

I laugh and walk towards my room. I stop when I see Leo in his, the door just slightly ajar. He's pacing backwards and forwards, running his hands through his hair. I can't help it; I stop walking and knock on his open door.

"Leo?" I ask, stepping in.

He stops pacing, and turns to look at me. "What do you want?"

"Don't be an ass. I'm just seeing if you're okay."

He stares at me, then sighs loudly. "No, I'm not fuckin' okay."

"Want to tell me why?"

"Don't talk to me like I'm one of your prisoners, Ash."

"Okay . . . What's happenin', yo?"

His lips twitch with a smile, and I give him a full-blown one in return.

"It's Evelyn," he mutters.

Ah, Evelyn. The girl he's been dating on and off. She's easy, she's expensive and she's up herself, in a big way. She's bad for him all round, but she's gorgeous. So he keeps going back.

"What's she doing now?" I ask, sitting on the small sofa in his room.

He raises a brow at me.

"What?" I say, throwing my hands up. "I'm trying to help."

He starts pacing again. "It's fucked up."

"And . . ."

"She's saying she's pregnant."

"Oh boy," I say, letting a puff of air whoosh out of my lips. "That is bad."

"You're fuckin' tellin' me. I got shit in my life. I'm a fighter. I don't have time for babies."

"Okay, take a few steps back. Are you sure it's yours?"

His eyes flash to me. "You sayin' she's fuckin' around?"

"What I'm saying is that unless you're sure she's not, then you might not be the father."

He mulls this over. "How am I supposed to find out?"

"Simple. If she's really pregnant, ask for a DNA test."

"*If* she's pregnant?"

"You need to see proof, Leo. You'd be crazy not to ask for it. Women make that stuff up all the time."

His eyes widen. "Why?"

I shrug. "Because they're desperate."

A look of disgust contorts his features, causing his lips to purse and his eyes to narrow. "That's fuckin' sick."

I laugh softly, standing. "Women can do crazy things if they fear they're losing something they want."

"Would you do that?"

I snort. "Oh no. *No, no, no*, I know how it ends."

"How?" he says, taking the hem of his shirt and pulling it off.

I stare for a moment before feeling heat creep up the back of my neck. I stare down at my hands. "I'm a girl. I've seen it go down plenty of times. I'm sure you can figure out how something like that would end."

"Yeah," he says, pulling on another shirt.

"Well." I clap my hands together, and turn towards the door. "Good chatting."

He chuckles. "Yeah, always fun."

I flash him a smile before exiting his room. I slip into my own room and sigh as my eyes go towards the shower in the en suite. Oh, I need one of those. I kick my door closed behind me, strip off and walk towards the shower. After turning the water on, I tuck my hair up and step in.

Heaven.

I sigh loudly as the warm water slides over my body. I wash my hair, shave my legs, and then reluctantly turn the shower off. I dry myself and then throw on a pair of grey sweats and a tank before joining Claire and Leo in the kitchen. They're arguing over what to cook for supper.

"Steak," Leo growls, shoving her out of the way and taking out the steak.

"Chicken," she snaps back, shoving him. He doesn't move.

"How about," I yell loudly, causing them both to turn, "you have both."

Claire rolls her eyes. "That ruins the fun."

Leo gives her a lusty expression, one that she always seems to miss. I don't miss it; it's loud and clear to me.

"Stop being difficult," I chastise her playfully.

"Fine," she sulks. "Let the Incredible Hulk have his steak."

Leo snorts and turns to her. "I'm glad you've finally learned your place."

Claire opens her mouth to respond, but I put my hand up. "Children, that's enough."

They both give me pouty expressions that have me smiling. I wave my hand. "Carry on, then."

I turn and walk out of the room, deciding to find a good book and curl up on the couch while they battle it out in the kitchen.

That's just a normal day for me.

Just how I like it.

CHAPTER THREE

The prison is quiet this morning. People are fluttering about, keeping to themselves, and the inmates aren't saying a great deal. They're all in their cells, most of them staring blankly at walls. The very idea of being trapped in a space like that for years on end has my heart tightening. It's one of my biggest fears.

There are a few prisoners in here who are wrongly convicted; it happens. It's a sad fact of life, but it's just how it goes. I don't see it a lot, and even when I do there's nothing I can do to help – after all, what could I do? It's not my job, and it's something that can't be changed. I just can't imagine how horrible it would feel. To be forever trapped for something you didn't do.

"Another early one, Ash?" Tristan says, appearing beside me as I reach security.

"You're here early," I say, checking the time. He doesn't usually do the morning shifts.

"Yeah. Just wanted to make sure the new prisoner was secured."

"Right." I yawn. "How's all that going?"

We reach security and start the long process of going through.

"You will see him today. You can check it all out when you go down there. He isn't saying a word."

"He doesn't really have to. Well, not to us, anyway."

"No, but it all helps," Tristan mutters.

"That's true. You want me to see what I can get?" I ask, shrugging off my jacket.

"Yeah. He won't speak, and I'm trying to assess him. His court appearance isn't for another few weeks."

"What have you got on him so far?"

"Not a great deal," he says, stepping through and stretching his arms out for scanning. "His name is Beau Dawson. He's the vice president of the Jokers' Wrath MC. Not married. No family. His sister died when they were both fifteen. They were twins."

"That's interesting," I say, stepping through after him. "Do you know what happened?"

He shakes his head. "Details are sketchy at this point, but I've got someone looking into it."

Someone looking into it? It's not really his job to have someone look into details such as that.

"Who is looking into it?" I ask.

He stiffens and shakes his head quickly. "Oh, just some other guards."

Something doesn't feel quite right, but there's nothing obvious enough standing out that I have the grounds to do something about it.

"Fair enough. Well, I'll stop by and see if I can get anything else."

He pats my shoulder. "You're awesome. Thanks."

I go through my usual routine of changing, logging in and pairing up with some other guards. Then I begin my rounds. We stop at Beau's cell first, because Tristan wanted me to see his reaction. I peer in, and my lips part as I suck in a breath, God, will it get easier to look at him? Surely it will?

"Beau," I say, though my voice doesn't come out as firm as it usually would.

Beau lifts his head, revealing those incredible grey eyes. They're lighter grey, like a storm cloud that has given off all its rain and is fading into the blue sky. His black hair drops over his forehead and his expression is almost murderous as he glares at me. They don't like being here; it's not abnormal.

"My name is Ash," I begin, "I just came to check in on you. I'm a guard here."

His glare doesn't waver; in fact, it's a little intimidating. He's lethal; it seeps off him.

"Have you had any troubles overnight?"

He doesn't answer; he just keeps his killer expression trained on me.

"Nothing?"

He doesn't move. It's unnerving.

"You're the vice president of the Jokers' Wrath MC. That must be a different kind of lifestyle?"

His eyes narrow, but he still says nothing. Interesting. It clearly gets a reaction out of him, even if he refuses to speak.

"I know you have no family. I suppose that's what they are? Would I be correct?"

His eyes flash and then harden. His jaw tics and it's clear family is a touchy subject. Just to test my theory, I ask a difficult question. I wouldn't usually do this, but Tristan has instructed that I get as much as I can out of him, so I go ahead.

"I was informed you lost your sister at a young age. Is that why you did what you did?

Like a flip is switched, he thrashes in his chains, his eyes wild and frantic.

"Shit," I curse under my breath.

He jerks, his large body arching upwards in what is clearly anguish. His entire frame is straining, his wrists jerking on the chains, his face going a dark shade of red with emotion.

"You're going to hurt yourself," I say, my voice tough, even though I feel horrible. "Calm down, Beau."

His fists are clenched so tightly they're white; his arms are bulging, ropes of muscle pulsing beneath his skin. He thrashes harder, panting. I turn to the Jeremy, who is already radioing it in. Only minutes later more guards arrive and we all step in. Blood is running heavily down Beau's wrists. If we don't stop him, it will get worse.

I take one of his arms, and the muscles flex beneath my fingers as I hold him firmly. Three other guards take different parts of his body. He growls and snaps, then he barks, "Fuck off, you cunts."

Well, then. It would appear Beau *can* talk.

"You don't settle down, you'll end up in bigger trouble than it's worth," Luke growls at him.

I didn't even see Luke come in.

Beau turns his eyes to me and bares his teeth. I glare at him, not showing any kind of emotion. He swings his body to the side, sending me flying backwards onto my ass. He did it on purpose, I know he did, and that makes me angry. It's not the first time this has happened; I'm always being knocked over. Anger swells in my chest all the same, because I still hate it. I might have upset him, but he doesn't need to push me around.

I get to my feet and walk forward, pressing my fingers down onto his shoulder and pinching a nerve there—I learned this in training. He roars in pain and lurches forward, landing on the floor. It hurts, I know it hurts, but it's an easy and effective way to take a prisoner down without the need for weapons.

I lean down, rocking on my heels as he stares up at me with rage in his features. In a low, growling tone, I say, "Don't touch me *again*."

Then I get up and leave.

They can deal with Beau Dawson.

~*~*~*~

"You look exhausted," Claire says when I drag my backside into the house that night.

I throw my purse down and shrug my jacket off. "Mentally exhausted, perhaps."

She pours a glass of the red wine she's drinking, and brings it over to me as I drop down onto the couch. "Here you are."

"Ohh, you're a champ."

She smiles and flops down beside me on the couch.

"Can I ask you something?"

I sip the wine, closing my eyes and groaning with delight. "Sure," I finally manage.

"I overheard Leo talking this afternoon."

My eyes pop open and I turn to her. "And . . ."

"And I heard that . . . Queen of Whoretown is pregnant."

I snort at her choice of words. "I don't know a great deal about it, but I did warn him last night that he needs to be careful."

"What does he see in a girl like her?" She pouts prettily.

"She's easy." I shrug. "Leo is complicated and she doesn't question him, she just gives him what he wants."

"Complicated is certainly what Leo is."

I nod, pursing my lips. "Does it bother you?"

She shakes her head quickly, too quickly, if you ask me. "No, of course not." She waves her hand and snorts. "He can do whatever he wants.

I grin at her, but choose to say nothing more. I wish those two would pull their heads out of their backsides and see that there's a serious sexual connection there.

"Did you get to see the crazy gunman today?" she asks, turning towards me with a curious expression. Her eyes are wide, her lips pursed.

"I did, nothing major happened," I sigh, leaning my head back.

"Your job sucks."

I laugh. "Some days I could agree with you."

"You up for pizza and movies tonight? I'm too lazy to cook."

I groan, kicking my shoes off. "Absolutely. I'm stuffed."

"I got that new movie, *The Fault In Our Stars*."

"Oh no," I groan, pressing a hand to my cheek. "I heard that one will make me ugly cry."

"Ugly, snot-pouring-out-your-nose, wailing kind of cry," she nods.

"Can't we watch something happy?"

"Trust me," she says, standing and skipping into the kitchen. "It'll be fun."

It's not fun.

Halfway through the movie I'm blubbering, clutching my wine to my chest, and wishing I had protested harder. This movie is so beautiful, but so incredibly heartbreaking. I can't deal with this sort of emotion.

It's ruining me. Claire is sitting beside me, making the occasional sobbing noise, her hand pressed to her mouth.

Damn her and her sad movies.

CHAPTER FOUR

"In a better mood today, are we, Beau?" I say, leaning against the cell door and staring in at the broody biker.

It's the third day, and they're still trying to figure out what happened—there really aren't enough details around it. He's up for a sentence, but witnesses are being very unclear. Apparently one said Beau was arguing with the man, but didn't shoot him. Another is saying that there was another man with him, and that he couldn't pin who it was. Security cameras went down before the shooting, so it was absolutely planned.

Beau is saying nothing. His club is saying nothing. Beau rarely speaks at all, and if he does it's to spit curses. Mandy said she couldn't get a word out of him, that he won't give her anything. He's protecting himself; I get that. But I also think it has a lot to do with protecting his club.

I don't know how, but it would make sense for him to keep quiet if they were trying to do something to change his sentence. After all, if he speaks, it could ruin anything they come up with. So, I continue on each day doing my rounds. Beau gives me the same, angry expression every time I stop at his cell.

I keep stopping there, though. Because, for some reason, I truly believe he likes it.

"The guards told me you don't sleep a lot?" I say leaning against his cell door, "You bein' picked on, Beau?"

He glares at me, and surprises me by muttering, "Do you ever go a-fucking-way?"

"That's not a word," I point out. "And no, it's my job."

"So I hear, *Wildcard*," he sneers.

"It appears you have a problem with me, Beau." I smile sweetly.

He smirks, his eyes growing even colder. "I have a problem with the fuckin' law."

"Well, that's apparent."

He shakes his head and turns away. "Maximus fuckin' makes a lot of noise at night. Go and sort that shit out."

"I'll talk to him."

"Do more than that, eh?" he grunts.

"Are you always so mean?"

He narrows his eyes and crosses his big arms. "Are you supposed to talk to me like that? Pretty sure you ain't."

I cross my arms, too. "I'm not disrespecting you, am I?"

He studies me. "What's a girl like you workin' in a place like this for, anyway?"

I tilt my head to the side. "I like it. It gives me something different to an everyday office job."

"I hear you're feisty," he murmurs, letting his gaze travel down my body. "I like them like that."

I shiver. Oh boy. I straighten and uncross my arms. "Good for you. I like mine outside of a cell."

With that, I walk away.

Concentrate. Focus. Remain professional.

~*~*~*~

I'm not meant to be here. My shift is over, and it's just past midnight. I'm running late, because I got caught up talking to Mandy about Beau. It seems to be a good thing, though, because if I wasn't here I would have missed the commotion that starts as I'm leaving. It begins with a faint noise, and it grows louder and louder as I near.

I step around the corner and into Ward D. I see Luke, Tristan and another guard named Peter in Beau's cell. They are holding him down, and Tristan lifts his hand and drives his fist into Beau's face. I yell out, not even thinking, and he spins around quickly, panting with rage.

"What are you doing, Tristan?" I cry.

He's not allowed to hit prisoners unless there's absolutely no way around it and he's lying on the floor about to die from an attack – even then, we learned how to defend ourselves properly in our training. There's no need for this.

"He attacked me when I came in here. I had no choice," Tristan barks.

"You need to step out and call it in," I demand. "I'll wait with him. You know the rules. Get out, Tristan."

Tristan turns, and Beau glares up at him. He has blood running down his mouth, so much so that it makes me wonder if he's been hit more than once. Tristan cuffs his hands behind his back and steps back, nodding at the other two guards. They both stare at me, and then exit the cell. Tristan pulls out his radio and calls it in as he passes me.

When they're gone, I step inside and stare over at Beau. He glares at me, his face a mess. I pull off my jacket and walk over, sitting beside him on the bed, and pressing the cotton material to his face. He growls but he doesn't make any move to attack me, which seems strange, considering they accused him of attacking them.

"Do you want to stay in here?" I mutter, staring at the split in his lip.

"Why are you fuckin' here?"

"Because you're beating my guards."

"Wrong," he growls. "They were beating me."

"Because you attacked them."

He leans in close, causing me to flinch, but I don't move back. He's trying to get into my space, trying to intimidate me. It won't work.

"Tough little thing, aren't ya?"

I shrug. "Just doing my job."

"Let me tell you a little somethin' about your job," he murmurs. "You got a whole lot of fuckin' criminals around you."

"No shit," I snort. "Last time I checked that's what's usually in a prison."

He narrows his eyes into a full-throttle glare. "Not what I meant. It ain't the criminals *inside* the cells you should be watchin'."

"What are you talking about?" I say, even though I've already had the same thoughts cross my mind. "You're hardly in a place to be making accusations."

He raises his brows. "That so? If anything, I think I am in the perfect position to be making them."

"How do you figure?"

He smirks. "Because I'm a criminal myself, remember?"

Asshole.

I say nothing; I just cross my arms.

"I'm guessing I have about five minutes before they come in here and lock me down, so here it is. Your boys, there, came in here and beat the fuck outta me. I was sleepin' in my bed, doin' nothin'. There is a reason for that, but it's a reason I'm not discussing while I'm in here. Just know those boys are up to no fuckin' good, and they're doin' some bad shit. Keep your eyes peeled."

I open my mouth to say something, but a group of guards enter the room. I stand, meeting Beau's eyes. He nods at me and I turn swiftly, exiting the room. His words play in my mind. Why would Tristan, Luke and Peter just go in and beat him? I've known Tristan a long time; he wouldn't just do something like that.

I'm paying no attention as I walk down the halls until I smash into Tristan's chest. His arms go around me, and he chuckles softly. "Are you okay, Ash? You were off in a world of your own."

I step back. I study him, and it's hard for me to see any change. However, the very fact that he's been off the past week is running through my mind. Could Beau be right? Is there something going on?

"Why were you in there, Tristan?" I ask. I can't help it.

His eyes harden, but he quickly wipes the expression away. "I told you, I went in there to check and he beat on me."

"Then you should have defended yourself and stepped out, you had no reason to put your fists on him."

He glares at me, showing me that I've hit a nerve and making me believe that Beau might just be right. "He's a big man, far bigger than me. He overpowered me. Now, I have a report to file. Are you finished?"

I narrow my eyes and then force a smile. I think I need to step away from this for now, because it's going to put me in a difficult situation if I get involved. My eyes are peeled, though. I'll be watching.

"I'm sorry," I say. "I didn't mean to jump on you. Is everything okay now?"

"No problem. Funniest thing, though," he says, running his hands through his hair. "The security cameras went down an hour ago; technical problems. We can't catch Beau attacking me, so there's really not anything I can do except put a report in."

My heart stammers. The security cameras never go down. It's just not something that happens. The only way they turn off is if someone does it themselves. I blink rapidly, trying to keep my expression impassive as all the details swim in my head. What the hell is going on here?

"That's too bad," I say, shrugging. "Are they moving him?"

He nods. "Of course. Kent believes me."

Kent is the head of the prison, and everything and anything goes through him. He makes most orders. Of course Kent would believe Tristan. Let's face it, who is going to believe a prisoner? Especially a biker who is accused of shooting and killing innocent people.

"Where is he going?"

"Solitary confinement. Forty-eight hours."

I nod, swallowing, trying to keep myself calm. "Well, I'm going to go. It's about that time."

He pats my shoulder. "Have a good night."

"Yeah," I say, turning. "You too."

Something is going down. I can feel it.

I just don't know what it is.

CHAPTER FIVE

A week passes without any further drama. Beau comes out of solitary and goes back into his cell, and Tristan seems to keep his distance. He's quieter than usual, and on the phone a lot, but otherwise it all seems to be going fine. There have been no more fights and no more issues between Tristan and Beau.

I'm busy doing my usual round on a Sunday morning, when I pass Beau's cell. He's staring down at his balled fists, panting. He seems angry about something, and I so desperately want to go in there and find out what but I don't. I just wrap my fingers around the cell bars and lean in.

"Something wrong, Beau?"

He jerks his head up and his eyes burn into mine. "Go the fuck away."

I narrow my eyes and see that he's shaking, just slightly. "Are you okay?"

"Did you not hear me?" he bellows. "Fuck off."

I meet his gaze and his eyes practically burn right through mine. His grey depths are turning a light shade of blue with his rage.

"I'm not the bad guy here. If there's a problem you can tell me what it is."

"So you can run to your supervisor, and tattle like the good little guard."

I frown. "You underestimate me, Beau."

"Stop fuckin' callin' me that."

"It's your name, isn't it?"

"Doesn't mean I want you to use it."

I sigh, but I don't argue. I just stand there, staring into his cell for long, long moments. He finally stands and walks over, stopping in front of the bars.

"Let me ask you somethin', girl," he says, his voice low. "Explain to me how you define a bad person, and a good person?"

I tilt my head to the side. "Bad people do bad things; good people don't."

"You think it's that simple? Are you goin' to tell me you're as absent-minded as the rest of these fucktards?"

I bristle but I don't react. Instead, I think about his question. Really think about it.

"It's not easy to define if a person is good or bad. Sometimes good people do bad things, because they're hurting, or because something bad has happened to them. Sometimes their minds play tricks on them, and sometimes their hearts don't speak up in time. It's not the same for a bad person."

He nods at me to go on.

"I believe if you're truly evil, then there isn't much that can change you. If you're sculpted into an malicious person from a young age, you have the hope of being better. If you're just evil for the sake of being evil, for the sake of taking things that aren't yours, such as others' lives, then you're unable to be saved."

He's studying me, his head tilted to the side. I keep going.

"Bad people choose to do the things they are doing, good people try hard to avoid being bad. They strive to be better, but, like I said, sometimes even good people can do bad things—it's just that they do it with a different heart."

He stares at me for so long I shift uncomfortably. "And what do you think I am?"

I'm shocked by his question. Yet I'm sure of my answer. "I think you're a good person who did a bad thing, because of something that happened."

He swallows and takes a few steps back before turning and walking to his bed. "Good afternoon, Ash."

His tone tells me we're done.

But my heart says otherwise.

~*~*~*~

I hear the uproar before I see any movement. I stand from the desk in the office, where I'm doing paperwork, and poke my head out of to see the guards dragging a struggling Beau down the hall. His face is dripping with blood, his eyes are swollen, and his fists are raw. My mouth drops open as they pass me.

I stand and rush out, running into Tristan.

"Out of the way, Ash."

"What happened?" I ask, pointing to Beau.

"He got into a fight. We're taking him to get cleaned up. If you can come and help out, that would be appreciated, because I'm putting in to get him moved. He's causing too many problems."

Too many problems? He's been rather quiet, to be honest. The only problem he caused was because Tristan apparently went in and flogged him. I don't have time to think about it. I hurry down the hall after the guards. We arrive in the medical office, and I step back as they chain Beau to the table, forcing him to sit.

"Where's the nurse?" a guard barks.

Tristan turns to me. "Have you seen Kaitlyn?"

I nod. "She was at lunch, last time I heard. Did you want me to clean him up while we wait?"

Tristan stares at me, then grunts, "Yeah, I need to attend to the other prisoner. Larry, Tuck, you two need to stay in here with her."

The other two guards nod, and Tristan pats my shoulder before disappearing out the door. I can still hear the commotion outside as I walk forward, gathering everything I'll need. I feel Beau's eyes on me as I move.

I place a tray of items far enough away from him so that he can't reach, and then I fill a bowl full of saltwater and dip in a washcloth, turning to him. He's messed up in a big way; his face is battered and bruised, and there's both dried and fresh blood coating his cheeks and his lips. His left eye is swollen, but still slightly opened. With a swallow, I step forward so I'm in front of him.

He's got his eyes trained on my face as I take another shaky step. My heart hammers as I lift the warm cloth to his eyes, gently placing it against his skin and wiping the grime away. I'm finding it difficult to breathe, my skin is prickling, and the thought of his eyes on me is giving me a flood of emotions I've never felt before.

It's unnerving.

I'm fully aware he's studying me. I try to concentrate on removing the dried blood, but it's getting more and more difficult the longer his eyes stay locked on my face. His expression is so hard, yet there's a depth to it that's showing me more than he's shown me in the last two weeks.

I reach down, taking his cuffed hands. I soak the washcloth, and then place it against his split knuckles. Whoever he beat, he did a good job of them, of that I'm sure. I notice as the blood is cleaned off his skin, that he's got tattoos across his fingers that read, *Lace*.

"That's a different tattoo," I dare to say, as I continue cleaning.

"It ain't none of your business," he mutters.

Of course it isn't.

I drop his hand and take the bowl, emptying it before refreshing the water. Then I take his other hand, cleaning it, too. I see he also has tattoos on these fingers, this hand saying *Krypt*. Interesting. I drop his hands and continue on with his face, focusing on the deep gash under his eye.

He flinches when I run the cloth over it, and I feel a puff of his warm breath hit my cheek. I realize I'm too close and go to step back, but he moves like lightning. His bound hands reach out and take one of mine, tugging me closer. His fingers are calloused and hard against my smooth flesh. I gasp and my eyes are wide as he brings me so close we're nearly nose-to-nose.

He says nothing; he doesn't need to. His eyes are on mine, his expression telling me everything he can't. It screams *don't mess with me*, as well as something else, something deeper—no doubt something about the guards that he wants me to know—and part of me wishes he could tell me. The guards jump into action quickly, jerking me backwards and securing him. His eyes don't leave mine, even as they recuff his hands, this time behind his back.

"Don't move again," Larry barks.

With a swallow and trembling hands, I step back and continue cleaning his face. I decide while he's here, and he can't escape, I might as well ask some more questions. "Do you want to tell me why you got into a fight?"

He glares at me, but I continue. "Did he say something about your family?"

A flinch.

"About . . . your sister?"

He bares his teeth at me in a snarl that has me taking a step back. His look is murderous, and it stuns me for a moment. I catch my breath and take the step forward so I'm close and only he can hear me. "I get it. I understand how it feels to be angry at the world, to want revenge. You might think I'm here to make your life harder, but I'm not. I understand what you said—I'm taking notice. I hope you know that I'd never let anyone hurt you if I had a choice."

Our eyes lock, and we don't move until the door swings open and Tristan enters with Kaitlyn following closely behind. I drop the washcloth, giving Beau a determined stare before turning. "I got most of the blood, Kait," I say, smiling at the young, redheaded nurse.

"Thanks Ash." She smiles back, taking over.

I walk over to Tristan when he beckons me, and lean in close.

"He say what happened?" he asks.

"No."

"He nearly killed the other inmate. Neither of them will talk so a decision has been made that he needs to be transferred to a higher-security prison. We don't have the facilities here to deal with this kind of violence. It won't be the first fight he'll get into."

I turn and look at Beau, whose eyes are still on me. I don't see this as being something he's gotten himself into, and it worries me. He really has no reason to be transferred, but there's nothing I can do to stop it. My argument is pointless in this situation.

"If you've got the morning free tomorrow, it would be good if you could accompany us. Two guards are off sick and we need extra hands. I know you don't usually do transfers, but in this case we don't really have a choice."

"I'm happy to," I say, giving him a forced smile.

At least I can get a feel of what's going to go down if I go.

He pats my shoulder. "Thanks, Ash."

I nod then glance back to Beau. He's watching me still, his eyes narrowed.

Why has this prisoner gotten to me in such a way?

Maybe it's because I truly don't believe he's a bad person.

CHAPTER SIX

It's a cold morning when I head out the next day. I pull on a coat, dragging the ties around my waist to hold it secure. I say goodbye to Claire and Leo, telling them my plans. They're too busy arguing over breakfast to hear me. With a wave of my hand, I leave.

The drive over to work is long; that would probably be because I'm spending my time pondering Beau and the issues going on around me. I've lain awake all night wondering why they're transferring him. It has to be orchestrated; I've seen prisoners do far worse and never get moved. Someone is behind this, and it scares me to think of why they'd be going to such an effort.

I arrive just as they're preparing the transfer vehicle. It's a large truck, with a fully secured back. In the back with Beau there will be two guards. He will also be fully shackled to the ground and walls of the truck, making sure he can't move. I'll be in the front with two other guards.

"Are you ready?" Tristan asks as I approach.

I nod, wrapping my coat around me even tighter. "Sure."

"I'm not coming, I have a meeting, but you're with some good guards."

He's not coming? That's strange. He always comes to these things.

"You're not coming?"

He shrugs, but I don't miss his eyes darting away for just a second. "It's a meeting I can't change, sorry."

"Okay," I mutter.

He pats my shoulder. "Let the security guys go over you, then jump into the truck. They're loading Dawson now."

I give him a fake smile as I head towards security. They make sure I'm not packing any weapons to attempt a prison break, and then I walk over and climb into the truck. Larry is already in the driver's side.

"Morning," he grunts, nodding at me.

"Hi," I say, feeling awkward. I cross my arms and tuck my knees up, waiting.

They load Beau about fifteen minutes later. Guards bark orders at one another, and then Peter jumps into the truck, staring over at me. He gives me a jerk of his head and then looks over to Larry. It's awkward being stuck in between them. "We're good to go."

Then we're off. Larry drives the truck out of the prison, taking us towards the highway. The high-security prison is about an hour and a half away, in the neighboring city. It's not that it's better than the prison I work at; it's just that they tend to be better equipped to deal with the more aggressive prisoners. *Not that Beau is an aggressive prisoner.*

I pull out a book when we hit the highway, and busy myself reading while Larry and Peter talk casually between them. The ride is smooth and easy, at least until the deep rumble of bikes comes sailing through the window. Larry turns and stares out his rearview mirror.

"That the motorcycle gang?"

I shudder. It's a club, for a start. Not a gang. And if it is, we're in big, *big* trouble.

The other thing that bothers me, is that he doesn't seem scared about it.

"What's going on?" I ask.

They ignore me as Larry continues to stare out the rearview mirror.

"They're early."

What?

My heart picks up and I turn to find Peter with a gun pointed at me. I reel backwards, confused.

"What's going on?"

"Shit, Peter," Larry barks. "It ain't them. It's the boy's fuckin' gang."

The boy's? Beau's? What's happening?

"What do you fuckin' mean it's the boys? How the fuck did they find out? It ain't meant to be them. Speed up, get off this road before they have the chance to get hold of us."

"What is going on?" I screech.

"Shut the fuck up," Peter barks, shoving the gun out the window and taking a shot.

I open my mouth to scream, but it's cut short when a bike lines up next to the truck. The biker, whose face is covered with a mask, raises his gun and shoots the tire, causing the truck to swerve off the road. Peter yells something, but I can't hear what it is over my scream as the truck skids further off the gravel. We're on a quiet stretch of road; there's no one else around. This is bad, very bad.

We're also on an embankment, and I know the exact moment the truck hits the edge, because it tips. My body is sent forward in a rush as it flips down the hill. I scream, but it's no use. Metal crushes around me, pinning me to the chair as the truck continues its descent towards the bottom.

When we hit, my head is jerked forward, and it hits the dashboard with a thud. By the time we stop moving, I'm barely conscious. My head is pounding, my body feels like everything is broken, and my mouth is filling with blood. I'm trembling all over, and I can't see.

I reach out, trying to feel something.

It's silent.

"Help?" I croak—both men are silent.

No one answers. I try to blink, but it hurts.

I hear the faint sound of voices yelling, and then two gunshots. They go off at the exact same time. I want to scream, fear coursing through my veins.

A loud, crashing sound echoes through the air, and the voices near closer. A door is jerked open and the voices sound as though they're in the cab with us.

"Dead," I hear someone say.

I want to scream, but I can't open my mouth. I can't even move. Fear is holding me still. A gunshot rings out in the cab and my scream finally breaks free, although it's hoarse and crackly.

"Now they're both dead."

Both dead? Both *dead*? Oh my God.

I open my mouth and make another gurgling sound.

"The girl is alive."

Oh God.

"Take her," a gruff voice says. Beau?

"That ain't a good decision, Krypt."

Who is Krypt? Confusion fills me. My body trembles and I make a whiny, broken sound as I try to cry out.

"Take. Her. She's innocent in this."

"Get her out." A growl from another male.

Hands curl around my arms, and things get shifted and shoved out of the way. I hear grunting and muttering as I'm pulled from the wreck. Pain shoots through my body, and I cry out as I'm jerked into someone's arms. I can feel every thump as he strides towards wherever it is they're taking me.

"Throw her in the SUV," someone orders. "We need to get the fuck outta here before anyone witnesses this."

Witnesses?

My head spins as I'm placed onto a cold, leather seat. Somebody reaches in, pressing a cool cloth to my eyes, wiping them. Pain shoots through my head and I find myself crying out, louder and more shrill this time.

"This is a bad fuckin' idea."

A low growl. "Just fuckin' trust me."

The door is slammed closed, and the car lurches forward. Panic seizes me, and I want so desperately to push myself up in a poor attempt to escape, but there's no hope. I can't move my body to even try to help myself. I'm in shock; I'm sure of it. Either that or I've got a serious back injury.

I blink my eyes a few times, attempting to open them again. This time I get a blurry picture. I can see the back of a seat and just over, a leather jacket that is wrapped around a very large man. He turns and looks over to me, and a strangled gasp leaves my throat. Beau? I shake my head from side to side, panic rising.

"Ash," he says, his voice low and husky. "Not how you expected this to go? Should have listened to me. Oh, by the way . . . I'm Krypt."

That's when I pass out.

CHAPTER SEVEN

I wake to the sounds of low, murmured voices. I'm in the back of what I'm going to guess is a van. White panels of metal that lead to a roof are all I can see. There are no windows and it's stuffy. I'm bouncing just slightly, as if we're going over a dirt road. I move my hands to wipe my eyes, only to find them cuffed.

This can't be good.

I blink rapidly, trying to clear my vision so I can get a better picture. I turn my head to the left, crying in pain as a sharp stabbing sensation radiates through my skull and travels down my neck. My entire body is stiff, and I can feel dried blood on my face so thick it makes moving my mouth slightly painful.

There's not a lot to see in here, just an empty space. I stare over at the back doors and see some chains. They're loose. I shift my body over to them, taking them in my bound hands. These could do damage, if I wanted them to. It's worth a damned try. If I have to stay here, bound and sick, I'll probably die. I've been taught some great lessons in fighting; I have a chance, even if it is only slight.

I pull the chains closer as the van continues to bounce. Then we come to a screeching halt, sending me rolling towards the back with a shout. Jesus. Ever heard of breaking slowly? The front door slams and I shove to my hands and knees, clutching the chains. I'll have to make this hurt for it to be successful. I have no idea what I'm going to face when these doors are opened, but I can't go down without a fight.

I just hope they don't kill me.

The door rattles and I brace myself, moving as close as I can get. I tighten my hands around the chains, holding them out, ready to lunge. The back door swings open and I don't think: as soon as I see the flash of a leather jacket, I leap out. My body screams in pain, agony ripping through me.

I land on a tall, solid man. I hook my arms and the chains around his neck, pulling back tightly. I'm half on his side, half on his back. "Motherfucker," he curses, reaching up with thickly ringed fingers and taking hold of the chain. It's at that angle I see the tattoos on his knuckles and realize it's Beau.

"You can't take me against my will," I growl, tugging back tighter. "I won't go down without a fight, you son-of-a-bitch!"

"Fuck, Rhyder, get this fuckin' woman off me."

I tug as hard as I can, causing a bellow to leave his mouth. He throws his head back, jerking his body, trying to flick me off. A large arm goes around my waist, pulling me backwards as Beau shoves the chains off his neck, and I'm thrown to the ground with a thump. I cry out, pain ripping through my body. It takes me a moment to roll, and I'm so angry when I do. How dare he? How fucking dare he steal me and think he's just going to get away with it?

"And to think I—"

I roll all the way over, ready to abuse Beau, but stop abruptly when I see around about twenty bikers staring down at me with angry expressions on their faces.

"Oh boy," I breathe.

"Yeah," Beau growls, leaning down and hurling me up. "Oh fuckin' boy all right."

He shoves me towards a large cabin and a huge shed that is behind the group of bikers. They part as I step through, some of them baring their teeth at me in not-so-nice gestures. I put my head down. That was a failure on my behalf, it would seem. Beau . . . or Krypt as he calls himself, keeps shoving me, forcing my aching feet to move.

Before we reach the door, a large biker steps in front of us. I stop dead and stare up at him, my mouth dropping open. He's huge. Like, mega. He's at least six-foot two, with shoulders bigger and thicker than any shoulders I've ever seen on a man. He's got the lightest blue eyes and thick, dark hair that is long and sitting just below his shoulders. I don't even dare try to count the tattoos winding up his arms.

"You better be sure this girl ain't gonna get us into trouble, Krypt. We don't need any more shit," he barks.

Krypt steps forward just as the other biker swings on his jacket, pulling it firmly over his massive shoulders. I see numerous patches on the leather, including one that states he's the "President". So he basically runs the club? I have read enough about bikers to figure that much out.

"She ain't gonna cause any more trouble," Krypt grates.

"She better fuckin' not, or I'll put her on her fuckin' ass."

With wide eyes, I gape at him. He flashes me a feral grin. "Yeah, babe, that's what I fuckin' said."

He steps past us, walking off to join the rest of the bikers. Krypt drags me inside, pulling me through the doors until we stop in the living room of the cabin. It's actually a nice space, surprisingly. There are polished wooden floors and a big wooden kitchen. The furniture is very masculine, all black and biker-ish.

"Why did you take me?" I ask as Krypt drags me down a hall.

"Because you're fuckin' evidence, and there ain't no way in fuck we're lettin' you go back and tell them what happened. There is big shit goin' down and you ain't goin' to ruin what we've put in place."

"I think this is the most I've ever heard you speak. I was starting to think you had a condition."

He snorts. "Code out here, woman. Don't speak when you're locked away."

"You killed people. It's your own fault you were locked away."

He stiffens and spins around, clutching my shoulders and shaking me just slightly. "You want to fuckin' survive?"

I open my mouth, but he cuts me off. "Well?" he barks.

"Yes!" I snap.

"Then shut your mouth, do as you're told, and don't fuckin' mention me or my club again."

"Your club?"

He growls at me.

"What are you going to do with me?" I ask as he turns and starts dragging me down the hall again.

"I have no fuckin' idea right now, but until I find out you're my prisoner."

Prisoner?

I want to gag.

"I'm hurt."

"Can see that. I'm not fuckin' blind."

"There's no need to speak to me like that," I bite out.

He spins to me again. "Don't feel fuckin' nice, does it?"

I recoil and flinch. "I've never spoken to you like that."

He chuckles, but his smile is cold and deadly. "Yeah, you were the only one."

I say nothing as he continues to lead me to wherever it is we're going. We stop at a room, and he shoves me inside. It's a big room with a double bed, a ragged couch and what seems to be a bathroom off to the side. He pulls me across the faded green rug on the floor, and forces me to sit on the bed.

"First thing," he says, reaching under the bed and pulling out a first-aid kit. "You even try to run, we'll kill you."

"You'd kill an innocent woman?"

He looks at me, his eyes burning into mine. "If she threatened our club and everything we've worked for, yeah."

A cold chill runs through me.

"You keep your mouth shut," he continues. "And we'll have no problems. This is a club life, and trust me, babe, it's not what your spoiled ass is used to."

"I'm not spoiled," I say, tugging on my cuffs.

He snorts. "Not spoiled my ass. Look at you. You're up yourself so fuckin' far you can't see your own head."

"That's not true," I protest.

"Ain't it, babe?" he snorts.

"I could put you on your ass in a matter of seconds, buddy," I spit at him.

"Is that a challenge?"

"I'll make it one when my ribs aren't broken."

He smirks. "You're on."

I refuse to answer him. He pulls out a cleansing wipe and reaches towards my face, but I flinch away.

"Don't touch me," I growl.

He glares at me, his grey eyes narrowing. "You got two fuckin' choices here; think carefully. You either let me help you, or you sit here in your own dried blood."

I stare at him, my expression filled with hate. "Fine," I grate.

He leans forward again, wiping the dried blood from my face. I keep my eyes trained on the wall beside us, not wanting to look at him. He cleans me up, and then puts a patch on the laceration under my eye. His face is still battered from his fight, and for a moment I think that we're matching with our eye gashes.

"You need to clean up and get some clothes on that aren't covered in blood."

Remembering Larry and Peter has my stomach coiling tightly. "You killed them?" I say, my voice shaky.

"They had it comin'. Believe it or not, babe, those men were bad guys."

"I'm starting to believe that," I mutter.

He nods. "Because of that, we need all evidence gone. We gotta burn your clothes."

I snap my head up. "This jacket was more than five hundred dollars. Look at it, it's epic."

Why did I wear the one jacket I actually loved today? That'll teach me. It's a biker jacket, too. All leather and spunk. Dammit.

He snorts. "Well, it'll make nice firewood then, won't it?"

I grit my teeth. "I have no other clothes."

"Plenty of women's clothes here."

"Why would there be clothes here? Is this your whorehouse?"

He smirks at me, showing me a dimple in his cheek.

"You got it right on, babe. It is a bit of a party house, lots of fucking."

"You're disgusting. You can play all you want, biker, but I know what you really are. I saw you in that prison; I saw what your *brothers* here didn't see. So act it up. I know the truth."

His eyes flash and I know I've hit the nail on the head. Who is the real Beau? It's certainly not this act he's putting on for me now. He hurts; he just won't admit it.

"Listen here, princess," he growls, a low rumble forming in his chest. "Don't pretend you know anything about me. I told you before, I won't fuckin' repeat myself: the reason I didn't give you fuckers anything is because any word I fuckin' say can be used against me or my club."

There we go with the *my club* again.

"You tell yourself whatever you want."

He opens his mouth to spit something else at me, but someone comes into the room. Another biker, this one is . . . I blink . . . that can't be right. I blink again. He's in . . . a wheelchair? Krypt sees me staring at the man and barks, "Take a fuckin' picture, it lasts longer."

I jerk and turn my gaze away from the man.

"Tyke," Krypt says, "watch her for a minute. I gotta talk to Rhyder."

Rhyder. Tyke. Krypt. Clearly these guys don't use their real names. The man in the chair wheels himself in, his strong arms rippling as he moves. Krypt shoots me a glare before leaving the room. I turn and stare at Tyke. He's a really, really stunning man.

He's equally as bulky as the other men, with rippling muscles running up his arms and no doubt continuing under his shirt. He's got messy russet-colored hair and deep, deep brown eyes. They're almost black. He's equally as scary and intimidating as the rest. I turn my eyes away when he holds my curious gaze.

"Never seen a man in a chair before?" he grunts.

I turn to him. "I, uh, yeah."

"Just not a biker?"

I shake my head, my cheeks flushing. "No, never a biker."

"Accident," he says. It's clear he's probably had to tell this story a lot, so now he shares it before the question is asked. I get that. "Fucked my legs. Crushed all the bones from my thighs down. Can't feel anything from just slightly under my knees. Enough that I can't stand real well, so I spend most of my time in this."

He pats his chair and I stare at it, unable to stop the smile creeping across my face when I see it's been decked out, Harley-style. Flames have been painted up the side, making it look like a gas tank. It has thick wheels with a whole lot of bling.

"Will you ever walk again?" I ask, feeling sorry for him.

He shrugs. "Probably—they tell me most of it's in my head."

"They?"

"Shrinks."

I scrunch up my nose. He wheels forward, using his big hands to pull the chair across the room. He goes right past me, leaving the door open. I'm not ashamed at my thought in that moment—*he can't chase me*. I never said it was right, but I certainly don't want to be stuck in this house with a group of bikers who are keeping me prisoner, for longer than I need to.

I don't think—I just do.

I run out of the room. Tyke doesn't yell right away, which tells me he hasn't seen me go. Adrenaline runs rampant in my body as I hurry down the halls. I reach a window and peer out. Krypt and the bikers are all out the front, talking between themselves. I turn, staring down the hall just as I hear Tyke bellow.

It's now or never.

I spin around and charge through the kitchen, slipping on something that has been spilled on the floor. With a curse, I push forward, my body aching and pounding with each step I take. I see a back door and I don't stop to see if anyone is behind me or in front of me, I just bolt right on out. I see a patch of grass before it disappears into thick, luscious mountain trees.

We're not close to any city, that much I know.

It's a huge risk, but there has to be a road close by. If I skirt around the trees and follow the driveway down, I might have some luck. I hear shouting and curses being flung about. I run forward, forcing my legs to move as fast as they can—which in the scheme of things is pretty fast, considering my condition.

I grit my teeth as pain shoots up my legs and right into my spine. My head pounds, and I'm struggling to breathe, but I push on. I force myself through the trees, dodging the thick branches pointing out of the massive trunks. I reach a clearing that boasts one hell of a gorgeous, crystal-clear creek.

I don't stop.

Mountains are all I can see ahead of me, and with mountains usually comes caves. I'm sure I can hide, at least for the night.

The wind is chilly, and I wrap my blood-stained coat further around myself, glad Krypt never got the chance to burn it like he'd said he would. Footsteps echo through the trees and I know they're close.

I keep pushing on, heading for the thick trees that surround the base of the mountain. When I reach them, I duck behind one, desperately trying to catch my breath. Fear and adrenaline battle inside my body, and my skin prickles with the knowledge that if they catch me it could end badly.

"I know you're fuckin' out there," I hear Krypt bellow. "I'll find you."

I have no doubt about that; it's why I push off the tree and keep running. His footsteps fade as I pick up my pace, getting deeper into the trees. Then I make the fatal mistake of tripping over a log that I try to jump. With a scream, I land on my face, sending a burning pain through my ribs that has me screaming in agony.

I push to my feet, desperate to keep going. Angry tears course down my cheeks because I know I'm about to fail, I'm about to ruin the only chance I have of escaping. Footsteps behind me come to a stop and I hear a cursed word before a heavy, booted foot lands beside my head. Krypt kneels down, pulling me up.

"You're fuckin' bleedin'," he growls.

Not the reaction I'd expected.

"You stupid fuckin' girl."

That's more like it.

He pulls me up and I wail in agony at the pain soaring through my body. I stare down and see that I am in fact, bleeding. I've obviously torn open a wound.

Krypt has one strong arm around my waist as he leads me out of the trees. I have no strength to fight, no energy left. That was all I had; I'm in too much pain to give more. If I weren't so hurt, I would have had a decent chance.

"Do you have any fuckin' idea what's in these woods?" he says as he leads me back to the house.

"Nothing that could be worse than staying here with you," I whisper, my voice gone.

He scoffs. "You would rather take on some feral mountain lion over me?"

I say nothing; he's got a point. I didn't think it through.

"You can't really blame me," I add. "You killed the people I work with."

He snorts, and his arm tightens around my waist. "You have no idea about the people you work with."

"I think you're wrong. I think I do have an idea. It still doesn't make it right."

Now it's his turn not to answer.

When we reach the house, he leads me inside and closes the door behind us. The 'President' comes charging over, his fists balled tight. "I swear to fuckin' Christ . . ."

"It's fine, Prez," Krypt says. "We got this."

"You're gonna get us all fuckin' killed with that brown-nose little bitch."

I prick up at his words. "Excuse me?" I yell. "Do you even know me?"

"You work with the rest of those little bastards. You're exactly like them."

"You're wrong. I'm nothing like them. I work there, I love my job, but I have a life outside of that place. I am a normal person; don't assume you know what I am."

He steps forward, leaning down into my face. "You're tellin' me that you wouldn't go straight to the cops if you got out of here?"

"Of course I would," I snap. "You killed people—some of those guards weren't bad."

"My point exactly," he steps back. "Krypt, she gets away again, I won't be so kind."

I glare at him as Krypt leads me past.

"Stop windin' him up," he mutters. "He's not a nice guy."

"He shouldn't pretend to know me; he doesn't."

Krypt stops, spins around and leans in close. "He runs things around here, and if you value you life you will fuckin' do as he says."

"He doesn't run me," I growl, standing my ground.

"You see what happened to your friends?"

My stomach twists, but I don't answer him.

"Well, did you?" he barks.

"Yes, I fucking saw it, you jackass."

"Then what the hell makes you think he won't do it to you?"

My next words are cut off as I realize he's right. Nothing is stopping him from doing it to me.

"That's what I fuckin' thought," he mutters. "Now move."

He walks me down the hall and back to the room. When we get in, he slams the door shut and turns to me. "Get in that shower and clean yourself up."

I don't bother to argue. Instead, I take the towel hanging off the bed and walk into the shower.

"Don't even think about climbin' out the window. It's barred."

Of course it fucking is.

I shut the door to the bathroom and turn the shower on, then slowly and very, very painfully I step out of my clothes. I'm covered in blood, and not all of it is my own. The very thought makes my skin crawl. I step under the warm water and cry out in pain as it hits the battered parts of my body.

I can barely stand it. The minute I'm clean, I step out. I pat myself dry and straighten to stare in the mirror. My face looks . . . *awful*. My usually sky-blue eyes are dull and bloodshot. My skin, which is really quite pale, is now covered in ugly bruises. My long, chocolate-brown hair is messy and matted. I sigh and step away, not wanting to look for a second longer.

I dry myself off and stare around the room, realizing I've got no clothes. With a groan, I walk over to the door and peer out. Krypt is leaning against the bedframe, arms crossed over his chest. Gosh, he's good looking. He flicks his grey gaze to me and it slowly moves down. "You need to get cleaned up before you dress."

"I don't think so, buddy," I mutter.

"You don't get a fuckin' choice, *Ash*."

The way he just said my name has shivers breaking out over my skin. I swallow and keep my arms tightly crossed. Krypt points to the bed. "Sit."

I stare at the bed, where the first-aid kit is lying. I know I'm an idiot if I don't go and let him help me. "Can I at least put some . . . undergarments on?"

His lips quirk. "Yeah, babe, whatever."

I flush and rush out past him, taking the pile of clothes on the dresser. I hurry back into the bathroom and pull on the bra and panties. I'm grateful the panties still have the tag on them, but that doesn't stop me from inspecting them to make sure they're clean. They're a little tight on my curvy body, but they'll do. When they're on, I pull the towel back over myself and walk out.

I sit on the bed next to Krypt, and he flips the first-aid kit open.

"You might need stitches in that wound on your arm," he says, nodding to the ugly gash near my elbow. It hasn't really stopped bleeding, even after my shower. A slow, thick rivulet of blood is already running down towards my wrist.

"You want me to let you put stitches in my arm?"

He meets my concerned gaze. "You want to die of infection?"

"No, but I'm not sure I won't die of infection if I let you do it."

He grins. God. Just, *God*. He's perfect. How can someone be such an asshole and yet be so damned good looking? It hurts to watch him. "You make the choice, babe."

"Don't call me *babe*, and fine, do whatever you want."

He flashes me a devilish grin. "You do know I'm goin' to put a needle through your skin, right?"

"I know what stitches are!"

"With nothing to numb your skin."

That has me swallowing. He sighs and turns, barking out, "Rex!"

Minutes later an older biker with a big, bushy beard comes in. "What?"

"Get me the whiskey."

"Whiskey?" I squeak.

He turns back to me. "It'll help the pain."

Oh God.

He reaches over and presses around the wound. "Definitely needs stitches."

Double oh God.

"Here ya go," Rex says, coming back in and tossing Krypt a bottle filled with amber liquid.

Krypt hands it to me. "Drink this while I clean the rest of you."

I stare at the alcohol.

"You scared it might bite you, princess?"

I jerk my head up. "Why the fuck do you think I'm such a princess?"

He doesn't answer, but his eyes are alight with humor. I get the feeling he's having a dig at me. I unscrew the bottle to prove my point, and take a long pull. It burns, but it's nothing I've never done before. Claire and I often go out drinking together, and shots are our thing.

I rest the bottle between my legs and meet his gaze. He's watching me, his eyes intense. He turns away and begins cleaning up any wounds he can get to while I continue to sip the alcohol. His fingers grazing over my skin have me breaking out into shivers. He's sending me over the edge, and I don't even know him.

I bite my lip and turn away, crossing and uncrossing my ankles. "Stop fidgeting," he mutters. "Shit, you'd think you've never had a man's hands on you before."

I don't look at him; I just keep my lip in my mouth and I turn my face away. His fingers run down my arm until he stops at the gash. "You ready for me to stitch this?"

No.

I take another long pull from the bottle before nodding sharply. I hear him rustling about, but I keep my eyes trained on the wall beside me. *You can do this. It's just a needle. You've got a tattoo, for Christ's sake. It's fine. It's okay.*

I take another sip when I feel him wipe my skin with something that leaves a cool sensation behind. I pinch my eyes closed, panting softly.

Fingers curl around my jaw and turn my head. My eyes pop open and I'm looking directly into his. I stop breathing.

"If you tense up, it'll hurt more," he says, staring at my mouth. *Why is he staring at my mouth?*

"Just do it," I grind out.

He lets my jaw go and reaches down to take a needle and some thread. I take a breath, another swallow, and turn away again. My head is swimming from the alcohol, but I still don't think it'll be enough.

He doesn't tell me when he's going to start; I just feel the sharp, burning pain shoot up my arm. I cry out loudly, but I don't flinch.

"Sorry," he murmurs.

Then comes the next raging hot prick, I bite my lip, desperately trying to stop the whimper that's threatening to escape. My entire arm feels like it's on fire.

Another pull of the needle and I give in to my cries. I make a strangled sound as he pops it out the other side.

"Nearly there," he says, his voice oddly calming. "I've seen men cry over this. You're doin' fuckin' good, babe."

Tears leak out of the corners of my eyes as he pulls the last stitch through. My entire arm throbs after the invasion of needle and thread. He ties the final stitch and then leans back. "You're done."

I turn and stare down at the three neat little stiches in my arm. "You . . . thank you," I croak.

He stands, nodding at me. He quickly cleans up and then turns and takes it all towards the door. Before he reaches it, he turns back to me. "I take it back." His voice is low and husky. "You ain't a princess at all."

My eyes widen at his words, but he doesn't see it. He turns and exits the room, shutting and locking the door behind him.

I guess that means we're done here?

~*~*~*~

I find myself dropping off to sleep on the double bed. I want to stay awake, but my eyes refuse to allow it. I'm exhausted and my body aches all over.

I lie down to just take the pressure off my arm and am out in minutes, drifting away from the unpleasant situation I'm in—even just for a moment.

"Hey."

I flutter my eyes open at the feeling of a hand on my arm.

"Wake up."

Wake up? I blink a few times and when I can focus, I see Krypt standing at the edge of the bed, staring down at me.

"Wha—"

"We gotta go."

Go? Go where?

I sit up slowly. My entire body aches. "Where do we have to go?"

"The cops are goin' mad. We can't stay here. We gotta go further up. We have a cabin in the mountains. We're goin' there until Maddox can sort it out."

"Who is Maddox?" I croak.

"The president."

Oh, so that's his name.

I process the information he's giving me, and as sleep leaves my body panic takes its place. Hang on; he wants me to go and hide out in the woods? Alone? With him? Because the cops are after him for murder and kidnapping? I shake my head and scoot back on the bed.

"I'm not going anywhere with you. It's bad enough being here but you're not taking me somewhere that you can end me as quickly as you met me."

He raises his brows. "Firstly, if I wanted to end you, I could do it right fuckin' now, and secondly, you don't get a fuckin' choice."

"You're a murderer," I whisper. "You killed people that I've known for a long time. Those guys in the back of that truck were innocent, some of them were my friends."

"Your friends?" he snorts. "You have no idea what they were."

I narrow my eyes. "And you do?"

"Abso-fuckin'-lutely."

I shift back further, but he reaches out and takes my arm, tugging me off the bed as if I weigh no more than a feather. I land on my feet and stumble forward. "I've already packed some clothes and shit for you, now let's move."

"You can't just take me," I cry, struggling.

"I can, and I fuckin' will."

He pulls me out the door and leads me down the hall. We run into a group of bikers just outside the front door. I notice Maddox right away, because he's so incredibly dominant. He turns and glares at me; I recoil behind Krypt. That dude scares the shit out of me.

"We got a big fuckin' problem, Krypt."

"What?"

"Seems there's more that are workin' behind the fuckin' scenes, Howard has another two boys we don't know about."

Howard? Who's Howard?

"Fuckin' who?" Krypt grates out.

"One called Tristan, another called Luke."

"I already knew that," Krypt grunts.

My eyes widen. "What?"

Maddox glares at me. "Anyone ask you to fuckin' speak?"

"You've killed my friends, you've kidnapped me, and now you're talking about people I care about. I'm not giving you a choice; I'm fuckin' speaking."

His eyes widen and he smirks.

Yeah, you bastard. I have sass.

"You know those boys, then?"

"Of course I know them. I worked with them."

He narrows his eyes now, staring at me. "You know Howard?"

"Who the fuck is Howard?"

"She ain't in on it, boss," Krypt says. "I can tell you that right now."

"In on what?" I demand, trying to jerk my arm free from Krypt's grasp.

Maddox ignores me and keeps talking. "We need to take them two fuckers out. They'll spill too much information."

"What?" I cry, thinking of Tristan. I saw some dodgy things going on, but that doesn't mean I want him killed.

Maddox storms forward, taking my arm in his. "Listen here, girl, and listen fuckin' good. Your boys are fuckin' bigger criminals than half the fuckin' bastards there."

"Maybe so, but it's not your right to hurt him. Regardless, he's my friend."

"He is workin' for a criminal; a fuckin' deadly one. If he's your friend, it's all a damned act."

"You're a liar," I cry, losing my patience.

I spin around and I twist my wrist so hard Krypt is forced to let it go. He steps towards me, but I divert him quickly with a swift punch to his stomach. He *oomph*s, and takes two steps back. Maddox grabs my arm and I spin around, lifting my knee and driving it right into his balls. With a bellow, he lets me go.

I take a step back, glaring at all of them. "I don't care who you are, or what fuckin' club you come from. Some of those men are my friends, and you have taken me from my life. I deserve to understand."

Maddox is panting, and shooting daggers in my direction. Krypt almost looks . . . impressed.

"Don't even start on me about your balls. It won't hurt you not to reproduce, you jackass," I bark at Maddox.

He straightens and walks towards me, his eyes flaring with rage. He lunges at me, wrapping a hand around my arm and jerking me so close I can smell his breath. "I've warned you enough times. Now I'm fuckin' pissed off."

"So do something about it," I spit back at him. "Kill me. You're going to anyway, aren't you?"

"Damn fuckin' right I am."

"Consider this," I growl. "You kill me, you're giving up the chance at some seriously good information. I know Tristan and I know Luke. I saw what went on behind the walls at that prison. So go ahead and shoot me; I fuckin' dare you."

Now he looks impressed.

"I thought you were a fuckin' pansy," he grunts, letting me go, and shoving me back. "You give me information, I let you live. You kick me in the balls again, I'll put a bullet right in your cunt, for revenge purposes."

I snort. "Fine. It's a deal."

"Fuck me," Krypt mutters from behind me.

"Seems you might have found a decent one, for once." Maddox smirks in the general direction that Krypt is standing.

I know there's something going down here, something even bigger than me. I need to know what that is. I need to understand because I'm curious. But I also need to keep myself safe.

"Krypt, tell her everything she needs to know on the way. We'll be around in the next few days; she can give us information then," Maddox says, turning away from me.

"Where are we going?" I ask Krypt.

He points towards the mountains. "Up there."

"Up?" I mutter.

"Up."

"On a . . . bike?"

He chuckles. "No babe, on the transport God gave us."

My eyes widen. "You want me to climb a fucking mountain?"

He grins at me. "It's a day's journey, if that, and yeah, I want you to climb a fuckin' mountain."

I point to my ribs. "Mountain plus climbing equals a world of pain."

"You'll be fine. It isn't steep."

"It's a mountain!"

He snorts. "Quit your whinin'. If the cops check out here and you're found, we'll all go to shit."

"That'll serve you right for kidnapping me, and shooting up a car full of guards."

He ignores me and reaches down to sling a bag over his shoulder. "Let's go."

"I don't have hiking shoes."

He snorts a laugh. "Fuck, you're a weird chick."

He drops his pack from his shoulder and pulls out a pair of sneakers. He hands them to me, and I put them on without argument. They're a size to big, but I'd rather take them then go without. He tosses a thick jacket at me. It's thick and warm. I push my arms through the sleeves and then we're off.

I follow him as he walks out of the yard, all leather jacket and fine ass. Damn his fine ass. Damn it. He moves like a tiger, sleek and powerful.

I hate that I'm going to be stuck with him in the mountains for a few days alone. It freaks me out. He's the kind of man that is hard to turn away from—let alone be stuck in a cabin alone with.

Fuck.

We head out to a path that leads into the thick trees. It's clear to me these guys have thought this out. They've picked a location for their cabin/clubhouse that is without a doubt in a tricky area. It's not in a public place, it's out and it's hidden. For police to get down here without being noticed, they'd have to come on foot. You'd be able to hear anything with that gravelly dirt road.

"Keep up," Krypt barks, jerking me from my thoughts.

Evening will fall in about three hours, and that's a little concerning for me. I pick up my pace, staying close behind him. "What are we supposed to do when it gets dark?" I ask him.

"We find somewhere and we sleep."

"Out here?" I say, eyes wide.

"Yeah, out here."

"You said there are cats. Big ones . . . that eat people."

He nods, trekking forward. "There are."

"And you want to sleep here?"

"Don't have a fuckin' choice. Besides, I got a gun."

"That makes me feel so much better," I say, staring around, my eyes scanning the trees. Well shit, now I'm freaked out.

My legs and ribs are aching by the time we're an hour in, and I desperately want to stop. I'm sore all over and my arm is throbbing. Not to mention I have somewhat of a pounding head from the alcohol I consumed. "Do you have aspirin?" I ask.

Krypt stops, turning around to stare at me. He's got a fine layer of sweat coating his skin, and God, does he look good. "You hurtin'?"

"Yeah."

He drops the pack and rummages through it, pulling out a couple of pills. He hands them to me with a bottle of water. I take them gratefully and swallow them down.

"Sit. We'll eat, and then we'll keep walkin' until we find somewhere to pull up."

I find a large rock and perch on it, watching as he pulls out a couple of granola bars. He hands one to me and I graciously accept it. I'm starving. We eat in silence, and nothing but the sounds of the wilderness can be heard for miles.

"This cabin, is it like your escape house?" I ask him once I'm finished chewing.

He nods, kneeling down and using the water bottle to wash his hands. "The only way in and out is to walk, so it ain't easy for any cops to find. None have found it yet. Besides, I'd hear them well before they reached us. It's in a good position."

"You want to tell me why we're going there yet?"

"You know why we're goin' there. The cops are all over my escape and your disappearance. They'll raid that clubhouse as soon as they locate it. We can't be there."

"That's not what I meant," I point out.

He stands, shoving the water back in the bag. "I know what you meant, babe, but I ain't ready to fuckin' tell you about it. We got tracks to make, so let's move."

With a sigh, I stand, and we begin walking again.

This is going to be fun.

~*~*~*~

We stop three hours later just as the sun is dropping over the mountaintops, and a cool breeze is trickling through the trees. Krypt finds a large overhanging rock that provides some great shelter. We both drop down underneath it, exhausted and panting. After a bottle of water each, we're able to catch our breath.

"I'll make a fire," he says. "But it has to be small. Don't want no smoke givin' us away."

I point further underneath the rock. "If you do it right back there, no one will see."

He stares at me, and my cheeks flush under his scrutiny. "You are smart, ain't ya, Wildcard?"

"Don't call me Wildcard," I mutter.

"Why not?" he murmurs, opening the pack. "It suits you."

I watch him unload a folded blanket, a couple of tins of food, and a flashlight. He lays the blanket out on a softer patch of ground and points to it. "Sit on that. It'll keep you warm."

I don't hesitate. I slide over until I'm on the thick, fleecy material. He joins me, sitting beside me so our legs are touching. I bite my lip, trying to avoid showing how much him being so close affects me. I don't understand this insta-attraction; I can only put it down to his looks and the fact that I haven't been laid for a long while.

"You hungry?" he asks.

"Sure."

Like someone skilled with nature, he creates a small fire and prepares some food in a small dish he had in his pack. I tuck my knees up to my chest and watch him work, the expression on his face is one full of concentration.

"So, are you going to tell me what is going down?"

He sighs, but keeps his eyes on the food. "We've got rivals, big ones, and they're causin' a problem for our club."

"Another MC?" I ask.

He raises his brows at my term.

"What? I know a little bit about clubs."

"Right," he mutters. "So then you'll know we take shit very seriously. This club is messin' with things they shouldn't be messin' with. Firstly, they put me in prison."

"But you shot and killed those people."

"Wrong," he says, his eyes hard. "I shot and killed Johan Reed, but it was all a big set-up."

"They set you up to kill someone?"

He growls, low and throaty. "Let me fuckin' finish."

I close my mouth.

"I had every intention of shooting that fucker, but it was set-up that I'd end up in the same place as Johan. I got a call out to there sayin' shit was goin' down with another club. Took another one of the boys and went to check it out. When I arrived, I saw nothin'. I went inside the coffee shop to check things out further and he was there, that filthy, motherfucker. I'd been lookin' for him for a long fuckin' time, and there he was. I lost my shit, pullin' out my gun and shovin' it at him. People freaked out, screaming and causing shit. I told them all to get down and stare at the fuckin' floor. I couldn't deal with them. I was wavin' my gun around like a mad man. It wasn't my finest moment."

My mouth opens.

"You need to understand I was blinded by rage. I didn't care about the people around me. They were all face-down when I shot Johan in the head, doubtin' anyone saw much—it's why witnesses were sketchy."

Makes sense.

"Screams broke out, Whiskey came in, and before I knew it shots were comin' in through the doors. They killed the rest of his family. Cops showed up minutes later, arresting me. The witnesses missed most of it, but there was enough evidence to assume I killed them all—

I was the one they saw wavin' the gun around, so why wouldn't it be me? I was arrested."

"What did he do to you that would make you so angry?" I whisper, eyes wide.

"That ain't any of your business. All you need to know is that I didn't kill the rest of them. I'm sure if they did their fuckin' research, they would see the bullets weren't from my gun." He snorts loudly. "Or maybe they were. Howard and his club are fuckin' clever."

"What you're telling me is that this other club shot the rest of his family, making it look like you did it."

"That's exactly what I'm tellin' you. They even cut the cameras so no one would see it. It was fuckin' crazy; people were everywhere. It wouldn't have been hard for them to slip shots in. I know Howard has some fuckin' good shooters. These people deal with bad shit. They have contacts with the cartel. They aren't the kind of people to fuck around."

"They said there was another man with you?"

He nods. "Whiskey, one of the boys, was checkin' out the café next door. He came in when he heard the shot. A few people saw him, hence why testaments were comin' through that another man was there. I'd already shot Johan when he came in. I made him leave before the cops arrived, but he took my gun with him – not exactly sure why. He got questioned, but said fuckin' nothin'. He won't say nothin' either, until this shit is sorted. Club code."

"Why?" I gasp. "He could have confirmed your story!"

"No," he mutters. "He needed to inform Maddox, and I didn't have time to get a call in. It was better that way."

I think about the witnesses that came forward, and how some of them were telling a very different story. His version makes sense, because logically, they would have missed the actual shooting part. It would be easy to assume it was Beau, since he was the only one they saw with a gun . . .

"What do the prison guards have to do with any of this?" I ask, narrowing my eyes as I try to piece it all together in my head.

"They're on the fuckin' inside. Howard paid them good fuckin' money to feed information. The prison transfer, it was all a big fuckin' set-up. They said they were movin' me for fighting? I had one fuckin' real fight; it wasn't enough to be moved. It was all set-up through the group of them workin' with him. They were plannin' an ambush, only they weren't expecting Maddox: they were expectin' Howard."

I shake my head, trying to clear it. "You're telling me they were expecting Howard? What was he going to do? Take you?"

"I have no fuckin' idea what he was goin' to do, but if Maddox didn't get in first, I would have found out."

"How did Maddox know?"

"Maddox is a fuckin' smart man. He has contacts everywhere. Not only did he manage to get hold of one of Howard's men's guns, he also shot those fuckers with it. When they search the club house they won't find me, and they won't find you, because it's goin' to look like Howard is the one at hand."

Oh God. My head spins with all this information.

"Why did Howard put you in prison, and then try to ambush them to get you out?"

He chuckles, but it's a deep, terrifying sound. "Don't you fuckin' see? He was tryin' to set the club up. I have no fuckin' doubt that man had the same idea we had, and was goin' to plant evidence to show it was the Jokers' who took out those prison guards—only we got in first. He probably would have then taken me and killed me, just for shit's sake."

"And in doing that he could have likely brought down hell upon your club."

He nods. "We would have had cops all over us. Fuck, more of us would have gone to prison. It would have caused an all-out war that would have ended fuckin' badly. He wants to put our club on the cops' radar, because they're tryin' to run some seriously bad shit through the town. If the cops aren't on their tail, they can do it easier."

"Isn't it going to cause a war now?"

"Absolutely," he mutters. "But if we go down, that little cunt is comin' down with us."

Oh, boy.

"And when they find you, won't you just go right back?"

"Not if we have the evidence to show that it wasn't me who pulled that trigger. If we set it up right, Howard will go down hard and so will his club."

"You still killed someone."

He looks away, not answering.

I can tell by the stiffness in his shoulders that this conversation is over. We sit in an eerie silence for a long, long time before he finally turns back and pulls the food off the small fire. He places it down and goes to open it, but ends up slipping and burning his fingers. He roars and leaps backwards, cursing loudly.

I don't think, I just rush forward and take his finger. I pop it into my mouth. My mom used to do this when I burned my fingers as a child, so it's just an instant reaction. The moment I realize that I have a big, thick finger in my mouth and a biker's eyes on my face, filled with shock and lust, my cheeks flush.

"You wanna be very fuckin' careful what your next move is," he growls. "'Cause baby, if you keep suckin' my finger like that it's goin' to be a long night for me and you."

Oh, boy.

I let his finger fall from my lips. The sexual tension is thick between us. "I . . ." I swallow. "I, ah . . . it helps take the burn out, I didn't think, and . . ."

His eyes are on me, and God, do I feel them burning into my deepest, darkest parts. "Been a good fuckin' month since I've felt a sweet pussy around my dick; best be careful about how you are around me. I've had a glimpse of what you've got goin' on underneath those clothes, and baby, believe me when I say I want a fuckin' taste."

Oh . . . my.

The air becomes thick around us, and I hear nothing but the faint sound of crickets chirping about in the trees. I swallow, and it seems like it takes forever to get the lump out of my throat. Krypt's eyes are on mine, intense and wanting, and fucked if I don't want to lean forward and capture his mouth with mine.

He's the one to move his eyes away first. He turns back to the food, pulling the can open quickly. I watch him, my eyes never moving from his large back as he pours the contents into bowls. He spins around and hands me one. I take it wearily, not meeting his gaze. We sit side by side, eating in silence.

"Are you hurtin'?"

I turn to stare at him, confused by his question. "Hurting?"

"Your arm? Your body? Is it hurtin'?"

I shift, feeling a dull ache in my ribs. I don't actually think I broke them, but I came close. "I am okay, thanks."

We fall silent again. I have so many questions eating at me.

"Hey, Beau?"

He stops eating, and flashes his gaze in my direction. "Yeah?"

"You're saying Tristan is a part of all this?"

He nods. "Tristan is most certainly part of all this."

"He's . . . I just . . ." I stop, gathering my thoughts. "He was my friend. If you'd asked me weeks ago, I would have said I trusted him one hundred percent. Then I saw stuff going down, and I doubted him . . ."

"Not your fault, babe," he murmurs. "It's clear you're a good chick, and a loyal one."

Was that a compliment?

"I know that, but I trusted him, and it hurts to know that he could use a prisoner for his own gain."

"He's bein' paid top dollar."

"He could lose his career," I whisper, meeting Beau's gaze.

He reaches over, running his thumb along my jaw. "Not everyone gives a fuck about their career, babe. People like you, who care about their jobs, and show the passion you do, are hard to find."

Tears burn in my eyes and I turn away, staring down at my half-empty bowl of the bad tasting tinned beans.

"He could have had you killed," I breathe. "That's never okay. It doesn't matter what a prisoner has done. It isn't his place, and it isn't his job . . . It would make him no better than half the people in that place."

"You're right about that, it's why he was hopin' never to get caught. He knows what he'd lose and he knows he'd quickly become one of them . . ."

"He deserves to be one of them," I growl.

"Hey," he says, reaching over and cupping my jaw in his hand. "Look at me, Ash."

My name on his lips has my entire body breaking out in shivers.

"You, girl, are a good fuckin' person. I saw it in the time I was there. I saw how those prisoners respected you. Don't you ever let that fucker bring you down. When you get outta here—and babe, you will get outta here—then you will go back and have your head held fuckin' high, because you're ten times the person any of those assholes are."

His words warm me in more ways than one. I like the fact that he thinks I'll get my job back, and I love that he's willing to make sure I'll get out of here.

"What do you think will happen to me when I go back?"

He brings my face closer, sending trembles up my spine. Warm puffs of his breath heat my lips as he speaks. "I'll make sure nothin' bad happens to you when you go back. You have my fuckin' word on that."

"Why?" I breathe.

"Because you're the only fuckin' real person I've met in the last ten years of my life. Because you gave me respect and put me in my place when I needed it. And because you kicked my president in the balls."

I laugh softly. "It wasn't my finest moment."

He grins, showing me a perfect, masculine jaw that transforms when his mouth moves. "It was a fuckin' great moment, babe. You showed him you weren't some pansy fuckin' bitch that he could push around. It showed him you were serious."

"He could have killed me," I point out.

"I don't fuckin' doubt that, but he won't now, so you're good."

I'm not sure if that comforts me, but I'll let it slide for now. Krypt lets my jaw go and turns back. He pulls out a blanket and lays it out. "It's goin' to get cold tonight. You got any issues layin' beside me?"

"That depends." I smile, unable to stop myself.

He raises a brow. "On what?"

"Well, are you going to try and have your way with me?"

He smirks. "That depends."

I laugh. "On what?"

"If you want me to have my way with you."

I flush and bite my lip, looking away.

"You want to be fucked, Wildcard? You keen to have my cock inside you?"

God, why is he so dirty? I'm supposed to hate him. He stole me, killed some guards, and has spilled some pretty bad information in the last few hours, and yet I don't hate him. It probably comes from the time we spent in the prison together. We'd developed some sort of bond, but all the same, it's a bad situation. I'm quiet for so long. He finally says, "You scared of me?"

I turn to him. "I kicked your president in the balls. What do you think?"

"Seriously, babe. Are you scared of me?"

I shake my head, keeping my eyes locked on his. "No. For whatever reason, I don't think you're goin' to hurt me."

"You're right about that," he murmurs. "I don't think I will."

I swallow.

He tilts his head to the side, studying me. "You know what I think you're really scared of?" he pauses for a moment. "I think it bothers you that you might actually want it."

I smirk. "Don't tell me you think I'm one of those women who will blush and turn away because you're putting me on the spot."

Oh, he has me pegged all wrong. This situation scares me, *he* scares me just a little, his president scares me a whole lot, but admitting to my needs has never scared me. I've always been one to say what I want.

He narrows his eyes. "Aren't you goin' to tell me that you can't stand me, and there's no way in hell I'm gettin' my cock near you?"

I snort. "You read too many books. No, I'm not going to tell you that. Firstly, I don't hate you, Beau. I don't know what your life is about, but there's a big story behind your stormy eyes, and I'm sure you have a reason for being the way you are."

His eyes darken, but he says nothing.

"And secondly, I haven't been fucked for over twelve months. I might be pissed at you for hurting me and dragging me into the wilderness, but I won't deny that the idea of fucking you turns me on."

He growls, like a feral, hungry beast.

It turns me on, big time.

"Shit. I've never met a girl like you, know that?"

I shrug. "I endeavor to be different. I've always been the girl that stands her ground. I was never going to be anyone's whore, but I was never going to be the girl that played coy, either. If I want to fuck, biker," I lean in close, "I'll fuck."

His eyes flash.

"And do you want to fuck, babe?"

I tilt my head to the side. "I haven't decided yet."

He makes a rumbling sound in his chest. "Let me know when you do, eh?"

I grin. "Yeah."

"Now get in here and go to sleep. It's been nearly twenty-four hours and you've only had two hours in that time."

He points to the made-up bed. He leans down and shoves the pack under the blanket, making a pillow. Then he turns to me and jerks his chin towards it. I stare at the space, and then narrow my eyes. "What about you?"

He shrugs. "Slept on worse."

I pull my coat tighter around me. I am tired. I position myself on the blanket and find a comfortable position. Krypt drops down beside me, pulling the blanket over us, then his big arms going up behind his head.

"Why a guard?" he asks suddenly.

I think about his question. "Honestly? I don't know. I wanted to do something different. I never wanted to be the office girl, or the checkout chick; I wanted to do something challenging that gave me access to all walks of life."

"Must be a tough job sometimes?"

"It is." I sigh. "Sometimes I wonder why I do it, but then I try to consider something else and fail."

"You're good at it; take it from me."

I smile. "Thanks."

"I'm still takin' you on when you're not hurtin'. I want to see you fight."

I laugh. "I'll bring you to your knees, biker, don't doubt it."

He chuckles. "Yeah, babe. We'll see. Get some sleep."

He doesn't have to ask me twice.

CHAPTER EIGHT

I'm cold.

No, that doesn't cut it—I'm so fucking freezing my teeth are rattling, and my entire body is shaking from head to toe. I can't feel my nose, and I certainly can't feel the rest of my body. I have rolled at least five times, trying to curl myself up to get warm, but there is no hope. My body is too sore to bend that much.

"Stop fuckin' wigglin'," Krypt barks.

"I'm freezing. Seriously, my nipples are going to drop off," I cry.

"Come here," he orders.

"What? No."

"You want your nipples to fuckin' drop off?"

"No!"

"Then get over here."

He reaches out and his warm hand curls around my cold one. He pulls back with a curse. "Fuck me."

"I told you I was cold. How are you so warm?"

"Leather," he mutters.

He reaches back out and pulls me towards him. The freezing air hits my skin as the blanket moves, and I cry out. Krypt takes me into his arms, tucking my hand under his jacket and forcing my face into his shoulder. He's so warm. My fingers are resting on his hard, muscled chest, and I can't help but notice how damned nice that feels.

"Shit. You're like a damned ice cube."

"It's not my fault. You were the one who dragged me up here."

He mutters a curse, and uses his arm to furiously rub my free shoulder. I find myself getting warmer right away.

"You know what they say about gettin' warm . . ."

"Don't even think about it," I warn.

He chuckles. "Can't blame a man for tryin' when he's got a girl in his arms."

"I bet I'm the only girl you've had in your arms that you haven't fucked."

"You're right about that," he snorts. "You talk the most, too."

"Be grateful. I could be screaming at you."

"Or—"

"Don't," I cut him off.

I know he's grinning, and if it were light, he'd know I was, too. I tuck my leg in his, and my body slowly begins to defrost. My eyes get heavy and his breathing evens out—then, before I know it, we're asleep again.

This time warm.

This time tangled in each other.

~*~*~*~`

The morning comes like a bad cold. My entire body hurts, and every muscle aches. I shift out of the hard, warm body I'm pressed against, desperate to pee. I roll and push to my knees, groaning quietly. Jesus, I'm never sleeping on the ground again. I look over to Krypt, who is sleeping quite soundly. He looks gorgeous during slumber, his big chest rising and falling softly. His dark lashes fan out over his chiseled cheekbones.

If I were a stupid girl, I'd take this chance and run. I'm not stupid, though. I know exactly how it would end: with me dead, or worse, mountain lion poop. Besides, with all this information that I've been fed in the last day, I'm not sure being home is the safest option for me right now. Something about Krypt makes me feel safe, like he's exactly where I should be right now.

Either that or my thoughts are clouded with lust and I'm fucked.

I push to my feet and step out of the overhanging rock area. The fog is so thick this morning that I can't see a foot in front of me. Great. I'm probably going to walk right into the jaws of mega lion. Swallowing, I tilt my head to the side and listen. I can only hear the sounds of birds, water and . . . nothing else. Thank God.

I walk forward, deciding to go with just walking in a straight line. I put my hands out in front of me, dodging trees. I turn back, hearing Krypt shuffling around. Nope, too close. He cannot, under any circumstances, listen to me pee. I keep walking forward. The trees thin out just slightly. I can hear the sound of trickling water.

I don't realize that the water is so close until I'm slipping down a bank, screaming, my sore body flying over rocks and jagged pieces of branch. I land in the cold water with a splash. It's freezing, as if tiny ice shards are stabbing me all over my body. I wail in agony, coughing and spluttering, splashing around as I try to find the surface. It's too damned foggy.

"The fuck? Ash?" Krypt yells.

"Help!" I squeal.

I hear his boots crunching as I struggle to get out of the water. I manage to pull myself up the bank, shivering violently. I reach the top and fall flat on my face. My entire body burns all over. It's so cold I can't even feel my injuries anymore. Krypt's boots pound through the silence, and I know he's getting closer. The fog is starting to clear, but I still can't see him.

"Where are you?" he yells.

"H-h-h-here," I stammer, my lips trembling.

I pull myself forward just as he comes into view. He stares down at me and his eyes widen. "What the hell are you doin'?"

"I was trying to pee!" I yell. "I didn't see the water."

He presses his lips together and I shoot him a warning look. "Do. Not. Laugh."

He clearly can't help himself, because he barks a laugh as he reaches down, pulling me up. "There are plenty of trees near the cave, and you walk all the way out here to piss."

"I didn't want you to hear me," I protest.

He wraps his arms around me. "You're fuckin' freezing. Come on, we need to get you dry."

God, I'm cold, and my legs are aching so badly they actually hurt. Krypt takes me back to the cave and sits me down. He lifts the blanket and then hesitates before saying, "Clothes off."

My eyes widen. "I . . . I . . . I . . . beg your pardon."

He leans in closer. "I didn't fuckin' stutter. Clothes off."

I stare at him like he's lost his mind. I mean, he must have, right? He can't expect me to strip.

"Either you do it, Ash, or I will."

"I'm not showing my naked body to you."

"Nothin' wrong with it, so I don't see why."

Oh he's being funny. I glare up at him. "There is something wrong with it. My ass does not look good outside of these jeans."

He grins. *Asshole.*

"I think I'll be the judge of that."

"Trust me, buddy," I snort, shifting, "you don't wanna see what I'm packing. I am not one of your skinny little Barbie dolls."

"What makes you think I want skinny little Barbie dolls?"

I glare at him. "Don't you?"

He kneels down in front of me, smirking. "You'll never know. Now get your clothes off."

"Turn around."

He rolls his eyes, but he turns around. I quickly strip out of my clothes and reach for the blanket. He lets it go easily enough. I pull it around me, and sigh at its warmth. He turns and stares at me for a moment before lifting my clothes. He lays them out over the other blanket near the fire. "Only you would wet your clothes when we need to get movin'."

"Well, I didn't know there was a damned river there."

He raises his brows. "You deaf, sweetheart?"

"Fuck you."

He grins and comes over, sitting down beside me. "You're freezing."

"No shit."

He reaches over, taking my shoulders and pulling me closer to him.

"Ah, what are you doing?"

"I'm warming you up," he says, matter-of-factly.

"No thank you."

He chuckles. "Wasn't askin' you, babe."

"You're trying to cop a feel, and it's not going to happen."

He pulls me so close I'm tucked into his side, his big arm slung around my shoulder. I can smell the leather of his jacket crossed with the scent of him . . . just man. All man. It's musky and a little dirty, and my body reacts to it. My skin prickles and I have to press my legs together as I feel my sex becoming damp.

"Fuck," he growls. "I can fuckin' smell you."

"What?" I gasp, horrified.

"You . . . you smell like fuckin' sex. It's like your body just flipped a damned switch and let me know what you're too scared to tell me."

"Don't flatter yourself," I breathe.

He makes a grumbling sound and scoots back, shifting so I'm between his legs. He wraps his big arms around me, bringing my back to his chest. I stiffen. Oh boy, this is some situation we're in right now. I close my eyes, clenching them tightly. I'm trying very hard to think about anything else right now.

"Stop it," he growls.

"Stop what?" I whisper. "I'm not doing anything."

"You're makin' me fuckin' hard with that smell."

Jesus.

Do I smell? Really?

I think it's bath time for me.

He parts the blanket just slightly, slipping his hand beneath.

"Whoa, hand out," I yell, only it comes out like a shaky, half-assed plea.

"Don't pretend you don't want my fuckin' hand in there. I'm not goin' to fuck you, babe."

"That depends on what you consider fucking," I whimper as his fingers find my belly.

"I consider it fucking," he murmurs, his breath against my ear, "when my cock is deep inside you, and you're screamin' my name."

"Okay then," I breathe. "Well, I consider anything entering my body, fucking."

I can nearly feel him grinning against my ear. "I don't have to put anything in your body to warm you up, Wildcard."

"H-h-h-how is this warming me up?"

His fingers slide up and down my belly, stroking the soft skin there, causing little shivers to break out across my skin. His hand inches higher, finding the swell of my breasts. He gently caresses the skin there, before sliding up and cupping my breast. I gasp and wiggle, but he uses his other hand to press firmly against my belly so I can't move.

"Believe me, in five minutes, you'll be warm."

I can't answer him. My entire body has come alive. It's been a while since I've been touched, and having this man's hands on me feels so erotic, so forbidden. I close my eyes, biting my lip so hard that I taste coppery blood. He shifts closer to me and I can feel his bulging cock in his jeans, pressing against my back.

All I can see of him is his booted feet by my side and some sexy-as-fuck black jeans. He presses his lips against my neck, and my nipples turn into little hard tips within seconds. He purrs against me, making a low, rumbling sound that has everything coming to life. In a big, big way.

"I can make you warm, baby. Just say the word and I'll make it all fuckin' better."

Oh I just bet he will.

"I . . ." I croak. That's it; it's the best I can do. That would be because his fingers are trailing down my belly towards my extremely aroused sex. His mouth is on my neck, his cock pressed against my back, and he's about to finger fuck me. Even I'm not that strong . . . I mean come on . . . Who could say no to that?

"Spread your legs for me," he growls into my ear.

My legs seem to do as they're told before my brain kicks in, and my knees drop open.

"Yeah, babe, that's the way."

His fingers dip into my sensitive folds and I whimper, arching my back. God, I'm so wet I can feel it coating him, making a slick passage for him to do as he pleases. He makes a deep, rumbling sound in his chest as his fingers find my clit and begin massaging it.

"Oh God," I whimper. "Yes."

"So eager," he hisses. "I'm goin' to fuck you with my fingers, babe. Are you good with that?"

Good? I couldn't be better.

"Yes," I breathe.

He releases my clit, which causes a groan to slide from my lips. He slips his fingers lower until he finds my entrance and then gently, he pushes one thick finger inside. I arch again and he uses his hand against my belly to keep me from going too far once more. Holy sweet mother of God, he feels amazing.

He tilts his fingers up as his lips graze over my neck again. "You're so fuckin' tight. Takin' everything inside me not to fuck you hard and fast right now."

Oh.

Yes.

I grind my teeth together as pleasure takes over. Oh . . . yes. He thrusts once more and I come, blissfully slow. My entire body shoots pleasure out in strands that start from my pussy, and work their way right up until my nerve endings stand on alert and my skin prickles. Krypt rewards me with a low, guttural moan that makes this so much better.

When I stop trembling, he slides his fingers from my depths and lifts them to my mouth. "Open."

"What?" I stammer.

"Suck yourself off me. Now is your time to suck my finger, baby."

I hesitate. I've never had anyone in my life be so . . . bold. He presses his finger against my lips and I close my eyes, parting my mouth. He slips his finger inside and groans as I close my lips around it. I suck, surprised that it's in no way near what I thought it would be. He thrusts his cock up against my back and I whimper.

"You're goin' to give me blue balls by the time we're done here," he growls.

I smile, and pop his finger out of my mouth. "Oh, didn't I tell you? That's the plan."

He chuckles and moves back. I turn and watch him adjusting his jeans before he leans down and takes my clothes. "They're dry enough. We gotta make tracks."

"So that's it? You're going to love me and leave me?"

He grins at me, big and beautiful. "Either that or I can pull my cock out, and you can suck this ache right out of it."

I flush and shove to my feet, taking the blanket with me. He laughs as I gather my clothes. "Didn't think so."

We finish packing and dressing, then we're on our way again. The track becomes narrow and ragged, barely recognizable. We climb over rocks and duck under trees—seriously, it would be hard for anyone to find this place. We don't talk a whole lot. Both of us are no doubt desperate for a shower and some shelter. The quicker we get there, the better. We only stop once when Krypt gives me some painkillers and food, and then we're back to it.

When early afternoon falls, I'm exhausted. I'm thinking we have to be close. God, I pray we're close. We're going extra slow, because of my sore body, so I know this has taken far longer than it usually would.

"Here we are," Krypt says, snapping me out of my daze. Well, I guess my prayers were answered, because ahead of us is a large, I mean . . . super large cabin sitting in amongst the trees. It's similar to the one below; only this one has two sheds either side of it and a barbed wire fence. Yes, a barbed wire fence.

"Why is there fence around it?" I ask.

"This used to a be a clubhouse, back when Maddox's dad ran the club. Once it had a track running up into it from the left, for bikes."

"Why did they change it?"

"For a few reasons," he says, pulling a key from his pack and unlocking the fence. "The first was it's so far out of town, and they were finding it hard to keep in the loop. Of course it had the bonus of being a secretive place."

"And the second?"

"T-Rex died."

"T-Rex?" I ask.

"Maddox's old man. He died, and Maddox wanted the club closer, but I think he just hated this place. He had a rough upbringing."

"Oh."

"So now we keep it in case anyone needs to hide out, and sometimes the boys come up just for a break. It gets used more than you'd think."

"How do they get up here?"

"Same way we did, babe." He smirks, swinging the gate open.

"They walk that far?"

"Clearly it wouldn't be just an overnight thing. They'd come for a week or so."

Interesting.

I stare ahead as we enter the massive space. While it's set amongst trees, it's been cleared enough to allow for the two sheds and the cabin. I take in the cabin first. It's old, but it's clearly held its age quite well. It's huge—I'd guess it has at least four bedrooms inside. The sheds off to the left and right are rusting metal, and are bolted with thick padlocks.

Krypt walks up the front steps of the cabin and I quickly follow him. The dusty porch is huge, and wraps around the entire thing. It's got some old furniture, old beer bottles and . . . boots. I raise my brows but don't ask; I just stay behind Krypt. The door is rickety and squeaks when he pushes it open.

At first glance, the cabin is quite nice. It needs a good dusting, and the furniture definitely needs updating, but it's nice. It's got a large, open living and dining area, which have been designed to incorporate pool tables, a few large lounges, and a bar. There's a small kitchen in the corner. This all narrows off to a long hall I see doors branching off of. I'm assuming those are the rooms.

"How many rooms are in this place?" I ask, peering around.

"Six."

"Six?" I gasp.

Krypt turns to me, and nods. "Yeah, six."

I'm shocked. I follow Krypt down the halls. The wooden floors creak as we move. I count all six bedrooms, a bathroom and toilet, a laundry, and a large storage closet. It is a massive place.

"Take your pick of the rooms, but take it from me: go with the first or the last."

"Do I want to know why?"

He smirks at me. "'Cause when the boys come, they like to bring whores."

"Whores?" I blink.

"Club whores . . ." he says, nodding, as if I'm supposed to understand.

"Club whores?"

"For Christ's sake, that's what I just fuckin' said."

I cross my arms. "Keep your shirt on, I was only asking."

"Club whores enjoy the men, and the men enjoy them. Most clubs have a group of them that hang around. They know what they are. They don't do relationships, though occasionally one of them wants to become an old lady."

"Does that ever happen?"

He swings a door open and points to the large space. "Yeah, it does, but she's usually gotta have somethin' different about her. Most whores aren't the kind us guys want for old ladies."

"Do you have an old lady?" I ask, stepping into the room and staring. It's massive, with a double bed, an old couch, and a desk, with a small bathroom to the left.

"Did I just have my fingers inside your pussy?" he asks.

I blink and turn to him. "What?"

"My fingers, sweetheart," he growls. "Were they in your pussy?"

"Ah, yes."

"Then no, I don't have an old lady."

I lean my hip against the doorframe. "I thought it didn't matter."

He raises his brows. "To some it doesn't; they'll fuck around. A lot of them have a piece of ass on the side, but most of them respect their old ladies."

"Right," I mutter.

"Don't believe me?"

I push off the door. "I do."

"You're a bad fuckin' liar."

I snort and stop at the bed, throwing myself down onto it. "Oh God, it's so soft."

"Best bed in the house."

I sit up, leaning on my elbows. "Did you fuck in this bed?"

His brows shoot up. "Who asks those kind of fuckin' questions?"

"Me. I want to know how many times I need to wash these sheets."

He shakes his head, running his hand through his hair. "Yeah, babe, I've fucked in that bed. About ten times. So have all the other club members. It's a *club*house."

"Ew," I say, leaping off it and quickly stripping all the sheets off the bed. "Tell me there's washing powder or something in this place?"

He smirks as I rush past him, and take all the sheets into the laundry room, shoving them into the machine, and tipping a heap of powder in. I set the machine and then turn. "There goes the idea of sleeping being the first thing I do."

He nods his head towards the kitchen. "Don't know about you, but I'm fuckin' hungry."

My stomach growls. "Is there even any food up here?"

He nods. "It's stocked."

"How?"

He sighs. "What do you mean *how*?"

"How is it stocked?"

"The boys stocked it."

"But how?"

He spins around. "For fuck's sake, woman!"

I cross my arms and stare at him. "Well . . ."

"Fine," he barks. "There is a track heading up here that can be accessed only by bikes, it may or may not be still open."

I gape. "Are you fucking serious?" I screech.

He groans and crosses his arms. "Here we go."

"You made me walk when we could have . . . rode?"

"Yeah, I did, because I can't fuckin' be on the roads."

Dang. He makes a point.

"We could have ridden with your brothers . . ."

"No, we couldn't. If they got pulled up, they'd be fucked."

I huff and walk towards the kitchen. "I hope there's some good food in this place."

We get into the kitchen and I pull open the fridge. There's a good load of food in there ranging from fresh fruit and vegetables, to deli meats and bread. My stomach grumbles. I'm exhausted, and I know for a fact I don't have energy to make anything special. I pull out some bread, ham and cheese and spin around, placing them on the counter.

"You eat this?" I ask, laying the bread out.

Krypt hands me a chopping board and knife. "I'll eat whatever you give me."

I prepare the sandwiches and grab a few sodas out of the fridge. We both drop down onto the couch and sigh. My legs are aching. I wish this place had a bath. Really, that would be awesome. I lift my sandwich and take a bite. Krypt has half of his gone in, like, three mouthfuls. I give him a disgusted look.

"What?" he mutters.

"That's wrong. Seriously."

"I'm a man. I eat; I don't nibble."

"I'm not nibbling." I pout.

"Yeah, you fuckin' are. Eat like a man, babe."

I roll my eyes and keep eating at my own pace.

"You're settlin' very well for a prisoner."

"It could be worse," I say. "You could have killed me."

"I was never goin' to kill you, Ash."

The sincerity in his voice has me turning and staring at him. He meets my gaze, and an intense silence fills the room. Oh boy. "You weren't?" I finally ask.

"I don't kill women unless it comes down to life or death, for me or someone I cared about. You weren't one of them; I knew that. I wasn't goin' to let you take a bullet. I was just bein' an asshole when I said the club would kill you." He winks.

I give him a weak smile. "Well, thanks."

"You trust me, don't you?"

I blink at him. "Pardon?"

"You trust me. I can tell you do. You're not scared, and you've only tried to run once."

I shrug. "I saw you in there; I never thought you would hurt me. I won't lie and say I wasn't terrified when your guys shot and killed the guards, but it didn't take me long to realize I was not in any immediate danger."

"You're in danger, though; you do know that, right?"

"How so?"

"There is a war brewin', and while you're with us you're right in the middle of it."

"It would seem I wasn't really that safe where I was, anyway."

"No. You were bein' used."

"Do you really think they were using me?" I ask, turning towards him and crossing my legs.

"Did you get asked constant questions about me? Did they ask you what I'd told you? What you'd learned?"

I gasp. Tristan asked me every day if I'd gotten new information out of Krypt. He was setting me up because he knew I had a connection with the prisoners? He was trying to use that connection to get information. Then he went out of his way to put me in that truck for the transfer. My chest seizes at the realization that someone I cared about had been using me and because of that, I was nearly killed.

"You okay?" Krypt asks.

"I'm fine," I say quickly, standing. "I'm going to shower."

"Ash," he calls out, but I'm already halfway down the hall.

The minute I get into my room, I press my hands to my head. I trusted Tristan; I'd considered him a friend, and all along he was just using me to feed information to a club on the outside. It was all a damned big set-up. Was any of it genuine? Did he care about me at all, or was he pretending with that, too?

~*~*~*~

I spend longer than needed in the shower. I wash my hair, shave my legs, soap my skin, and then spend an hour brushing my brown locks out. I pull on some of the clothes left for me: a pair of short shorts and a turtle-neck sweater. I don't even want to think about the fact that these could be some club-whore's clothes.

I head back out to Beau, and find him on the phone at the kitchen counter. My eyes widen when I take him in, and I stop, unable to take another step. He's standing with his back to me, phone pressed to his ear. He's not wearing a shirt, and all I can see is one hell of a muscled back and a massive—no, scratch that—gigantic tattoo.

I squint, trying not to take in the way his jeans hang low on his hips, or the tiny dimples on his lower back. Instead, I focus on the tattoo. It's a gorgeous piece of artwork of a girl. She's only young in the picture, maybe ten. She's got long, golden hair and a gorgeous, dimpled smile. Underneath the tattoo, there is one word: *Lace*.

Like on his knuckles?

Interesting.

He must hear me, because he turns his body, taking me off-guard. I straighten and quickly force my eyes up to his. He narrows his, studying me. His body distracts me, far too quickly. Holy mother of

God, it's like he was built to be a statue. Rippled abs, a broad chest with a light scattering of hair that's just barely there, biceps to make your mouth water and a *V* that you want to lick all the way down to his . . . oh God . . . I'm staring at his cock. I jerk my head up to meet his smirk. Shit; he caught me. I flush and turn my gaze away, staring at the painting on the wall.

"Yeah, got it," he mutters into the phone.

Silence.

"I said I fuckin' got it, Maddox. I'll sort it out as soon as I can."

He grunts.

"Yeah, bye."

He hangs up the phone and takes a step towards me. I quickly focus back on him, and gasp when I realize just how close he is. He reaches out, taking a lock of my damp hair. He twirls it about, staring down at me like he wants to eat me alive.

"Did you enjoy the view?"

I snort. "What view?"

He chuckles and tugs me closer. "I saw you starin' at my cock. How long has it been since you've been fucked, sweetheart?"

I shove him back. "You already know that answer," I huff. "Go and jerk yourself. It's clear you're struggling."

He grins and winks at me, before stepping back and throwing his phone and wallet onto the counter. "I'm showerin'. Stay here. Don't try and run or you'll get eaten alive by some wild creature."

"You're an asshole," I say, leaning my hip against the counter.

"Never said I wasn't, babe," he scoffs, turning and walking down the hall.

I watch him go, and the minute I hear the shower start, I breathe a sigh of relief and turn, taking hold of his phone. Honestly . . . he just left it here. Maybe it's a test? I don't really care; I'm taking the bait. I unlock it and my heart flutters when I see it has no passcode. Silly, silly man.

I dial Claire's number.

"Hello?" she answers after three rings.

"Claire, it's me."

"Ash!" she cries. "Oh my God, Ash!"

"It's me, I'm okay."

"We didn't know," she says, her voice shaky. "We've been looking for you. They found dead bodies and . . ." Her voice croaks before breaking off.

"It's okay," I soothe. "I'm okay."

"Where are you? What happened?"

"I'm . . . I can't really say right now, but I just want you to know I'm safe. I needed you to hear that."

"I've been so worried," she sobs. "I thought you were dead."

"I'm okay," I say again. I feel like it's all I can say.

"Should I call the police?"

"No," I say quickly. "No, it's fine. I . . . things are going down, and right now I don't know what's safest. Just sit back; I'm okay, and if I need to I will contact you again."

"Put. That. Fuckin'. Phone. Down."

Beau's voice is like a whip, lashing across my nervous system and causing my hands to shake.

"I have to go, I love you," I whisper, hanging up the phone.

I turn slowly to see him standing at the entryway, towel wrapped around his waist, his body still damp, hair dripping down his forehead. He obviously heard me, because it's clear he's just jumped out of the shower and hasn't dried himself. I slowly put the phone down, placing it on the counter. Beau storms towards me. "What the fuck is wrong with you?"

"I needed my friend to know I was okay. I didn't call the police."

"You fuckin' idiot," he roars. "You didn't need to call the police; all she needs to do is go to the cops and they'll fuckin' tap her phone, find where the call came from."

"I . . ."

"You don't fuckin' think," he barks. "Do you think I stole you just for any good reason? That I just thought 'hey, this'll be a fuckin' hoot'.

Fuck me, Ash. Shit is goin' down, big shit that could put your life in danger. I have you here for your protection, when I really could have left you in that fuckin' truck."

"Oh no you don't," I growl. "You aren't protecting me. I was in the wrong place at the wrong time. It's the only reason I'm here."

"Fuckin' shit," he snarls, crossing his big arms across his chest. "I pulled you in here because I wasn't goin' to let them put a bullet in you. I coulda left you there; don't you fuckin' forget that."

"My family need to know I'm okay, do you understand me? She won't call the cops. I made sure of it," I yell, throwing my hands up.

"Fuckin' women," he hisses, storming forward and taking the phone. He picks it up and dials.

"Maddox, it's me. We got a problem."

His jaw tics.

"Ash made a fuckin' call."

I hear Maddox blow up on the other end.

"Yeah, it was my fuckin' fault. I left the phone, it won't happen again. She didn't call the cops."

He sighs and closes his eyes. "I fuckin' know. The phone will get smashed."

A deep breath.

"I fuckin' know," he bellows. "She said her friend won't ring the cops."

I shift, feeling a little guilty.

"Well, I have no choice but to believe her."

He growls once more and then ends the call, spinning to me. "Get in your room, now."

"Not sure that's a good idea," I say, taking a step back.

He lunges for me, catching hold of my wrist and hurling me so hard against his body he loses his towel. I squeal, but he keeps his arm pinned around me, pressing my thighs against his very naked body. His cock is resting on my belly. Even though I can't feel the skin, I can feel its presence there.

"Your . . . your . . ."

"My fuckin' cock is on your stomach. If you keep misbehaving I'll find a better place for it."

Shit.

"Get it off me," I yell, squirming.

It twitches against my belly.

"Oh my God, stop it!"

He snorts, spinning me around. He presses my back to his chest and shoves us forward, heading down towards the room. The moment we reach the door, he pushes me inside. I stumble forward, landing on my knees. I turn without thinking, and come face to face with his cock. His very large, thick, pierced cock.

My eyes widen at the piercing. It's a big barbell going right through the head of his cock—I mean in one side, out the other. That would have hurt like a bitch. When I realize I'm staring, I throw myself backwards with a squeal.

"Jesus, do you want to take a fuckin' picture?" he growls, finding some jeans and jerking them on. "That's the second time you've looked at my cock."

"Well it was right in my face," I yell. "It was kind of hard to look away."

"Just admit it," he mumbles, lifting me up and throwing me on the bed. "You want it."

"Kiss my—"

"With pleasure, babe."

Asshole.

He leans over and ruffles through some drawers, and takes out a set of handcuffs. Oh hell no. I launch myself off the bed, but his hand wraps around my ankle before I get the chance to even get off. He jerks me backwards kicking and screaming, and then he flips me over effortlessly as if I'm merely laying here. He throws his body over mine.

He jerks my hands above my head and wrestles the handcuffs on. "Get off me," I screech, bringing my knee up to hit him, but he presses his body over mine so hard I can't get it high enough.

"You want to disobey me, you can stay attached to this bed."

"I didn't disobey you," I grunt, squirming. "You never told me I couldn't use the phone."

"You're a prisoner. When do prisoners ever get to use the phone?"

"I'm not a prisoner," I protest. "Prisoners don't get finger fucked."

He laughs, the piece of shit.

"Good point."

"Get off me," I wail angrily.

He shackles me down and then stares down at me, grey eyes on blue. "You comfortable?"

"I hate you."

"Can I get you anything?"

"Eat a big dick."

"Water? Food? A cock to shut that pretty mouth?"

"You even so much as think about putting that thing near my mouth and I'll—"

He kisses me.

He fucking kisses me.

And I like it; I can't lie. His lips are soft, his stubble scratchy in the best possible way against my cheeks. His tongue is forceful, yet sweet as hell. He kisses me until my mind is spinning and my heart is pounding. He keeps going until I'm wet for him, aching for him to slide between my legs and fuck me until I'm screaming his name.

Then he pulls away.

Asshole.

Mega asshole.

"Now, go to sleep and start behavin'."

He gets off me and leaves.

Leaves.

Jesus. It's going to be a long night.

CHAPTER NINE

I was right. It is a super long night. I toss, turn, groan and ache. By the time morning sheds its light through the window, I'm more exhausted then I was the day before.

Krypt comes in the room first thing, his hair ruffled with sleep, his jeans unbuttoned and hanging low enough that I can see the touch of hair poking out the top.

"Sleep?" he murmurs, lifting his hands, causing his muscles to flex. He runs them through his hair and down over his face.

"No, because I'm cuffed and sore."

He stares at me. "Why didn't you yell out?"

"Seriously?" I gape. "You put me here. I didn't think I had a choice."

He sighs and shakes his head. "Come on, I'll get you some food and then you can sleep some more."

He walks over and uncuffs me. The minute my hands are free, I shoot my fist out and I hit him in the side of his jaw. It clearly takes him by surprise because I get a decent, hard hit in. He roars and stumbles backwards, tripping on the rug and landing on his ass. I throw myself out of the bed, groaning in pain as my sore body moves.

"That's what you get for cuffing me, you big jerk-off," I growl, stepping over him.

"You'll fuckin' pay for that."

"Yeah, yeah, tell that to my fist."

I grin all the way down to the shower. I turn the water on and step underneath it. I groan and close my eyes, the warm water easing everything. Then suddenly, it turns freezing cold. I squeal and reach over to adjust the temperature, but it makes no difference. Then I realize that Krypt has obviously turned another tap on, probably a few, making the water run through cold.

"You piece of shit!" I bellow. "You'll pay!"

"Tell that to the washing machine." He laughs from down the hall.

I leap out, turning the taps off quickly. I wrap a towel around myself and charge out and down the hall. I step into the kitchen and without thinking, I speed towards him. He's grinning, his arms crossed over his chest. I don't even look at the rug on the floor, and just my luck, I topple straight over when my foot gets caught.

I land on the ground with a thump, and in my haste to get up my towel drops off. Literally, it just drops off. I squeal, grabbing for it, but Krypt is quicker. He reaches down and tugs it out, dangling it in front of me with a wicked laugh as I try to cover all my bits.

"I'll kill you," I cry. "Kill, slowly, with a blunt knife. I'm going for your eyes first, I'm going to pop them out and squash them. Give me my towel."

"Nice ass, babe." He chuckles.

"Fuck you," I bark. "You piece of shit."

I crawl towards him, hoping he can't see what I have to offer.

"Fuckin' nice tat, too."

"I'll stab you."

He kneels down, dangling the towel in front of me. "Best you reach up and get it."

I shove my hand out and I hit him clean in the nuts. He roars and topples backwards, and I take my chance to snatch my towel and turn to scurry away. He rolls, catching my wrist and pulling it out from underneath me. I land on my face with a cry. He throws himself towards me, taking my hands and flipping me over.

Then his body is over mine.

"Are you finished?" he breathes, staring down at me.

"Not even close," I growl.

"Then we'll stay here all fuckin' day."

"Get off me, you—"

"Do I need to kiss you again?" he asks, cutting me off.

"Fuck you."

"I can do that," he says, lazily making circles with his finger on my cheek. "All it would take is a quick jerk of my jeans, and then my cock would be sinking deep inside you. And trust me, sweetheart, I fuckin' want it there."

"You're a pig."

He leans down, bringing his lips so close to my ear. I shiver. "Don't pretend you don't like it. You would have loved to know I stroked over my cock last night, thinkin' of your sweet pussy. And baby, when I came, it felt so fuckin' good."

Oh God, why does he have to arouse me so? The very idea of his big, thick hands stroking over his cock, his abs clenching, his muscles pulling, has everything inside me coming to life.

"G-g-get used to your hand. It's all you'll get."

"We'll see about that."

His lips brush over my ear and I helplessly whimper.

"I think you'd like me to fuck you right now."

"You're wrong about that," I groan as he rocks his hips, pressing his jean-clad cock against my exposed pussy.

"Think I can make you come like this?"

"Don't even try it."

God, I sound so breathy. Like I'm not even trying to fight him off. He rocks his hips again, pressing against my core, causing my clit to jerk to life. I wish I could protest, but I can't fight the bolts of pleasure shooting through my body. He tucks his arm under my head and brings my lips up to his, gently brushing over them.

"I think I can make you come. I think I can make these pretty lips part for me."

I keep my lips pressed together, even though his are softly resting against mine. He keeps rocking his hips, the friction of his jeans causing enough pressure for my clit to begin that dull ache that I know will lead to extremely explosive things. He rubs his lips over mine.

"Come on, baby, open up. Let me kiss you."

I shake my head, keeping my lips pressed together. He keeps stroking his hips against mine, and the friction suddenly becomes too much. I squirm, trying to escape him. He's surrounding me, his warm body is crushed against mine, and his cock is taking me to the edge without even touching me.

"Yes, come," he growls.

I throw my head back, and I do just that. I can't stop it, I'm not even sure I want to. I push my chest up into his, my nipples grazing across his taut chest as my orgasm rocks me. I cry out his name, pulsing shamelessly as each burst of pleasure shoots through my body. The moment my lips part, he presses his tongue inside, giving me a mind-blowing kiss.

I give it all back. I kiss him so hard, so deep that our tongues become one as they dance together. His lips feel like heaven, and his stubble is scratchy against my cheek. I don't care, not even a little bit. I kiss him until it hurts. By the time he wrenches his mouth from mine, we're both panting.

"My cock fuckin' hurts for you right now," he breathes.

My body is alight, and my hand starts moving before my brain kicks in. His eyes widen as I reach into his jeans, curling my fingers around his throbbing length. It's long and thick, but not too thick that it would be considered painful. It's perfect. I rub my thumb over the piercing and he growls.

Mmmmm, I like the feeling of his cock in my hand.

I squeeze him, and then begin to gently stroke. His cock swells in my palm and his entire body goes tight.

"Fuck, you're goin' to de-man me in my own fuckin' pants."

I shift and reach down, shoving his jeans down. "No. I'm going to de-man you on my skin."

"Mother. Fucker."

I move with long but firm strokes. He winds up tighter and tighter with every pull. My entire body is aware of him; it's taking everything I have not to moan his name and beg for him to end this inside me. I pick up the pace, jerking him harder and faster until he's grinding out my name through clenched teeth.

"Coming, fuck," he barks out.

His cock swells, and then he releases with a ragged growl. Hot spurts of come land on my belly, and I gasp with delight. It feels amazing, warm and soft, evidence of his arousal. His entire body shakes over mine as I milk every, last drop from his cock. When he begins to soften in my hand, he lets his body relax.

"I've never had my dick pulled for me, but shit, remind me to do it a few more times before I die."

I laugh softly. "You haven't had someone jerk you off?"

He shakes his head, pressing his lips to my shoulder. "No, babe, all the girls I fuck are whores, and they're more than keen to just do what I want. No man wants a hand when he can have a mouth or a pussy."

"Ouch."

He nips my flesh, causing me to shudder. "I'd take your mouth or pussy over your hand any day, but babe, that was fuckin' amazing."

I slide out from underneath him and snatch my towel. "I have talented hands, what can I say?"

He snorts. "Talented enough to make breakfast?"

"You're pushing it, biker."

I shove to my feet and disappear down the hall to get some fresh clothes on. I go for a pair of jeans and a tight, black top that dips low at the front. I throw my hair up into a ponytail that is loose and messy, and then I make my way back out. Krypt is on the phone again, so I decide to attempt breakfast.

I'll make it clear: I'm not a good cook, but surely I can whip some eggs together. I mean honestly, how hard can it be? I open the fridge and pull out eggs, bacon and some tomatoes. I decide to scramble it all together, so I chop the bacon and tomato into small pieces, crack a few eggs in, and then mix it all with salt.

Krypt watches me, leaning against the doorframe as I mix the eggs over the stove, and then make some toast. When it's all ready, I place it on the table. He finishes his phone call and walks over, staring at the food. "Looks good," he murmurs, sitting down and resting his elbows against the table.

"I think I did pretty good." I smile, shoving my fork in.

He's quicker than me, scooping up a big bite and shoving it into his mouth. His face twists immediately and my fork halts just before it slips past my lips. I watch as Krypt's eyes widen and he shudders all over, as though he's going to vomit. He leans forward and spits the eggs out.

"Oh fuck." He gasps, poking his tongue out and rubbing it, fucking rubbing it, with his fingers.

"What?" I cry, dropping my fork.

"Did you put the whole fuckin' container of salt in? Holy shit."

I give him a sheepish smile. I don't know how much salt to put in; I don't cook. I just tipped a few teaspoons, assuming it would be enough.

"Shit, I think I need to wash my mouth out."

He stands and rushes off down the hall. I lift the eggs to my nose and breathe in. They smell nice. I poke my tongue out and just touch it on the fluffy, yellow goodness. The salt burns my tongue and I drop the fork quickly, scrunching up my face. God, yuck.

"My guess is that you can't cook?" Krypt says, joining me at the table again.

I look down at my plate. "No, sorry."

"No problems, babe," he says, standing and gathering our plates. "I got it."

I feel like an idiot, but I don't say any more. I am suddenly feeling fragile, the reality and weight of the situation piling on me. I stand and leave the room, needing some fresh air.

I step out the front door, inhaling as I go. It's crisp and clean up here, no gas from the city or pollution; just fresh, sweet air.

I sit on the front step, staring out. My eyes well with tears. I guess breakfast was just a way of taking me back to reality, and back to the fact that I'm stuck here with a man I hardly know, in a difficult situation. What's going to happen when I go back? Will I ever be able to trust the people I work with? What's going to happen to Tristan?

"Shit is gettin' to you, isn't it babe?"

Krypt sits down beside me, resting his hands on his knees and looking towards me.

"I'm fine," I croak.

"Hey," he says, reaching over and taking my chin, turning me towards him. "You don't need to pretend you're fine."

I blink back my tears, hating that I'm showing him such a fragile side. "It's not that I'm pretending. I feel as safe as I can in this situation here with you; it's just the hurt over Tristan and the things that were happening right in front of me, and I didn't even know."

"You were doin' your job; you thought they were your friends. You don't find bad shit if you ain't lookin' for it."

He's right about that; I had no reason to suspect anything. Not until he came in, anyway.

"I worry about my job when I go back," I admit, staring into his eyes.

"Don't," he growls, low and deep. "Because if anyone bothers you, I'll make it hurt, babe, don't doubt it."

"Why would you do that for me?"

He shrugs. "Because you're a good girl, and I like you."

"You don't really know me."

He pulls my chin so I come closer. "You gave me a chance when no one else did; you believed in me. It's enough."

I swallow, staring at his lips, wanting to taste him again. Our moment is interrupted when the phone rings in his pocket. With a curse, he pulls it out and stares down. I can see Maddox's name flashing across the screen. He presses a button and puts it on speaker.

"Yeah?"

"We got a problem, Krypt."

I pretend I'm not listening, but the fact is I am. Krypt quickly takes the phone off speaker, but it's so quiet out here I can still hear the conversation.

"What's the problem?" Krypt asks, flashing his eyes towards me before focusing back on his conversation.

"Cops have done a raid, which is fine, they found fuck all, but last night we got a fuckin' homemade cocktail bomb thrown through the window."

"What?" Krypt growls. "Fuckin' who?"

"Take a guess."

"Anyone hurt?"

"Santana was in the room, Krypt. Scared the fuck outta her, but she's okay."

Who is Santana?

"What are you goin' to do?"

"We are goin' on lockdown, but we can't do it here. I don't think it's goin' to be the first attack, and until we can get the information we need, we best stay low."

"You're comin' here, aren't you?" Krypt sighs.

"Just for a bit. I can't risk anyone in my club gettin' fucked up over this until I know what's goin' on."

"Right. When are you comin' up?"

"We'll be there soon."

Krypt hangs up the phone and turns to me. "I hope you're ready to see club life, babe, because you're about to get front-seat tickets."

I bite my bottom lip and ponder it, before asking, "How many of them is there?"

"Twenty, give or take. Most of them will stay in the sheds. Maddox and a few of the guys and girls will stay up here."

"Girls?"

He smirks. "There's Santana, for a start. She's always with Maddox. And they'll bring pussy; it's how they roll."

I scrunch my nose. "Pussy?"

He winks at me. "Pussy."

"Great. Who is Santana?"

He leans back, staring out at the beautiful scenery. "Santana is Maddox's pain in the ass."

I narrow my eyes. "His daughter?"

"No, babe. Santana grew up in a tough life; she was homeless at a real young age. Maddox found her convulsing in a street about five years ago. She was only sixteen, and when he got her help, he realized she had no one. Her family is dead. So, he took her in. Let's just say their relationship is strained. He thinks he owns her, and she doesn't like being bossed around. The sexual tension is huge."

I frown. "Isn't she like . . . his adopted daughter? He must be a great deal older than her, if she's only twenty-one."

He snorts. "She ain't ever been like a daughter; she just gives Maddox a run for his money. He thinks he's the boss of her because he saved her. And he ain't all that much older, Maddox is only thirty."

Fair enough.

"Well, at least she isn't a club whore. I really don't want to spend the next . . ." I scrunch my nose up. ". . . however long, with a group of girls who can't keep their legs closed."

He laughs. "Yeah, well, Santana is good value. You'll like her. And as for the whores, you won't see much of them."

"They'll be underneath a biker, no doubt."

He leans in close. "Absolutely."

"And that will include you?"

His eyes scan my face. "That depends?"

I smirk. "On what?"

"Are you going to be under me?"

I flush. "That depends."

He gives me a full-throttle grin, causing his dimples to pop out. "On what?"

"Are you going to make it worth my while?"

He reaches up, wrapping his fingers around the back of my head. "Oh, absolutely."

Now I can't wipe my grin off my face.

~*~*~*~

The guys from the club arrive about five hours later.

I managed to get some sleep and a decent shower before they showed up. I heard the rumble of bikes for a fair while before I saw them pull into the lot. I am sitting on the chair out the front, watching them all get off their shiny rides. I see Maddox first, and watch in fascination as he pulls his helmet off and throws his leg over the bike.

He's massive; the man is daunting. His eyes fall on me and he smirks, I throw him my own classy smirk back. I notice a girl behind him, and I train my eyes on her as she throws herself off the bike and pulls her helmet off. Wow, she's gorgeous. She has long, black hair that falls in soft curls right down to her bottom. She's only a tiny girl, no bigger than five foot. She has olive skin, and beautifully slanted eyes.

I focus my attention on the other bikers, and smile when I see the side-cart that holds Tyke. The biker riding gets off and helps him up, and Tyke supports himself on the bike while they unload a wheelchair. Maddox reaches the bottom of the stairs and I turn to stare at him. He's still smirking at me.

"Nice to see you again, Maddox."

From this angle, with him looming over me, he reminds me somewhat of Heathcliff from that remake of *Wuthering Heights* in 1992. He's got that long, thick dark hair and the lightest blue eyes. He's so broody, so scarily stunning. When he smiles, it's like a lion baring its teeth before making a kill.

"I see you're fittin' in just fine. You got information for me?"

I ignore him, staring at his thick legs. "How are your balls?"

He snorts. "Workin' just fine."

"Shame."

The girl, who I'm assuming is Santana, appears beside him. I look up at her, and wow, up close she's absolutely gorgeous. Her eyes are so dark brown they almost look black. She's like a new-age Pocahontas. Her eyes meet mine and she gives me a warm, welcoming smile that surprises me.

"Hi," she says, and her voice is like melted honey or something. Jesus. No wonder Maddox is hung up on her. "I'm Santana."

I stretch my hand out, taking hers. "Ash."

"Ash is short for . . ."

"Just Ash." I smile. "I know, it's strange but my parents liked it."

She flashes me a smile that brings up two dimples in her cheeks. "I like it, too."

"Well, you girls can go ahead and get comfortable, because I got shit to do," Maddox says, stepping past me. "San, we gotta talk about last night."

He doesn't look at her as he speaks, but she glares at his back as he passes. "No thanks."

He stops and turns, glaring at her. "Do as you're fuckin' told."

I turn and look up at Maddox. "Someone is broody today. Go sort your 'shit' out. We're going to get to know each other."

I stand and take Santana's hand, dragging her off before he can say any more. We pass all the bikers as we walk down towards the back lot of trees. I notice some of the bikers have girls on their bikes. Some, I assume are old ladies, others I'm assuming are whores.

"Thanks for that," Santana says as we reach the trees.

I wave a hand. "No problems. He's a jerk-off."

She laughs. "He can be hard to live with. Did Krypt tell you what happened with me?"

I nod. "I hope that's okay? He just gave me a brief run-down."

She shrugs, reaching up and tying her hair into a loose ponytail. "It's no biggie. Most people hear the story. I don't really have anything else, and getting a job is hard with no skill, so Maddox and the club is all I have."

"Krypt says it gets tough with Maddox?" I ask, finding a rock and perching on it.

She nods, sighing. "He's so controlling."

"It sounds like he's hard because he cares."

She snorts. "I've seen Maddox with that many girls, it's not even funny. He doesn't care about me; he just likes the control that I allow him to have. My own stupid fault really."

"You're probably right." I laugh. "I'm just glad to have another female here that isn't pinned underneath a biker."

She grins at me. "Tell me about it."

We spend the next hour talking, and it warms me to know I have someone else like me around. I don't honestly know how long I'll be here, but knowing I have the chance to make a friend out of Santana is enough to keep me at ease.

We just don't know when the next move will be made, or what kind of affect it will have.

And that scares me.

CHAPTER TEN

TRISTAN

I pace up and down the small length of the office, my hands pressed behind my back, my mind spinning. This all went wrong. It didn't go to plan, and now everything is fucked up. Ash is missing, and no doubt has every intention of revealing anything she knows when she comes back. I knew I should have never let her near Dawson; it was a stupid move on my behalf.

I won't make that kind of mistake again.

"I'm late, I know."

I turn to see Officer Davies entering the room. I call him that here, but to me he's just Dan. Dan Davies. Criminal. Police officer. The kind of man people fear. He's tall, over six foot, and is as broad as a linebacker. His powerful frame and deadly cold eyes make him a fantastic cop, a fantastic *corrupt* cop.

He's been a part of this from the start. He's been friends with Howard from the Tinman's Soldiers MC since they were just kids. It's an operation so big, so deadly, that they have cops running against cops, guards gone wrong and people on the inside in places they shouldn't be. Tinman's Soldiers is a lethal club, and shit is about to get worse.

"I don't have time to fuck around in here," I mutter, running my hands through my hair. "We need to sort this shit out."

Dan walks over to his desk, his large body casual, as if he doesn't have a care in the world. As if he isn't running a criminal organization while fighting crime like a pretend hero. People around this place would have no idea that he's corrupt. He's cherished, loved and damned good at what he does.

"Where's Luke?"

"Here."

We both turn to see Luke entering the room, his eyes darting around. Dan nods at him and he shuts the door, locking it, before joining me at Dan's desk. We all sit. Tension is thick in the air.

"We have more than one problem," Dan begins. "But the first problem is the girl that got away. If the club has fed her any information she could blow this out of the water."

Ash. He's talking about Ash.

Sweet, loyal Ash.

I'd love to say she wouldn't bring it all into the light, but that wouldn't be the case. Ash loves her job, she's loyal and fierce, and there is no way she would let this go unnoticed. I considered her a friend, but I have no doubt that if she knows about me now, all of that has changed.

"Do you think she's alive?" Luke asks.

Dan nods. "She is. A phone call was made from her to Claire, her roommate, just days ago. We are still trying to track the location, but I have no doubt the girl is breathing."

"If we can get her back, I'm sure we can talk her around—"

"No," Luke says, cutting me off. His eyes are hard and empty. "Ash is a risk to us now; there's no way she's going to just let it go. We can't risk her being involved. Everything is planned out, and we can't afford another blowout."

"What are you saying?" I ask, already knowing the answer, but needing to hear it anyway.

Luke shrugs. "It's simple. We have to kill her."

"And we have to make it look like it was them," Dan adds, his face equally as stony.

Fuck.

I'm sorry, Ash.

~*~*~*~

ASH

It's been five days since the bikers arrived, and it's been quite chaotic. If they're not drinking, they're fucking, and if they're not doing both of those things, they are plotting shit we don't have any idea about. My injuries are mostly healed now, and I'm able to walk without any pain. Santana and I spend the days wondering around in the trees surrounding the house, just exploring nature and getting to know each other.

She hasn't revealed a lot about her story, but I've no doubt it's something life-changing. You can see the pain behind her eyes; it runs deep. Krypt spends most of his time with Maddox, formulating a plan to take down the Tinman's Soldiers. It would appear a war is on the way, and I have no doubt it's something I don't want involvement in.

Krypt and I are full of sexual tension. I can't look at him without feeling it sizzling between us. I'm doing everything I can to avoid it, to stay away from him, to find some inner strength, but each day it gets harder and harder. I don't want to involve myself with a man I know I could so easily fall in love with.

"Ash!"

I'm out in the trees, just weaving through them. The sun is out today, bright and beautiful, sending rays of warmth through the thick leaves that are poking out from the gorgeous stumps of the trees. I'm soaking it up, loving the outside air. At the sound of his voice, however, I find myself turning, and squinting to see what the problem is.

"Ash!"

It's Krypt. His voice sounds frantic. Why is he frantic? I rush out of the trees and I notice him right away. He's standing on the patio, his eyes scanning the area to find me. When his gaze falls on me, I'm sure I can see him breathe a sigh of relief. He charges down the stairs, stopping when he reaches me.

God he looks good today, like he belongs in a museum for women to fawn over. His big shoulders are covered with a tight, black T-shirt and his jeans hang low on his hips. There are no chains today, but he is wearing those sexy-as-sin black boots that make everything inside me clench. His eyes are darker than usual, which I've noticed happens depending on his mood. If he's angry, they almost go as blue as Maddox's, but when he's relaxed, they're a dark, stormy grey.

"We got a big problem," he says, taking my arm and pulling me inside the house.

"What?" I pant, following after him.

He leads me into Maddox's 'domain', which is just a bedroom he's converted into an office so he can do all his private stuff. Maddox looks up the minute we walk in, and he nods at Krypt, who closes the door. Well, this can't be good. It's like being in the school principal's office again; you know you're in for it when the door closes.

"Sit down," Maddox orders, and I slink over and drop into the seat.

Krypt stands behind me, his big hands resting on my shoulders. I feel a little dominated in this position and I shift, uncomfortable.

"So?" I ask, my voice low and quiet. "Care to tell me why I'm in here?"

"You're in danger," Maddox says, not holding back any punches. He just gives it like it is.

"What do you mean?" I ask. A shiver runs up my spine, and Krypt squeezes my shoulder.

"I mean I have people everywhere, just like that no good—"

"Get to the point, boss," Krypt urges.

"I have word that you have a death sentence."

My stomach turns, but I manage to stutter, "W-w-what?"

"I didn't think they'd let you go so easily. You have too much information, and it's going to ruin what they've created. They aren't going to do it themselves, though, no. My guess is they'll put it on us. 'Cause that's how these fuckers roll. Which means they're goin' to take you out, but they're goin' to make it happen in a place where we are. You can imagine why. They need the heat to stay off them, and what better way to do it than to have news flashin' around that we killed our hostage?"

I'm going to pass out; I just know it. My head spins and I swallow over and over to try and keep the contents of my stomach in. I didn't ask for any of this. Being a prisoner to this club is one thing, but suddenly becoming the hunted is another.

"They don't know where I am, right?" I whisper.

Maddox looks to Krypt, and he squeezes my shoulders again. Oh God, they do.

"You said this was a safe location," I croak.

"It is, but there's a chance they were trackin' Krypt's phone. It ain't hard to do. If that's the case, they could show up here. The advantage we have, at this point, is that we can hear anyone comin'. I'm putting watches on every entrance; we will make sure we catch anyone who comes close."

That's not enough; it's not. They're asking me to just trust that they can keep these men away from me; we all know that isn't the case. It never works like that. The girl always gets taken. I close my eyes and shove to my feet, my entire body shaking. I can't be here; I don't want to be here. The only place I'm safe is in a police station, possibly in a cell where no one can get to me.

I turn and rush out of the room.

"Ash!" Krypt calls, but I don't dare stop. If I do, there's a chance I'll hurt him, and I don't want to do that. Or maybe I do. I don't know.

I run to the room I've been using and swing the door open. I reach the drawers in a split second and pull out a fresh pair of clothes before jerking mine off. I need something clean on to leave.

I can get out of here; I'll find a way to safety. It can't be any worse than staying here with a target painted on my back.

The door squeaks and then closes, but I don't turn, I already know who it is. He can't talk me out of this; he can't convince me that he's safer for me. He can't, and he won't. I'm leaving. If I have to shoot him, I will. There are plenty of guns lying around this place.

"What're you doin'?" he asks, stepping behind me and putting his hands on my shoulders. I stiffen as he turns me to face him.

"I'm fucking leaving."

His eyebrows shoot up. "You lost your mind?"

"Lost my mind?" I screech. "It isn't me who has lost my mind, it's this fucking place, and all the shit around it."

"Calm down, process what Maddox told you, and get your shit together. Runnin' is dangerous, and you'll be killed without hesitation."

"You want me to stay here," I growl, shoving my finger into his chest, "with a bunch of men who kidnapped me? And trust that when it comes down to it, they're going to have my back?"

He reaches up, tangling his fingers into my hair and pulling my face forward. The air crackles between us as he lays his intense expression upon my face. "Yeah, I fuckin' do."

"Well, I don't. I'm a walking fucking target. You can't ask me to stay here, and just roll over and wait for a bullet."

"You don't get a fuckin' choice."

I shove him in his chest. I don't think it does a great deal until I see him struggle for air before composing himself and jerking my head back, causing a sting to radiate through my skill. "Listen to me, girl. You ain't runnin' out of here because I'm not goin' to have your death on my hands. If I have to chain you up, I'll fuckin' do it."

"Let me go!" I screech, raising my knee and hitting him so hard in the balls his entire body drops to the floor.

He growls in pain and barks, "What the fuck is with you and balls?"

I leap over him, but his hand shoots out and catches my leg. He tugs me so hard I land flat on my face. Angry tears course down my cheeks as I kick and push forward, desperate, needing to get out of here.

"I don't want to be here with you," I bellow, my voice cracking just slightly. "It's your fault I'm here. It's all your fucking fault. I didn't ask for any of this."

"I know you didn't," he growls, his voice low and clearly pained. "But there ain't no way I'm lettin' you get killed for it. You have to fuckin' trust me, Ash."

"I don't want to," I scream. "I should fucking hate you."

He slides up over my body, his chest pressing against my back. His mouth drops to my ear and he murmurs, "But you don't fucking hate me and it kills you, because you know I'm the best thing for you right now."

He's right; deep down I know that, but it doesn't mean I will accept it easily.

"I will go to a police station, and—"

"Ash," he growls into my ear. "They're in on it, too. You wouldn't be safe."

"What?" I squeak.

What sort of horror are these people running?

"Right here is the safest place you can be right now."

"I don't want to die, Krypt," I whimper, my voice low and pathetic, like a whiny child's. "I didn't ask for any of this."

"Look at me," he demands, moving off me and rolling us so his body is settled over mine. Our eyes lock. His are determined, like he's sure nothing will ever happen to me. "I won't let anythin' hurt you. I will lay my life down before anyone touches you."

"Why?" I whisper.

"Because innocent people don't deserve bad things. They don't have a choice."

I stare up at him. "Is that all?"

My heart picks up and I swallow, wanting to dart my eyes away, but instead I hold his gaze.

"No," he says, his voice low and husky. "But that's the only reason I'm tellin' you right now, because the rest of it . . . I'm goin' to show you."

I don't get the chance to answer, because his mouth comes down over mine. His jaw flexes and pulls as he kisses me, deep and powerful, taking all the bad away and replacing it with heaven. Krypt is my little piece of heaven, the fantasy I can't have but I *want*. When I'm with him, I forget that he can *never* be mine.

His kisses fog my mind, his body floods my heart, and his presence makes me forget to breathe. I can't protest, there's nothing left to say. The fact is I want Krypt as much as he wants me, wrong or right. And if being here with him, feeling him over me, is how this moment is going to go, then who am I to stop it?

Our bodies grind against each other in frenzied passion as our tongues dance. The piercing in his lip tickles my skin as he devours me. His hands find my stomach and slide up beneath my shirt, splaying out across my warm flesh. My cheeks burn; I'm not a skinny model, not like most of the women I have no doubt he fucks.

"Don't touch me there," I breathe into his mouth.

"Give me a good fuckin' reason why not," he rasps against my lips as his hand slides up, searching for my breasts.

"I'm . . . I'm not skinny, and . . ."

"I'll tell you this once, so listen fuckin' close. I don't want no skinny, bony-assed woman. I want a woman with flesh, something for me to appreciate. I want curves that make my jaw tighten, and my dick hard. I want to see beauty that only a woman with curves can accentuate. You, baby, are what a woman should be. So, I'm goin' to keep my hands on you, I'm goin' to suck your nipples, I'm goin' to squeeze your ass, and then I'm goin' to put my cock deep inside you—purely because you're the most beautiful thing I have ever seen."

Oh, God.

When he puts it like that, there really is no way to say no.

"There's somethin' else." He nips at my lower lip. His hand finds one of my breasts, and he squeezes it with a firmness that has my back arching.

"W-w-w-what?"

"I like it rough, darlin'."

"Don't they all," I mewl, sliding my hands under his shirt and feeling the hard, yet silky smoothness of his skin against my palms.

"No, sweetheart," he grates out, sliding his hand around my back to unclip my bra so he can find my nipples. Oh God, yes.

"Then elaborate," I pant, squeezing his hip with my fingers.

"When I fuck, I like to fuck with a raw ferocity most women can't handle. I don't make love. I want you up against a wall, my hands tangled in your hair while my cock is driving in and out of you. My hands won't be gentle; my cock won't be gentle; and baby," he growls, "I won't be fuckin' gentle."

"Give me all you've got, biker," I challenge breathlessly.

"Fuck," he hisses. "Never had one so eager."

"Just one question," I moan, writhing beneath him as he pinches my nipple so hard that pain shoots through my spine, and pleasure floods my pussy.

"Only one?" he murmurs against my mouth. "Go."

"Will you put your hands on me in an aggressive way that will be forever scarring?"

He pulls back, his lips swollen from our kiss. "It's your turn to elaborate."

"Will you hit me?"

He narrows his eyes. "Fuck no."

"So you just like angry sex, you don't like . . . sadistic sex?"

He smirks. "I'll hurt you, baby. But it'll be with my mouth as my teeth sink into your flesh. There will be no brutal violence. I'm not fucked up. I don't like it like this because I've got deep, dark issues. I like it like this because there is a certain thrill that comes with sex that is rough and angry. I know you won't get it because you're a chick, but it's how I like it. Not all the time, of course. But eh, I'm a biker and a bit of rough and tumble is fuckin' hot."

I stare up at him, and a slow smirk creeps across my face. I believe Krypt has underestimated me. I have a sex drive wilder than most men; I love it. I am forever wanting to find different ways to do it, often fantasizing about more than one scenario. I reach up, stroking his jaw. His eyes soften—at least, until I pull my hand back and slap him.

"You fuckin' . . ." he growls, taking my hands in one of his and shoving them above my head. "Don't do that again."

"You want it rough, Krypt? Then do it properly."

His eyes flare with need, his mouth slackening as if he's just discovered something he has dreamed about his entire life.

"Well?" I hiss up at him. "Are we going to lay here, or are you going to fuck me and make it count?"

A slow, wild grin spreads across his face. His eyes flicker between grey and blue as the light shines in over us. Then, before I can say another word, he has me flipped on my stomach. He presses himself over me, his hands taking hold of my shirt and sliding it up. He shifts his body and rips it off as if it didn't have to clear my head and arms first.

He leans down, biting the flesh on my back, causing little moans of pain and pleasure to escape my lips. Using one hand he tucks my arm underneath me, pressing his face down to my ear. "I'll make it count, baby, don't you fuckin' worry about that." He nips my earlobe and then his lips are sliding across the back of my neck, pushing my hair out of the way.

I whimper shamelessly, pushing my backside up into his already hard cock. "Uh, uh, uh," he chastises, pushing it back down. "I'll be the one to decide when you get that."

His weight goes off me for a second while he takes my pants and quickly pulls them down my legs. He puts his hands under my hips and raises my ass into the air, revealing my tiny G-string, which thank god was brand new; I made Krypt assure me of that. He leans down, and his warm breath penetrates the thin cotton to warm my damp sex.

"I love how you fuckin' smell," he rasps against me. "So fuckin' sweet. Have you ever had your pussy licked from behind?"

I shudder. Oh, God.

"Didn't think so."

He tears my panties off with a loud rip, and then his mouth is back against my ass. He breathes me in, a long, slow inhale that has my cheeks flushing. Then his mouth is against my exposed entrance, his tongue slides along the damp flesh. I drop my head, my eyes fluttering closed as he presses his entire mouth against me, his tongue sliding out to find my clit.

"Oh God," I whimper. "Shit."

All that heat covering me sends me over the edge. I press myself against him, wanting him to put his fingers inside me and fuck me while his lips are against me, but on this angle, I know it's not possible.

Krypt makes it possible.

His tongue penetrates me as a finger would, and I cry out so loudly I shock myself. It feels oddly amazing, so soft and yet hard. His fingers go up and he strokes my clit while his tongue fucks me in a way I've not been fucked before. I thrash my head from side to side as an orgasm rises.

Then he pulls back.

It takes me a moment to realize what has happened, and it isn't until the cool air hits my exposes skin that reality kicks in and my orgasm dies. I turn around, and he's rocking back on his heels. He's squatting as he rocks, a smirk on his face. He's got no shirt on, and his jeans are unbuttoned. His cock pokes out the top, the head an angry red, like it needs to be freed.

"Are you proud of yourself?"

He winks at me. The fucker. I lunge at him, knocking him clean over. He lands on his back with an *oomph*. I drop over him, straddling his hips. I take his hands and shove them above his head. He grins up at me, amusement dancing in his eyes. Effortlessly, he throws me off him. My entire body is aware of him as I crawl forward quickly.

I hear shuffling behind me as he crawls after me. His hand lashes out and catches my hip, pulling me backwards. I drive my elbow into his ribs, before spinning around and raising my hand to shove him backwards. He catches it, slamming it against the wall behind him. He slides his body up against mine, pressing me against the cold surface with no way out.

"I win, sweetheart."

"I wasn't even trying," I pant.

He thrusts his cock up against me, and I can feel the soft skin against my belly. It's clearly freed from its confinements. He presses his forehead against mine, while his hands hold my hands above my head. He continues to thrust his hips, sliding his length up and down my belly, warming me.

I lower my head; scattering little kisses down his jaw. He groans and his eyes close as I slip my tongue out and lick the soft skin beside his mouth. I move down his neck, kissing and sucking, loving the way his flesh tastes. When I reach the little nook between his neck and shoulder I open my mouth, and I bite him so hard my teeth nearly puncture his flesh.

He stumbles backwards with a roar, and with a smirk I get to my feet, backing up towards the bathroom. He glares up at me like a feral animal as he pushes to his feet and stalks towards me. He looks like a maniac, his hand pressed to his neck and his cock jutting out of his jeans, the piercing glistening in the light.

"You'll pay for that."

"You have to catch me first," I taunt.

He lunges at me, but I step to the side, skirting around him. He spins, his hand lashing out and catching my wrist. I spin too, taking a step forward and wrapping my hand around his exposed cock, squeezing.

"You hurt that, baby," he hisses, "and there'll be no fun for you and I . . ."

I stroke it, a little, and then give it a hard jerk.

His jaw tightens as he backs us into the bathroom.

I stoke again, and a hiss escapes his lips.

"Be careful," he warns.

I squeeze, and his cock swells in response. His eyes burn with an intensity that tells me he's going to fuck me hard, and he's going to make it unforgettable.

Cold porcelain is a shock against my back as he presses me against the bathroom sink. He lowers his eyes and grins, spinning me around, forcing his cock from my hand.

"You're goin' to watch me fuck you."

My cheeks burn red as I catch a glimpse of us in the mirror. My hair is wild, flowing down over my shoulders in dark waves. My eyes are bright, and my lips are puffy from being kissed. Krypt looks like the devil behind me, his eyes intense, and his jaw tight. He's ready, and he's going to make it count.

I shove my head back, hitting his mouth. He lets off a feral hiss and a droplet of blood appears on his full lips. Something comes alive inside me. His eyes flare as he reaches up, tangling his hand in my hair and shoving me forward, pressing my cheek against the glass. "You're a bad girl, Ash," he purrs against my neck. He thrusts his cock against my ass and I whimper. "You want my cock here, deep inside your sweet, plush ass?"

I stomp on his foot and he lets out a long, wicked laugh. He reaches down, taking his cock in his hand and rubbing it up and down my ass. Heat floods my pussy and my clit throbs for more. He still has my face pressed against the glass as he torments my ass with his thick length.

"You protected, sweetheart?" he growls against me.

I nod.

"Clean?"

I nod again.

"Good," he rasps. "So am I."

Oh boy.

"It's goin' to burn, baby, but I can promise you this. By the time we're done here, you'll never see anything but *me*."

Then he plunges forward, sinking his cock deep into my pussy. I cry out loudly, my flesh burning and stretching around him. He feels like he's twice the size and thickness when he's inside me like this. My body struggles to accommodate him. His lips touch my shoulder as he slowly slides his cock out and thrusts it back in, harder this time, so hard our skin slaps together.

"Motherfucker," he gasps. "As sweet as I knew you would be."

"Oh God," I whimper. "Krypt, it hurts."

"It's meant to hurt," he growls. "Pain makes pleasure feel so much fuckin' better."

He releases my face and stretches his arm down to find my clit. He gently strokes while he pulls his cock out and slowly inches it back in, letting me feel the burn. A fire ignites inside me with each slow thrust, and soon my clit is throbbing for more.

"I'm goin' to make you wetter," he snarls, pulling his cock out and spinning me around. He takes my hips in his hands and he lifts me onto the sink, spreading my thighs.

"Look at you, Ash," he admires, his voice husky and low. "Look at your sweet arousal coating your legs."

I stare down and he's right; my thighs are damp from my arousal. I bite my bottom lip as he lowers to his knees in front of me before pressing a soft kiss to my clit. Then he's sucking it. The man goes from ice to fire in a matter of seconds, and it beats me to know how he does it. He can be so hard and cold, and then suddenly he's making everything disappear until all I can breathe is *him*.

He licks my pussy, devouring it, sucking, and licking until I'm shamelessly screaming his name. Then he slowly rises until we're the same height again. He leans forward and I can see my arousal dampening his gorgeous lips. "Suck it all off, Ash. Now."

My eyes widen. "W-w-w-what?"

"Suck your sweet taste off my lips."

Oh my God.

My mouth drops open as I stare at myself on his lips. Then I think about taking his bottom lip into my mouth and sucking. My entire body shoves me forward, not giving my brain a chance to kick in. I am millimeters from his lips when I look up at him; his eyes are on me, his expression fierce. His gaze tells me to move it, so I close the gap.

I take his bottom lip first, sucking it into my warm mouth. He groans and his hands find my hips so he can pull me closer, until my exposed pussy is pressing against his belly, coating him. Oh God. This is so erotic, so dirty, and so indisputably wrong in the best possible way. Tasting myself on his mouth has everything in me wanting more.

I release his bottom lip and snake my tongue out, running it over his top one. His growls turn into feral hisses. Impatient, he pulls my hips forward more, and then he's inside me again. A throaty moan escapes my lips as he begins fucking me; real fucking, not the tedious kind. No, this fucking is raw, brutal, hard and dirty. His hips slap against mine, his cock bringing the perfect kind of pleasure and pain. My nipples rub against his chest as I bring myself closer.

I take hold of his bottom lip, loving the way his chest rumbles in appreciation as he fucks me. I suck, lick, and devour myself off him while he takes me in a way I've never been taken.

I find my orgasm first. Heat begins rushing up from my toes until my entire body is hot, desperate for release.

With one more perfect thrust, I come. I come so hard my teeth sink into his lip and our feral cries fill the room. Then, in a blur, I'm being flipped around and bent back over the sink. His hands fist in my hair and he fucks me so hard my pussy aches in the most delicious way. I can see us in the mirror; we look like wild animals on the edge of frenzied passion.

"Watch me come," he barks. "Watch me fucking come inside you."

My eyes are on his at the exact moment he explodes inside me. His eyes almost roll with pleasure, hazing over as he goes off into another world. His lips part and his head drops back, feral hisses and groans escaping his lips as his thrusting slows, until he's dragging his cock in and out lazily.

"Holy shit," I breathe when he stops thrusting and his head finds my shoulder, his big body stretching over mine.

"Holy shit, all right," he pants. "I've decided somethin', right here and fuckin' now . . ."

"What's that?" I whisper.

"I'm fuckin' keepin' you, Ash. Because there is no way I can go through my life without feeling that kind of intensity again."

My heart feels like it stops beating.

He wants to keep me?

What if I don't want to be kept?

CHAPTER ELEVEN

Cleaning up is interesting. I have our arousal all over my body, and so does he. His chest is still damp from having my pussy resting against it. We're a stunning mess. Showering is the best option, so we both get in, our hands discovering each other's bodies as we lather up and get clean.

When we're done, I dry and dress, and Krypt pulls on a pair of clean jeans and nothing else. My breath comes out in a whoosh as I watch him moving around the room, his body so darned sensational I want to take my tongue to it and lick every single perfect inch. He's divine, like heaven wrapped up in tattoos.

"You hungry?" he asks when I come out, still drying my hair.

I nod.

He tilts his head to the side. "I scared you, didn't I?"

"What?" I say, shaking my head. "No."

"When I said I'm keepin' you. It scared you."

My cheeks flush. He walks forward, cupping my jaw in one of his rugged, rough hands. "I've never wanted a woman to be my old lady, and I've had enough of them. The minute I saw you, the minute you opened your mouth, there was something about you I'd never seen in a lady before. It's not just about the fucking, Ash—it's about the fact that you give me somethin' no one else ever has."

"You don't know me, Krypt."

"No," he murmurs. "But I'm going to."

"No," I whisper, pulling my jaw from his chin. "You're not."

"You tellin' me you won't get to know me, and consider bein' with me?"

"Why?" I bark, taking a step back. "You're feeding me bullshit that I've heard from enough men to know it means nothing. You don't understand me, Beau. Not even close. You don't know what I'm scared of, or what makes me cry. You don't know what makes me laugh or what I love and hate. All you like is that I'm sassy, and I made your dick feel fucking good. That isn't enough for me, so don't ask me to be something I can never be to you. I never have and never will be someone's possession."

I turn and walk out of the room, giving him no more.

I rush out of the house and past a group of bikers who fucking cheer and wink at me. Well, I guess the house has thin walls. I push through the front door and I see Maddox sitting on the stairs, watching Santana who is sitting on an old chair, staring out into the wilderness. He turns when he hears me, and his eyes narrow.

"Hey," he yells as I rush past him.

"Eat a dick, Maddox."

His boots crunch on the gravel as he follows me, and it takes everything for me not to turn and kick him in the balls again. His hand curls around my arm just before I reach the thick trees that I'm enjoying so much lately. He spins me around, and my face bumps into his massive chest. I shove at him, causing him to take a few steps back.

"Don't touch me."

"You and Krypt fightin'?"

I stop and glare at him. "Since when did we become friends? Newsflash, we're not. I hate you. I hate him and I hate this place."

Yep, that was petty of me, and I sounded like a small, pathetic child.

"You done?" he asks, leaning against a tree and crossing his arms over his chest.

I sigh. "Yeah."

"Good. Now are you gonna tell me why you're runnin' outta there and he ain't followin' you?"

"No reason. It's fine."

"Darlin'," he smirks, "the entire house heard the fucking he just gave you. Now I'll ask you again: Are you gonna tell me why you're suddenly runnin' out the door?"

"He . . . he wants to keep me," I say, meeting his eyes.

His brows go up. "He wants you to be his old lady?"

"He wants to get to know me more, so he can make me his old lady, yeah."

"And you don't want to."

It's not a question; it's a statement.

"No, I don't want to."

"Why?"

I shake my head. "What do you mean why?"

"Why is bein' his old lady not good enough for you?"

"Oh for fuck's sake," I snap, throwing my hands in the air. "It's not that it's not good enough for me, it's that it isn't me."

"How would you know?"

"Jesus, Maddox, because I am not like the rest of those girls. I am free, I am independent, and I don't do well with being told what to do."

"You talked to the rest of those girls?" he asks, his voice still causal.

"No."

"Maybe you should."

"What good would that do?"

He steps forward, leaning down close. "A biker doesn't just consider anyone to be his old lady. Especially not bikers like Krypt; he has never asked a girl to be an old lady. It's a fuckin' honor to be given such a role, and it's not to be taken lightly. There are girls that would give up everything to be noticed."

"I'm not one of them," I whisper, staring into his eyes. "And I never will be."

"Then you don't deserve him, so here's what I'm goin' to tell you: if it's what you really want, then you stay the fuck away from him. Krypt doesn't need shit like this in his life; he's lived through enough. You decide you're too good for him, then you don't put your pussy near him again."

"I never said I was too good for him, Maddox," I protest.

"Then what are you sayin'?"

He turns and walks off, not letting me answer. I drop my head against the trunk of the tree, suddenly feeling like an asshole for acting the way I did. It's not that I don't want to be with a man like Krypt, because that isn't the case. It's just that the idea of giving up everything to spend my life on the back of a bike . . . I just . . . I can't.

"Hey."

I lift my head to see Santana. She's giving me a gentle expression. "Are you okay?"

I shrug, turning my face away from hers.

"I heard what Maddox said. He's not right, Ash."

I turn back towards her. "Isn't he?"

She shakes her head. "No, he's not. Being an old lady isn't for everyone, and it doesn't make you a bad person."

I stare at my hands. "I care about Krypt, but he's not given me the chance to need more from him. He took me from my life, and now I'm stuck here and I'm confused. I don't know where I'm at. Then he loads me up with that, and it freaked me out. I am an independent woman, I love my job, and I love having a life. I don't think being cramped up as an old lady is where I want to be . . . but it doesn't mean that Krypt isn't every-fucking-thing, because God knows, he could be."

She smiles, touching my arm. "You don't need to think about all this right now. The fact is, you don't know him or the club well enough to make that decision. Get to know them while you're here, but in the end, it's your choice, Ash."

"And if I fall for him?" I whisper.

"Then maybe your choice will be easier."

I shake my head.

"You know what? Let's go and get drunk. We both need it."

I tilt my head to the side and smile at her. "You want to get drunk?"

She gives me a wicked grin. "I love to do what I'm not supposed to."

I grin back. "I'm all in."

~*~*~*~

Santana goes to the house and returns five minutes later with a bottle of tequila. We sit in the trees taking shot after shot, until we're laughing and giggling like schoolgirls.

"I heard them saying you can fight real good?" she says, leaning against me.

"I can. I had to learn with my training."

"I want to see you beat one of them . . ."

I laugh. "Ohhh, that would be fun."

We fall silent for a minute before she shoves to her feet. "Maddox will have a fit when he knows we're out here drinking."

I raise my brows, standing too. "Why?"

"Because he's an over-controlling asshole," she deadpans.

I giggle. "He is."

"Let's go inside and torment the whores."

I throw my head back and laugh, and then we both weave out of the trees and head back towards the house.

There is a drinking session going in full-swing when we enter. There are bikers everywhere and girls with no tops. I let my eyes scan the room until they fall on Krypt. He hasn't noticed my entrance because there's a woman serving him a beer, pressing her breasts against his face and giggling as he bites her flesh.

My heart twists.

Why is it twisting like that? I just told him I didn't want anything, and now it's hurting. God dammit, I'm one of those girls. I shake my head, turning to Santana. She's giving me a sympathetic expression that I refuse to acknowledge. Instead, I walk over to the large pool table in the living area and I take a cue.

"Who wants to play? I'll take my top off if you win. If you lose, I get to kick your ass?"

A bunch of bikers laugh gruffly, and three stand up. I've not been introduced to them. One is an older man, around sixty or seventy. He's got a long, grey beard and kind eyes. The other two are younger, both extremely handsome and buff like Maddox and Krypt. One has blond hair and dark brown eyes, and the other has long, brown hair and hazel eyes.

"We're in." Hazel Eyes grins.

"Are you sure about that?" I smirk, slinking over to the table. "I'm good at pool."

"So am I, babe."

My smirk widens and I flash him a wicked smile, before reaching for the pool cue. "What's your name, handsome?" I ask Hazel Eyes.

"Ray." He winks.

"And you?" I say to Brown Eyes.

He gives me a long, sultry smile. "Grimm."

"Like the Grim Reaper?"

He nods.

"Nice."

I catch a glimpse of Krypt as I round the table, and he's watching me with a feral expression that makes it clear he's not happy. I take the first shot, sinking some good balls, and the game kicks off. Ray is good, he wasn't lying, and he manages to outdo me in the first ten minutes. We've bet on the best out of three, but he isn't going to let me off easily.

"New rules." He smirks. "Each time you lose, something comes off. Shirt off, sweetheart."

I grin, drunk and no longer caring. I take the hem of my shirt and slowly, while swaying my hips, slide it over my head. I picked a good bra that pushes my breasts up. The bikers whistle and cheer as I lean over the pool table and keep playing. I win the next round, smirking with victory and doing a little sexy dance around the table.

"Last round." Grimm smirks. "If we win, you get naked. If you win, you kick our ass . . . though I fuckin' doubt you have it in you."

"Oh," I say, hitting a ball and sinking it. "I have it in me."

I win, like I knew I would. My cheers fill the room and shots are handed my way as the guys grin. Either way, they're winning. They get to put their hands on me—at least, they'll try. It won't last long. I've been wanting to kick some ass since I got here, and now my injuries are healing, I think it's time I prove I can.

"Who is first?" I ask, jumping from foot to foot.

It's surprisingly Grimm who steps forward. He smirks at me and leans down, putting his hands on his knees. "Let's see what you got, little darlin'."

I kick him, swift and fast, hitting his shoulder and sending him tumbling backwards. I leap at him before he has the chance to get up, landing on his chest and taking hold of the pressure point at his neck. He roars and flips me off him, rolling towards me. People are scooting out of the way and cheering as we roll across the floor.

"Good fuckin' move," he grunts, flipping his body onto mine. "But you will lose."

I grin up at him, and then I jab my thumb into his eye. He makes a strangled sound and while he's dazed, I hook my feet in his and wrap my fingers around his arms, twisting until his body falls to the side. I force myself back up into a standing position as he pulls himself up and glares at me.

"You play dirty. I can play dirty."

He winks at someone and an arm goes around my neck from behind as he walks forward. Using the strength of my body, I lift my legs into the air and I kick him in the stomach while the person holding me has my weight. He takes a few steps backwards, and while he does, I reach back and I take hold of whoever has me by the nipples and I squeeze so hard he bellows in pain.

I spin around and see it's Ray. He stares at me in agony while he rubs his nipples. Then another set of arms goes around me. These arms are bigger, and far sturdier. I notice the rings and the tattoos, and I know right away it's Maddox. "Time to fight a real man. It seems my boys are makin' fools out of themselves."

"They're going easy," I pant. "They don't want to hurt a girl."

He chuckles. "I'll hurt a girl. Three seconds." He lets me go and shoves me forward, counting down. I spin around and consider my moves quickly. Maddox walks towards me, smirking, ready to go. I know he wont' give in to me easily. The moment he reaches for me, I duck and spin around behind his back. I'm gifted with a speed Maddox doesn't have, and I'm going to use it.

I drive my fist into his lower back, and as he spins, that same fist finds his balls. Again. Bellowing in pain, he lunges forward, capturing my wrist as I pull it back. He twists it around so I'm forced to go with it, dropping to my knees. I still have my other hand, and when he's close enough I throw my elbow back into his shin as hard as I can.

"Fucker."

I drop and roll out, knowing he will grab for me again. He smirks at me when I come up, and stalks towards me once more. "You're a feisty little shit, but I will win this."

"You think?" I grin, shoving to my feet.

I bounce from foot to foot as he looms in on me. He takes me by surprise by launching his foot out and hitting my knee, sending me back down to the floor. I groan in pain but roll towards him, grabbing for his foot. It isn't the best move, because he drops down on me, trapping me on my side by sitting on me.

He presses a hand to my face, forcing it to the floor. He's being reasonably gentle—I know he is, because I've been in a similar position before, and it hurts.

"I could get used to this chair."

I close my eyes, taking in a deep breath before twisting my body with everything I have until I'm flat on my back. He's still sitting on me. He takes my hands and shoves them above my head, one of his big hands fully capturing both of mine. "What are you goin' to do now, little girl?"

"Kick your ass, Maddox." I grin.

He's not watching my legs, and I'm flexible enough that I launch my knee up, sending him forward just slightly as he loses his balance. He falls forward, his hands releasing mine and dropping either side of my head. I move quickly, wrapping my fingers around his big arms and finding those pressure points again. I pinch them hard and he barks a curse, trying to shake me off.

He pushes up so he's on his hands and knees over me. His hands move quickly to pin down my shoulders, but my hands are in the perfect position to twist up and grab him by the cock. I do so, reaching up quickly and grabbing him so hard he howls. Holy shit, Maddox is something to grab hold of.

The bikers burst out laughing as I twist Maddox's cock in my hand. "We have two choices here." I grin. "You let me go and admit defeat, or you let me keep twisting your cock. It's impressive, by the way."

His jaw is tight, but there is something in his eyes that tells me he isn't backing down. And he doesn't. He moves his knee quickly, lifting it, causing a howl to escape his throat as the movement causing my grip on his cock to tighten, and then he brings it down over my girl parts.

"Motherfucker!" I bellow.

"I told you I'd kick you in the cunt for revenge. Now let me go," he growls.

"Fuck you."

He presses his knee harder, and because I'm tender from Krypt, I hiss in pain.

"Let me go," he orders.

I twist him harder and he presses harder.

"One of us has to give in," I bite out. "And it won't be me."

"I like my cock bein' pulled, baby," he spits. "So it won't be me either."

I really don't want to hurt him in a bad way, even though I know I could. Our eyes are locked in a furious mental battle, neither of us wanting to give in. Realizing that the man isn't about to be beaten by a girl in front of his club, I finally release him. I could make it hurt, but I'm a nice person. He grins down at me, moving his knee. He leans right down until our lips nearly touch.

"You fight good, but you'll never beat me."

"Eat me."

He laughs and pushes off. He reaches his hand out and I take it, standing. The bikers cheer, and thrust drinks at me as I pass. I might not have beaten Maddox, but motherfucker . . .

I owned that fight.

CHAPTER TWELVE

I stumble down the hall. I've had far too much to drink. Seriously, what the hell is wrong with me? I find the bathroom and step in, only to come across a biker balls-deep in a whore who's bent over the sink. "Really?" I snap. "I need to pee."

The biker turns, glaring at me. "Fuck off!"

I mutter something profane and turn, walking down to Krypt's room. His room has the only other toilet in this house, and there's no way I'm going to pee outside. I swing his bedroom door open and shove in, not stopping to consider that he might actually be in here with someone.

He is.

I skid to an abrupt halt as I see Krypt sitting back in his bed, arms up behind it, watching a whore dance and strip in front of him. His eyes swing to me lazily when I step in, and a slow smirk appears across his face. Oh, he thinks it's funny, does he? I have no doubt that this is his way of bringing revenge down on me for earlier.

If I didn't need to pee so badly, I would charge over and smack him in the face.

Instead, I step past the drunken, naked whore, and slip into the bathroom. My anger swells in my chest as I pee. I can either go out there and make a scene, or I can give him the same arrogance he's giving me. I finish up, and by the time I've washed my hands, I know exactly what I need to do.

I step back out, shoulders back, a smirk of my own plastered across my face.

The whore is crawling on the bed towards him, her breasts swinging as she nears. He's got no shirt on, and his hands remain behind his head as he watches her. Before she reaches him, I step beside the bed and glare at her. She jerks her head up at me, confused.

"Get out," I say, my voice smooth yet demanding.

"I beg your pardon?" she slurs.

"I said . . . get out."

She pouts and turns to Krypt. "Who is she?"

"Who I am is beside the point," I say, leaning in and glaring at her. "It's what I'll do if you don't get out now."

She stares at me for a moment and then mutters, "You're the fighting girl."

"I am." I smile. "Now scoot, or I'll practice on your oversized boobs right there."

She huffs and rolls off the bed, not bothering to put any clothes on as she walks away. I turn to Krypt. He's not said a word; instead he keeps his arrogant smirk as he watches me. I walk around to the end of the bed and take hold of my shirt.

"You want a whore, Krypt? I'll give you exactly what you desire."

His eyes grow lusty as I begin to move my hips from side to side, while I slowly unbutton my shirt. I throw it off before making light, yet sexy work of my pants, until I'm in nothing more than my bra and panties. Krypt stares at me, his expression giving me nothing.

I reach up, fingering my bra and running my hand over my breast lightly. "You want me to take this off?"

Krypt grins, but doesn't answer me.

"Did you turn into a mute, Krypt?"

He places his hand on his muscled belly and tilts his head, studying me. I watch him sitting in that position, and my lip slides into my mouth. Imagining him with his cock out, stroking it, has wild ideas filling my mind. I remove my hand from my breast and in a sultry voice, I rasp, "Jerk yourself."

His eyebrows shoot up.

"Don't act like it shocks you. Do it, or I won't take my clothes off."

He shakes his head, shifting and staring at me.

"No?"

He smirks.

"Fine. It won't be me taking my clothes off for you tonight then," I say, turning and walking towards the door.

I'm nearly there when I hear his zip, loud and clear. A slow, sensual smile curls my lips as I turn back to see him jerking his jeans down and releasing his cock.

"Make it good," he says gruffly.

He wraps his large hand around the head of his cock and begins squeezing it gently. I watch it grow in his palm, stretching and swelling until it's ready. I stand at the end of the bed, watching him with a clenching pussy as I slowly run my hands over my bra while swaying my hips.

He keeps squeezing his cock, clearly saving the pleasuring part for later. His eyes narrow and go lusty as I reach around and unclip my bra, flicking it off. I cup my breasts, moaning as my thumbs graze my hardened nipples. Krypt begins to stroke his length, slow and deliberate, his eyes fixated on my nipples.

I slide my hand up and pop my finger into my mouth, sucking it with a little moan before reaching down and swirling the moisture around my nipple. A little gasp leaves my lips and my pussy swells. I love the fact that he's watching me while stroking himself; it's erotic, in the most amazing way.

I run my free hand down my body, over my belly, and to my panties. I take the elastic in my fingers and pull it out, lowering it just enough for him to get a glimpse before letting them go. He grunts angrily, his eyes wild, his dick so hard it looks almost purplish from this angle. "Hands on your pussy. If I'm showing you, then you need to show me," he orders.

"Maybe I just want to make you suffer," I purr.

"Now, Ash, or I'll bend you over and fuck this come right out of myself."

I grin, but my heart picks up a few beats at his words. I take hold of my panties again, lowering them down and shuffling out of them. Then I stand, fully naked in front of him. He sucks in a breath, his hand stopping as he takes me in. "You're so fuckin' beautiful."

My cheeks heat as I slowly begin moving again, running my hands over my body, stopping at my breasts to squeeze every now and then. "Fuck. Dance for me, baby. Show me how good it fuckin' feels to be naked in front of me," Krypt groans, stroking his cock harder and faster.

I dance for him, swaying my hips from side to side, letting my hair cascade down my back as I tilt my chin back, moaning while my hands explore my aroused body. I can feel how damp I am between my legs. I let my fingers slide down, swiping through my arousal.

"Fuck," Krypt rasps. "I can see how wet you are. Put your finger in your mouth, gorgeous, suck it off."

I lift my hand to my mouth, sliding my finger past my lips. I close my eyes and moan, so completely turned on. I suck myself clean before letting my fingers wander back down to my pussy. I slip them into my depths, relishing in the damp warmth there. My eyes are on Krypt, watching his hand slide up and down his cock, watching his body tense with need.

"Play with your pussy," he growls. "Fuck, yes."

I stroke my clit, moaning at the heightened sensation that travels through my body.

"Spread your legs. Let me see your sweet cunt."

I stare around, noticing a chair close by. I bring it closer before placing one of my legs on it. In doing this, I expose myself fully to him. My cheeks flush crimson at the realization that he can see all of me. I dare to glance at him, and once again he's stopped stroking himself. He stares at me, his lips slightly parted, his eyes so full of lust they almost burn through me.

"Holy fuck," he breathes. "That's the sexiest fuckin' thing I've ever seen."

I tentatively push my fingers back into my folds, finding my clit again. I stroke, dropping my head back as everything comes to life. It feels so good, so damned amazing. Knowing Krypt is watching makes it that much more erotic. My clit swells beneath my finger, becoming a hard little nub.

"Oh God," I whimper.

"Yeah, baby, yeah," Krypt grates out, his hand stroking his cock so hard his muscles bulge in his arms.

"Krypt," I mewl, rubbing harder, moving down to slip a finger inside my heat.

"Shit, fuck, baby, come for me."

"I . . ." I cry out. "Oh God, I want to."

"Come," he barks, his hand working over his cock in a frenzy.

Everything swells inside me before exploding out. I scream his name as my orgasm rocks me, taking me over the edge. I don't even hear

Krypt move, but before I can finish my high he's in front of me, his hand around my hip. He thrusts inside me, so fucking hard it burns.

"You're . . ." he grunts and he thrusts.

"So . . ."

Thrust.

"Fucking . . ."

Thrust.

"Perfect."

He's fucking me like a wild animal, his hand on my hip, his cock driving in and out of my wet flesh. His other hand is tangled in my hair, and he's tugging me hard with each stroke of his cock inside me.

"Fuck, Ash," he roars as he finds his release. His cock swells before exploding. I feel every pulse as he empties himself into my wanting sex.

"Krypt," I whimper, pressing my lips to his sweaty neck.

He stops thrusting, but he doesn't move away from me. He holds me there for the longest time, until both of us can breathe normally again. Then he pulls back and stares down at me, his expression sated. He leans down, pressing a light kiss to my lips before pulling back and letting me go.

"You're goin' to be the fuckin' death of me, Ash," he says, jerking his jeans back up.

"I could say the same," I whisper, leaning down to find my clothes.

He sits on the end of the bed, watching me dress.

"About earlier," he begins.

I put my hand up. "We don't know each other, Krypt. Can we just . . . can we just go with it for now?"

He stares at me, his eyes intense. With a sigh, he nods. "I can go with it, sweetheart, but know this." He stands, and leans in close. "I won't be waitin' forever."

I swallow as he steps past me, and walks towards the door.

"Krypt?" I call out.

He turns.

"Don't think that it wouldn't be an honor to be with you like that. It's just . . ."

"I know," he grinds out. "It's just it ain't for you."

He walks out without another word.

Well, if I'd never felt used before, I certainly do now.

CHAPTER THIRTEEN

Krypt avoids me the entire next day.

That's fine; I'm still deliciously sore because of our actions. Each time I move I'm reminded of his heated length sliding into me, fucking me into oblivion. Just the very thought of it has my skin tingling. He might think he's not for me, but he's very wrong. He's all I can think about. He's consuming me.

"Get her up here. It's not safe for her down there."

I hear Krypt's voice as I move through the halls the next evening. I stop, pressing myself against the wall. Who is he talking about?

"She's not goin' to be happy with that, Krypt," Tyke growls. "She doesn't want to be in this life."

"She ain't gettin' a choice. It's dangerous, and if Howard figures out she's lookin' for me, he'll jump at the chance to take her."

"Fine, but you ain't gonna be the one to go and get her."

"Think I don't know that?" Krypt barks.

I wonder whom they're talking about. My mind spins with the possibilities. An old flame? A sister? A friend? A niece? The shuffling of boots has my body launching off the wall. I crash right into Krypt's hard, muscled chest.

"Oh, sorry," I mumble, pushing back. "I was just, ah, I was . . ."

Shit.

I look up to see Krypt smirking at me. The arrogant jerk. His eyes flash with humor; he's finding it amusing that I'm stuttering like a small child in front of him. I take a breath and straighten my shoulders, turning on my heel and disappearing down the hall.

"Good to see you, Ash." He chuckles.

I throw my finger up over my shoulder and his laughing intensifies. He can't see it, but I have a huge smile on my face. I duck around the corner into the kitchen; I haven't eaten all day. When I get in, a few of the club whores are gathered around, making sandwiches. They look up when I come in. Three of them give me sour expressions, and I recognize one of the ladies as Krypt's striptease. Yeah, I outdid you baby. The fourth one is softer, her face less tense.

"Ladies," I murmur, walking past them.

"That's Krypt's whore," one mutters.

I snort. "I'm no one's whore, honey. I fuck because I want to fuck, not because I'm desperate for attention."

"Bitch," another grunts.

"Tell yourself whatever you want." The third laughs.

I ignore them, listening to them leave the room. I turn, thinking I'm alone, only to see the fourth, quieter girl watching me. She's pretty, and not in the cheap kind of way. Her body is curvy, sure, but it's not slutty or fake. Her long black hair falls over her shoulders in curls, and her eyes are a soft green.

"Why are you here?" she asks, her voice small.

I tilt my head to the side, watching her. "I don't really have a choice."

"You're not a whore?"

"No, of course not."

I realize how rude that sounded and go to correct myself, but she jumps in.

"Don't say sorry." She gives me a sad smile. "It's not for everyone."

I narrow my eyes. "What's a pretty girl like you doing being a piece of ass for a biker, who really doesn't treat you the way you deserve to be treated?"

"They don't treat me so bad," she whispers. "I'm the one they treat most gently, for whatever reason."

I can see the reason. She's softer than the rest; it's clear by the way she holds herself.

"Why do you do it?" I ask, stepping closer.

She contemplates this for a while, before saying, "They make me feel . . . important."

"But," I hesitate, wanting to word this correctly, "but they are treating you like a sex toy."

"Not all of them." She smiles coyly. "Some treat me better than that."

"Even so, they're never going to give you what you want, so why do you stay?"

Her eyes grow dark. "Because, even in their worst times, they're the best I have."

My heart breaks for her. "I understand that," I say, smiling weakly.

"They take care of me, even if I am only a piece of ass. That's something."

"You're right." I nod, understanding. "It is."

"Anyway, I have to go. Tyke is waiting for me."

"Tyke?" I ask.

She flushes. "Yeah, Tyke. He's good to me, probably the best out of them all."

I flash her a quick smile as she slips out. When she's gone, I turn and make myself a sandwich before heading down the hall, eating it. The bikers are out in the shed, so the house is quiet. After a slow lap, I finish up my sandwich and decide to go and read.

I'm passing Maddox's room when I hear a moan. A throaty, deep moan. I stop, turning my head to see the door is cracked slightly open. I bite my bottom lip and hesitate. *Don't be a perv.* I shake my head and go to walk away when I hear Maddox's guttural, "Fuckin' suck it harder."

I can't help myself. I look.

My cheeks burn when I see Maddox sitting on the couch, his jeans jerked down, his cock freed and settled in one of the whore's mouths. She's sucking him furiously, her hands tied behind her back. I open my mouth, but only a little whimper comes out. I've never seen something so erotic in my life.

Maddox's jaw is tight, his long hair loose around his shoulders. He's got his hand on the base of his cock and he's stroking in swift jerks as the top of his cock is devoured. *Oh boy*. I squirm, knowing I should look away, but not being able to bring myself to turn. It's so erotic. Like real-life porn.

A hand wraps around my hip and I jerk, going to spin, but a firm grip stops me. "You dirty little girl." *Krypt*. It's Krypt. My cheeks flush when I realize that he's just caught me watching Maddox getting his dick sucked. I try to take a step back, but his hands pin me in place.

"Do you like watching his cock getting sucked?" he purrs in my ear.

"I, I was just passing and . . ."

"Answer me, Ash. Did you like watching it?"

I swallow before whispering, "Yes."

"Oh, baby," he growls, his voice throaty. "I think you just made me want you more."

I did?

His hand slides around my hip and edges towards my jeans.

"What are you doing?"

"Making you come."

"Krypt, no . . ."

"Shhh," he murmurs into my ear. "If you make too much noise, Maddox will see you watching him. And then you'll be left to explain that to him, and let me tell you, Maddox is an erotic little fucker. He wouldn't hesitate in throwing you over his couch and fucking you while that whore there sucked on your tits."

Oh my God.

I whimper.

Krypt chuckles.

"My girl is bad."

His hand slides into my jeans, slipping straight past my panties and into my soaked pussy. He makes an appreciative sound when he dips his fingers into my arousal. "God, you're so fuckin' wet. Do I need to take you in there and fuck you in front of him?"

"Oh God," I whimper.

"Maybe let him suck your tits while I fuck you hard."

"Krypt," I mewl as he begins rubbing my aching clit.

"Or perhaps you can suck his cock while my dick is deep inside your ass."

I jerk and my pussy clenches, causing bolts of pleasure to shoot through my body. I'm on fire; I want to come so hard. Krypt swirls his fingertip around my clit, sending me higher and higher. My eyes are on Maddox and the whore, watching her suck him, and watching his handsome face as it fills with pleasure.

I can't lie. The idea of being in a Krypt-and-Maddox sandwich doesn't have me cringing; it has everything inside me pulsing. Krypt rubs harder and faster, his lips at my neck. He sucks and nips, bringing my blood to the surface before moving on. I can feel his hard cock against my back as he rubs it against me.

"Fuck, my cock is so hard."

"Rub it against me," I plead. "Come hard against me, Krypt."

"Baby," he growls.

I reach around with my hand, rubbing it over his length hard and fast. He hisses as his fingers work my clit, bringing me to the edge. My entire body is prickling with a sensation I've never felt as I watch Maddox's hips push off the couch in pleasure when he nears his release.

"Krypt," I pant. "I need to come."

"Come, you filthy little bitch. Fucking come."

His words make a strangled sound rip from my throat, enough to have Maddox shoot his head up and his eyes lock on mine. I don't think he can see Krypt, but I have no doubt he's figured out I'm not alone. I'm not whimpering like this without touching myself. A slow, sexy smirk appears on Maddox's face when he realizes what's happening.

"He . . . he . . . he saw me," I gasp.

"Let him watch you come, baby. Let him watch me make you scream."

My mouth drops open as he flicks my clit, taking me to the edge. I rub his dick harder, using friction to bring him to the same point.

"I'm going to, oh God," I yell.

Maddox makes a rumbling sound, his eyes still on me as he barks his release. The whore struggles to take all of him, licking and sucking each drop as he thrusts his cock into her mouth. Krypt hisses beside me as I rub harder and faster. My release pours through me, my vision blurring as my body trembles.

"Fuck, you're going to unman me," Krypt pants. "Fuck, Ash."

"Come for me," I demand. "Now, Krypt."

I squeeze him and he snarls a curse as I feel his cock pulse in his jeans. He shudders, tightening his fingers on my hip as he uses my back and hand to rub every drop from him. Maddox stands, untying the whore and jerking his jeans up. Then he makes his way towards us. When he reaches me, our eyes meet and he takes my chin, jerking my face up.

"Did you like that?"

I swallow, but nod. Maddox's eyes flash up to Krypt's.

"Maybe it's time we share this one, Krypt."

Krypt grunts. "Fuck off, Maddox."

He smirks and looks back down to me. "I like to share." He leans in close, grazing his lips over mine until I'm shivering all over. "You convince Krypt there to let me in, and we'll fuck you until you can't fucking breathe."

Then he shoves me aside and steps past me.

Holy mother-fucking shit.

I think I just wet my pants.

CHAPTER FOURTEEN

I hide for the next few hours, my entire body still on fire over what just happened. Where did that even come from? I mean, I won't deny I love sex, but to do that, openly, with Krypt's hand in my pants . . . that's just . . . wow. I am almost sure I have only done those things in my fantasies. I really didn't think I'd turn those fantasies into reality.

"Hey!"

I look up from the sofa in my room to see Santana. She skips in, dropping down beside me.

"Hey." I give her a shaky smile.

"What's up?"

I shake my head quickly. "Nothing. What about you?"

"I'm bored. Want to come outside and learn how to ride a bike?"

I laugh. "No thanks."

"Krypt will be all over that—you draped over his bike . . ."

I snort. "He will not."

She giggles. "Bikers love nothing more than the women they want slinking all over their bikes."

I grin. "You're an animal."

"I try." She winks. "Hey, can I tell you something?"

I nod, turning to her.

"You won't tell Maddox?"

"Why would I tell Maddox?"

She shrugs. "Well, you know, because he's all protective and shit."

"Still, I'd never tell him."

She smiles and leans in close. "I'm . . . I'm kind of seeing someone outside the club."

My eyes widen. "You are? Won't Maddox have a shit fit?"

She shakes her head, a saucy little grin on her lips. "Not if he doesn't know."

"Okay," I say, slightly concerned, but figuring it's not my place to lecture her. "So tell me about him?"

She leans back. "He's really sweet. He has taken me on a few dates. Oh Ash, he even opens doors for me."

I smile. "He sounds nice. What's his name?"

"Alec."

"That's a nice name."

She nods. "He's a really good guy. He hasn't tried anything. He's not bossy and best of all, he's not a biker."

"Bikers bother you?" I ask, shocked.

She shakes her head. "No, not at all. But Maddox is always on my case, making me feel like I have no life. Alec lets me be whatever I want. I don't have to answer to him."

"Do you think it's going to bother Maddox when he finds out?"

"Maddox doesn't like his control being taken away," she says, her voice soft. "I'm his little puppet. The girl he saved. He thinks I owe it to him to be his little dog toy. But I'm tired of it."

"Do you care about Maddox?"

"No," she says quickly, far too quickly if you ask me.

"Sure about that?"

She gives me a hard expression. "He is horrible to me. He treats me badly, and he won't let me have a life. There's nothing to care about."

"Okay," I say. "I believe you."

"Alec is different." She sighs, smiling. Maybe she really does like Alec. It sure looks like it, judging from the stupid love-struck expression on her face. "He is so sweet."

"What does he look like?"

She squeals happily, throwing her arms around me. "He's gorgeous, Ash. Like sandy-blond hair, and blue eyes . . . gorgeous. He's got a killer bod."

I beam. She deserves happiness. "So are you going to see him again soon?"

She pouts. "While we're on lockdown, I can't. Maddox would never let me out."

"No, you're right about that."

"Anyway, come out front with me. Penny will be here soon."

"Who is Penny?" I ask, following her out the door.

"Krypt's little angel."

I stop walking. "What?"

She laughs. "Don't be jealous, they haven't been a thing for ages."

My mind swims as I walk out the front with her. Krypt's little angel? What is that supposed to mean? They *haven't* been a thing *for ages*? Meaning there was a time they were? We stop on the front steps and sit down, but my mind is too foggy to have decent conversation.

Commotion brings me back to here and now, and I blink a few times to shake the intense thoughts from my mind. I look up and see Maddox coming through the gate with a girl behind him. I gasp as I take her in. She's beautiful, in the sweet-and-innocent kind of way. She's nearly an exact replica of that actress Amanda Seyfried, with her long, slightly wild blond hair, and light blue eyes.

She's wearing a white dress that ties up around her neck and flows prettily around her knees. I swallow down the lump in my throat as I watch her eyes scan about for Krypt. Santana is right; she sure does look like an angel. *Krypt's angel.* I shake the thought from my head just as I notice Krypt coming out of the shed.

He's got the smile of all smiles on his face as he approaches her, dimples and all. When he reaches her, his arms encircles her waist and he flings her around, causing an angelic little squeal to leave her lips as she wraps her legs around his waist and her arms around his neck. Her lips slide over his, rather quickly, but it's a kiss all the same. He grins, pressing a kiss to her head, on top of the one she just gave him. Jealously punches me in the chest like a hammer, and I find myself backing up.

I need to get out of here.

I turn and rush back into the house, dodging bikers as I go. I run through the building, and straight out the back, heading down the yard until I find a thick cluster of trees to disappear into. I lower myself, squatting on the floor and capturing my head in my hands. I steady my breathing, telling myself to stop it.

You said no to him.

You said no.

I know my jealousy is uncalled for, but I didn't say no to Krypt because I didn't want him. God, I barely know him, but the raw fact of the matter is I do want him, more than I'd first thought. This is all too much. Everything is too much. This wasn't meant to happen to me. God dammit, it wasn't meant to happen.

"Hey, are you okay?"

I hear Santana's voice, but I don't look up.

"Ash."

She kneels down, placing a hand on my back.

"I'm okay," I pant, but I can't catch my breath.

Don't have a panic attack now, Ash. Breathe.

In.

Out.

I can't catch up. Everything from the past week catches up on me, hitting my chest like a sledgehammer. I sob loudly, tears streaming down my face as I struggle to breathe.

"Shit," Santana says. "Ash, breathe."

I sob loudly again, rocking backwards and forwards on my heels, thumping my chest to try and get my lungs to work.

"Just hang on."

She gets up and rushes off, even though I attempt to squeak out a no. I don't want anyone to see me like this. I don't want them to witness my pathetic breakdown. I stand and stumble further into the trees, gasping for air as I go. My eyes are blurred with my tears, and so much is running through my mind.

Krypt.

Penny.

Tristan.

Death.

Trapped.

I begin singing in a wobbly voice. My doctor taught me this method years ago when I first started having panic attacks. It helps; it forces my lungs to strain and work. I sound like a hysterical loon as I stammer out the words to Taylor Swifts "Sparks Fly". I hear boots crunching, and then I hear Krypt's, "Fuck."

I shake my head and keep singing. My entire body shakes and tears thunder down my cheeks. Krypt's arms go around me, and he crushes me against his chest. His hand goes to the back of my neck, holding me close, pressing me against him so he's all I can feel.

"I got you," he says gruffly.

I keep singing, keeping my eyes clamped shut. Krypt holds me there, rocking me just slightly as I have a complete mental breakdown. I cry for everything, but mostly I cry because I'm such a goddamned idiot. I should have never befriended Krypt. I should have just left it. Left it all alone.

"Breathe for me, Ash," he says, squeezing the back of my neck. "Come on."

I struggle to take a breath, my lungs seizing the moment I try to fill them.

"Come on baby," he encourages. "Big breath."

I open my mouth and gasp. It's not much, but it's air.

"That's my girl. Keep going."

I do it again and again until my shaking has subsided, and only my tears continue. Krypt pulls my head from his chest, taking hold of my chin. He forces me to look at him. I blink away my tears as I try to focus on his gorgeous, rugged face.

"You with me?" he asks.

I nod.

"What the fuck happened?"

I dart my eyes away.

"You saw Penny, didn't you?"

I don't look back.

"Fuck, Ash."

Now I feel like an idiot.

"You care about me?" he says, his voice low and husky.

I refuse to answer that. Instead I croak out, "I don't know you."

"Stop your shit, and answer the damned fuckin' question."

I don't. I won't.

"Fuck, you're a stubborn woman."

I close my eyes, taking a deep breath. "It wasn't that. It was . . . it was just everything."

He knows I'm lying. I know I'm lying. Neither of us say anything.

"Come inside. I'll give you a shot of whiskey. It'll sort you out."

He pulls me to my feet and leads me through the trees.

"Krypt?" I whisper.

He stops and turns to look at me, his eyes zoning in on mine.

"Thank you."

He gives me a jerky nod, and we continue on through the trees.

When we get inside he takes me to the bar, and hands me a damp cloth and a shot of whiskey. I wipe my face before swallowing the shot. He hands me another one, his eyes firmly on mine. I take it, too, before looking up at him. He studies my face, his expression unreadable.

Neither of us gets the chance to speak before Penny appears beside him. God, she's even more beautiful up close.

"There you are." She smiles at him.

Krypt drags his eyes from me, and smiles down at the girl, who could only be around twenty-three, or twenty-four.

"Penny, I want you to meet Ash."

My eyes widen. Not what I was expecting. I probably look like a snotty mess. I wipe my face again before plastering a smile on my face.

"Hi Ash." Penny smiles, extending her hand.

I take it, hesitantly. "Hi."

"Ash is a friend of the club's. She's not a whore, so you don't need to hesitate in talkin' to her," Krypt adds.

I scrunch my nose in disgust at his introduction, but I squash it down.

"How refreshing. It's usually just Santana and I."

I swallow and smile again. "Well, now you have me."

She beams and turns to Krypt. "Take me outside for a walk. I want to catch up with you."

He turns his gaze back to me. "You good?"

No, but I'm not about to tell you that.

"Of course," I rasp. "Go."

He turns to Penny. "Hang on a minute."

He walks around the bar and over to me. His hand curls around the back of my neck in that dominating way again, and he leans into my ear. "We're not done with this, you hear me?"

I swallow.

"You *will* tell me what made you cry, and you *will* be honest about it."

Another swallow.

"And if you even try to escape me, I'll put you over my knee and spank your beautiful ass."

Oh, God.

He pulls back, not looking at me as he turns to Penny. "Let's go."

She stares at me curiously, but smiles and hooks her arm through Krypt's. When they're gone, I close my eyes, and let out a whoosh of breath.

Well that didn't go very well, now did it?

~*~*~*~

Santana fills me in on Penny while Krypt is outside with her. It turns out Penny and Krypt were together for about four years from the time she was eighteen until twenty-two. They only split about two years ago, so that must make Penny around twenty-four, as predicted. They grew up together, and were close for a long time. She is four or five years younger than Krypt, but their families were close.

From what Santana tells me, Penny didn't want the biker life and made the choice to go into the city and study, leaving Krypt behind. He was devastated, but knew it was for the best. They were never going to work. He was a biker; she was a soft, gentle woman who wanted a white picket fence and two-point-five children.

They're good friends now, and have been since the break-up.

It kind of makes sense to me now why Krypt didn't like me saying I wasn't going to be an old lady. I'm the second woman who has rejected him for his lifestyle. I feel bad about that. Really bad. But it won't change my mind. I barely know Krypt, and I certainly don't know much about the biker life.

Obviously, Penny did.

"I overheard that she wants to reconsider things with Krypt," I overhear as I'm walking back to my room that night.

"Me too. I hear them talking outside. She said she wanted him back, and he was hesitant."

I stop, listening to the voices coming out of the kitchen.

"I bet that Ash girl won't like that."

"Fuck her. She's a bitch anyway."

I roll my eyes and walk off, wondering if what they're talking about is true. Is Penny here to get Krypt back? I slip into my room and shut the door behind me. I walk over to the bed and flop down, exhaling loudly.

It shouldn't matter to me if she wants him back, I won't even be here long. I have a job and a life to go back to.

I'm staring at my hands when my door opens. I look up to see Krypt. He flashes me a smile before shutting the door behind him and walking in. I don't say anything as he shrugs his jacket off, and crawls onto the bed beside me. Why is he even here? I don't understand.

"You're brooding," he mumbles, taking my body and pulling it underneath his.

I don't bother to protest. Krypt gets what he wants, protests or not.

"I am not," I scoff.

"Baby." He smirks. "You so are."

"Fuck off, biker."

"I like you mad," he murmurs, dropping his head into my shoulder.

"Can you get off me?"

"No."

"Now!" I snap.

"Ah . . . *no.*"

I growl and drive my fist into his ribs. He chuckles.

"I thought you were tougher than that, darlin'."

I hook my legs through his and lean up to bite his chest. He barks a curse and flips us over so I'm on top of him. He captures my hands and smirks up at me. "Cheater."

"You want to dance, biker? I'm in the mood to dance."

He chuckles, throwing me off him. He rolls off the bed and stands, wiggling his fingers in that *come and get me* kind of way. I smirk and leap off the bed too, looming towards him.

"We can dance, baby. But make it count, because if I beat you, I'm fucking you, and I'm not going to be nice about it."

"And if I beat you, then you have to put me in the bath and wash me from head to toe. Then you're going to lick my pussy and get nothing in return."

His chest rumbles at my words and a slow, sexy smile appears on his face.

"It's a deal."

I grin.

I take a step towards him, and he dances off to the side. Oh, Krypt likes to play. I swing at him, missing his belly by mere millimeters.

He's fast. He jumps towards me but I duck quickly out of his way, popping up behind him and throwing myself onto his back. I press a smacking kiss to his cheek. "One for me."

"That was just the beginning, honey." He chuckles, taking my arms and bending forward, flipping me over his back.

I squeal as I land on the floor. I roll before he gets the chance to sit or lie on me. It's hard to move a man that lies on you. Instead, I drive a fist into his shin. He bellows and presses a booted foot over my hand lying on the floor. Not hard, but hard enough so that I can't move it. He stares down at me with lusty eyes.

"Oh, my dick is going to make you sore, little girl." He smirks.

I arch my back up, using my leg to connect with the back of his knee, bringing him down. I roll, pushing up to my hands and knees. "My pussy is going to relish in every lick your tongue gives it." I grin.

He turns, on his hands and knees as he crawls towards me. He's like a caged animal that's just been freed. He backs me up to the wall, smart man. He pushes up to his knees and grabs my waist pulling me flush against him. "Your pussy will pay when I'm done."

I use my arms to flick his off me, and then wrap my arm around his neck, forcing his head down. He lets out a long chuckle, using his arm to wrap around mine and flip me over. I land with a thump, but use my knee to stop him coming down over me. I drive it right into his belly.

He grunts and leans back, giving me enough room to lunge upwards. I latch onto him like a little monkey, keeping my arms around his neck and my legs around his waist. "What ya gonna do now, biker?"

He reaches down and pinches my ass so hard I let him go with a squeal. He laughs loudly. Asshole. He captures me in a headlock, pulling me against him. "Mmmm, I can feel it already. Your little pussy squeezing me until I'm coming hard inside you."

I shudder.

"Five seconds, baby, or I win."

My hands go back for a shot at his nipples, but he captures them with his free hand. "Uh, uh, uh."

I shoot my leg back quickly instead, hitting his knee. He growls and loosens his grip, so I do it again, forcing him to release his arms so he can take a step away from me. I swing around, ducking low and driving my head into his belly, shoving him hard against the wall. I bounce back as his hands swoop down to catch mine.

"That all you got?" I mutter, bored.

He lunges at me, catching me around the waist and slamming my body to the ground. Then we're tackling, fierce and wild, hands hitting and pulling, legs kicking, teeth biting, laughter sounding out through the room. We roll about, knocking lamps down, and shoving furniture out of the way. I give it my all, but Krypt is a big man.

Finally he pins me on my back.

"I win."

"Fine," I pant. "You win."

He smirks.

"How are you going to take me, sir?" I flutter my eyelashes at him.

"I changed my mind. Your pussy on my lips is exactly what I need right now. My hands pinning you down as you squirm."

"Or," I breathe, "I could lay on top of you with your cock in my mouth as you suck my clit."

He growls.

"Baby, it's like you're one with me."

He brings us up so we're sitting. I reach forward and take his jeans, popping them open. I reach in, feeling the hot skin of his cock as I curl my palm around it.

"Fuck, yeah."

We make light work of our clothes, kicking them off until we're both naked. We're equally hungry for each other. Krypt lies down, pulling me over him. Well, pulling my ass over him. I rest on my elbows, his cock brushing against my cheek. I try not to think about the fact that my ass is in his face right now. He hums against my pussy, causing a little shiver to slide through my body.

I reach down, curling my fingers around his cock. I stare at it, deciding to go with licking his piercing first. I snake my tongue out, sliding it over the little ball. He groans, and slides his tongue through my heat. Oh, boy. It's going to be hard to concentrate. I take him into my mouth, closing my lips around him.

He sucks my clit into his.

I take him deeper.

We do this until we're a frenzy of hot mouths against each other, kissing, sucking, licking, and nipping until we're both bucking, needing release.

Then someone knocks at the door.

"Krypt?"

Penny.

Seriously.

Right now?

Krypt hisses and then lets out a long, feral groan against my pussy before wrenching his mouth away. Fuck him. I'm not going to stop.

"Ash, stop," he grinds out. "Stop."

No.

"Ash," he pants. "Don't want her hearin' this. Don't want her thinkin' . . ."

I keep sucking, hard and deep. Fuck what she thinks. If he didn't want to do it, he shouldn't have started.

"Krypt?"

"Yeah?" he barks.

"I . . . I wanted to ask if you . . . um . . . wanted to have dinner with me?"

Fuck off, Penny. I've got his cock in my mouth, and I will be making him come.

"Ah, yeah," Krypt says, his voice husky.

He tugs on my hair. I don't stop. I suck, and I suck hard. He hisses, and his breathing becomes ragged.

"Fuck, Ash," he whispers. "Fuckin' stop. You don't understand. I care about her, fuck. Stop."

Anger swells in my chest and I suck him harder, using my teeth to graze over his head. The fucking asshole.

"Could I come in . . . or are you busy?"

Oh, he's busy.

His body jerks and I feel the first hot spurt of come hit the back of my throat. He tugs my hair harshly, causing a burning pain to radiate through my skull.

"I . . . I'm coming," he manages.

Oh yes, he is.

His cock pulses over and over, until there's nothing left. When I'm done, I get off him, wiping my mouth and smirking at him. I pull my clothes back on and walk towards the door.

"Ash, don't you fuckin'—"

He doesn't get to finish because I swing the door open. He pulls a blanket over himself with a curse. Penny stares down at him, then looks to me. I give her a smile, and step past her. "Later, Krypt."

Then I disappear down the hall.

It's only when I'm alone that I let my hurt shine through. I lift my hand and drive it into a nearby wall with a yell.

Goddammit.

CHAPTER FIFTEEN

I hear Krypt's bellow before I see him.

I'm sitting with the guys in the bar. Tyke has been chatting to me for the last hour or so, and Ray and Grimm have been feeding me drinks. I like these guys. Their old ladies have been interacting with me, too, which is odd. There are only three of them, but they seem to keep to themselves in the sheds most of the time.

I think at first they'd thought I was a whore.

Sara, Indi and Petra belong to Grimm, Zaid and Rhyder. I haven't had the chance to get to know Zaid and Rhyder, but I do know Grimm. His old lady, Sara, is a really nice girl. She's in her thirties, and has a super sweet nature. I'm glad to be speaking to some of them and getting to know the club, considering I've been here a week now.

"That bellow sounded somewhat like your name." Tyke smirks.

"That broody motherfucker can suck my—"

Krypt bellows again; definitely my name. I smirk and lean back against the bar, waiting for him to show. He does, his face wild with anger and his fists balled. He storms over, stopping in front of me.

"Evening, Beau." I grin.

"Don't you fuckin' *evening* me. Stand up. We are going to talk."

"Ah, no."

"Ah, fucking yes."

He doesn't give me a choice. He leans down, shoving his shoulder into my stomach and lifting me up. I squeal and slap his back. He charges through the house and out the door. He takes me down to one of the sheds before setting me on my feet and barking at the few lingering bikers. "Get out."

They all stand with muttered curses, and leave.

Then Krypt spins to me.

"What the fuck were you thinkin'?"

"Excuse me?" I snap. "Me? What were *you* thinking?"

"I've spent the last fuckin' hour calming Penny down, because she was beside her-fucking-self."

"No offence, Krypt, but if you didn't want to do it then you shouldn't have."

He leans in close. "What I do is my business. If I wanted everyone to know I was fucking you, I would have taken you out and done it in front of them."

Ouch.

"If you're so ashamed of the fact that you're fucking me, then why are you doing it? If you don't want Penny to know, then you shouldn't be sticking your dick in me."

He growls. "She matters to me."

I get in his face. "Obviously not enough, because as I recall, your cock was inside my mouth when she was at the door and you came, hard."

He snarls, baring his teeth at me. "I told you to stop."

"And I didn't want to!"

"She matters to me," he roars. "I never wanted her to see me like that. I asked you to stop. You should have fuckin' stopped."

"So you could have dumped me on my ass and run out to her?" I laugh bitterly.

"Exactly," he snarls. "Because she means something to me, and you fuckin' don't."

Slapping me would have hurt less than those words.

My head spins and tears burn in my eyes.

I wish there was something I could say, but there's a knot deep in my chest that is stopping me from breathing normally.

Krypt's eyes soften just slightly, and I know he realizes what he said was harsh, but the thing about saying something is that you can't take it back. I turn, walking towards the door.

"Ash, don't you fuckin' . . ."

I spin around, my eyes wild. "Here's something for you, Krypt. Go and fuck yourself, because I sure as hell won't be doing it again."

I shove through the door, running towards my safe place—the trees. When I get to them, I slide down a trunk, not caring that it scratches my back. I drop my head and struggle for air. I should have known better. I was never meant to be here, and now I know why. I sob loudly.

I want to go home.

CHAPTER SIXTEEN

I sit out there in the cold for a solid few hours.

Then I know I have to go back. There is nowhere for me to run. I can't go into the wilderness at night, because that's risking my life, and I won't do that. So, I do the only thing I can. I get up, take a deep breath, square my shoulders and walk back into the house.

The bikers are in full swing when I get inside. There are half-naked girls, beers being shoved around, and laughter filling the small space. I walk straight past them, heading towards the hall. A hand lashes out and grips my hip as I pass, and I look down to see Maddox with his hand on me.

"Let me go, Maddox."

He tilts his head to the side. "What crawled up your ass and—"

He doesn't get to finish his sentence, because I shove my hands on his chest and shove him back. "Do not finish that sentence. I have had about enough of you bikers for a lifetime."

He takes my wrists and pulls me down closer so I fall onto his lap. "That's a piss-ass answer, stop your bullshit and pull yourself together."

"Oh, bite me."

He smirks and leans in, doing just that. I squeal loudly as his mouth closes over my neck and he bites me. The motherfucker makes it hurt, too.

"Ow," I scream. "Maddox, you bastard."

He laughs as he pulls away, and I can't help but grin back.

"There we are, pretty smile returned. Now get off me or I'll change my mind and bite you in other places."

I smile at him, not because he's being sexual again, but because I think it's the first nice thing he's done for me. I shove off his lap and stand, catching a glimpse of Krypt standing at the bar. His eyes are on mine, fierce and deadly. I lose my smile and walk off down the hall, giving him nothing.

It's clear we're done.

He's ashamed of me. He doesn't want his precious Penny to know about me, and that's fine, but I don't have to accept it.

I *won't* accept it.

~*~*~*~

I'm woken in the morning to a high-pitched scream.

I jerk up out of bed as footsteps pound down the hall. I rub my eyes, trying to listen, terrified to even move. That wasn't a good scream, it was the kind of scream you hear when someone finds a dead body.

"Fuck, shit, get her inside," I hear Maddox bark.

"What is it?" another voice yells.

"Howard left us a present. Where's Ash?"

Krypt's voice.

"Sleepin'. Who is that?"

"I don't fuckin' know, but he's in a bad fuckin' way."

He?

I get out of my bed, pulling a pair of jeans on before walking through the house and out the front door.

What I see has my entire body skidding to a halt.

There is a man slumped outside of the gates, but all I can see of him is blood. He's covered in it. My eyes widen, and I begin to tremble as I force my legs to take me closer. The bikers are rushing about, some of them on the phone, others standing back and watching with disgust.

Maddox and Krypt are leaning down, touching the man, no doubt checking for a pulse. Santana is standing to the left, her hand pressed over her mouth. Penny is beside her, her face pale.

I turn my attention back onto the man that's been dumped. As I near, I see his arms, that tattoos winding up them. I freeze in horror when my eyes fall on an all-too-familiar tattoo of a skeleton with a name wrapped around the skull.

I scream before I think, running full-throttle towards the body.

Krypt spins around, and so does Maddox. They both stare at me in confusion for a minute, until they realize my eyes are trained on the body. I am sobbing wildly by the time I skid to a stop. I drop to my knees, reaching out. "Leo?" I whisper.

"You know this man?" Maddox asks.

"Yes, oh God. Leo, honey, wake up."

His entire body has been beaten; he's covered in blood. His eyes are puffy and there is a split under his cheek that's gaping and dripping with blood. His lips are busted up. He looks terrible.

"Leo," I croak.

"Get her inside, now," Krypt suddenly yells, an urgency in his voice that has me panicking.

"Krypt?" Maddox questions.

"Fuck, now!" he roars.

Someone runs towards me, standing me up and jerking me towards the house. I don't know what's happening.

"Krypt?" Maddox yells again.

"Don't you fuckin' see? They knew she'd come out here, which means . . ."

He doesn't get to finish, because the sound of gunfire rings through the trees. A bullet zooms right past my head. I scream and begin running towards the house. Another shot rings out, and a burning pain rips through my shoulder. I drop to my knees, crying out in agony.

"Get her in, now!" Krypt roars.

Someone leans down, lifting my body and dragging me through the front door. Another shot hits the pole beside my head as we pass it. When I'm inside, I'm rushed down the hall until whoever has me reaches a bathroom. I see it's Grimm, when I manage to focus through my pain. He lays me on the floor, pulling out his gun. He lays me directly under the window, so that I can't be shot through it.

He pulls a towel off the rack and presses it against my shoulder. "It's goin' to be okay."

"It hurts," I wail.

"I know. Stay still. You can't afford to move right now."

"Krypt," I croak.

"They've got this."

I hear more gunshots, doors slamming, and girls screaming, before everything falls silent. I am still shaking through the pain, my vision blurring as my body threatens to drop into darkness.

"Oh God, it hurts," I scream.

"Hush," Grimm says again. "It'll be over soon."

My head swims and my eyes flutter closed. I'm still screaming, but soon darkness clutches me and takes me with it. I let it, too. I need the escape from the pain, because the pain is too much, and I feel as though I'm going to die if I don't get away from it for just a second.

"Ash," I hear Grimm say as I sink further. "Ash wake up."

Then I hear nothing.

~*~*~*~

"Motherfucker, she's bleeding," I hear through a foggy haze.

"Stitch her, fast. If you don't, she'll lose too much blood. The bullet is gone."

"Fuckers. I'll kill them all."

"Just focus, Krypt."

Krypt?

I open my mouth and try to squeak his name. A hand strokes over my face, only barely there. "I got you, baby. We're goin' to make this better."

"Load her up, Krypt. It's goin' to fuckin' hurt."

Maddox.

"You want me to fuckin' drug her?"

"You got a better idea out here?"

"Fuck."

Everything goes quiet as I drift back into my unconscious state, but before I'm fully out, I feel a needle being plunged into my arm. Then everything goes black again.

~*~*~*~

I wake again. This time I'm bouncing. Like I'm in a car.

Everything hurts.

My tongue is dry.

I cry out hoarsely, desperate. Where's Krypt? Where is he? I want him. I need him.

Krypt.

"I got you baby," a soft voice says. "I got you. You're safe."

Krypt.

I reach out, my fingers desperate to feel him. My mind is spinning, but I know I need him, almost frantically. I clutch at anything I can, my fingers curling around something soft.

"It's okay," he murmurs, placing a warm hand over mine.

"Krypt," I wail. "Krypt?"

"I got you."

"Krypt."

"She's hallucinating. Just hold onto her."

"Who's there?" I cry, hearing the faint voice and feeling my panic rise.

"Ash, I got you honey."

Krypt?

I cry out for him, reaching around frantically again. I feel a chest, but I don't know whose it is.

"I'm sorry, Krypt, I'm sorry. Don't leave me out here. Please don't leave me out here. I want you. I do want you."

"Hush, you're going to be fine. Just hang in there."

"Krypt!" I wail. "Please don't go."

Another sting pushes into my arm, and once again my world is taken from me.

CHAPTER SEVENTEEN

I wake to the sounds of voices. I shift. I'm on a bed. I can feel the soft mattress beneath my body. I let my eyes flutter open. I have to blink rapidly to gather my bearings. I stare, confused. I've never seen this room before. Where am I? I try to swallow, but my tongue feels like a dead weight, dry and scratchy.

"Krypt?" I croak.

Nothing.

I try to sit up, only to cry out in pain and drop down again. I turn my head and stare down at my heavily bandaged shoulder. I got shot. Oh my God, I got shot.

Leo.

"Leo!" I cry, trying to sit up. "Leo."

The door opens and before I can say another word, Krypt is beside me, his big arms steadying me. "He's at the hospital; he's okay. You're okay."

"Oh Krypt," I rasp. "Oh God."

"Hey," he says, turning my chin towards him. "I swear it's okay."

"I got shot."

He stares at my arm before turning back to me. "You did, but I promise you it's not as bad as it seems. It's only a small wound, now it's been stitched. You're going to be fine. We got some antibiotics. So long as you take them all will be fine."

"You stitched me?" I croak.

"After we got the bullet out."

"I had a b-b-b-bullet?"

He strokes my cheek. "It's okay, Ash."

"W-w-w-where are we?"

"At the clubhouse."

"But . . ."

"Hey, it's fine," he murmurs. "It's the safest place for us. We thought being up there was, but how fuckin' wrong we were. We couldn't hear them coming in. Out here we can see from all directions, including a clear view of the road. We're goin' to end this, Ash, don't you doubt it. Those fuckers will pay for what they did to you."

"Claire!" I suddenly shriek.

"What?" he asks, narrowing his eyes.

"If they got Leo, that means they could have Claire. Oh God Krypt, no."

"Calm down. Tell me where I can find her."

"G-g-g-give me your cell."

He hands me his cell and I unlock it quickly, dialing Claire's number. It rings and rings. When it answers, I breathe a sigh of relief.

"Claire, oh my God, I'm so glad you're okay—"

A low chuckle sounds out, making me pause. "I wondered when you'd call, Ash."

That voice. I have never heard it, but I already know it's bad.

"Who is this?" I say, my voice low.

Krypt reaches for the phone, but I shake my head, needing to hear for myself.

"My name is Howard. I'm sure you've heard of me. I delivered that package to you, did you get it?"

"Fuck you," I spit.

He laughs again. "That's no way to talk to the person holding your friend."

"What do you want?" I growl.

Krypt reaches for me again, but I shoot him a warning glare. He snarls but he doesn't push.

"I wanted you dead, but that didn't work out so well. You see, I can't have you around, ruining my plans. That club will get what's coming for them, but while you're in the way, threatening to ruin it all, it just won't happen."

"Just say it," I croak.

"You for your friend; the decision is yours. A life for a life. If you want her to live, you will meet me in three days time at the Southside wharf. If you don't want her to live, don't show up. The choice is yours. Think long and hard about it. Oh, and Ash, if you call the cops or bring those fuckin' bikers in, I'll slit her throat. But," he laughs bitterly, "I'll fuckin' rape her first."

Bile rises in my throat as he hangs up. The phone slips from my hand and I struggle to catch my breath.

"What happened?" Krypt demands.

"H-h-h-h-he has Claire."

"Shit," he snarls, standing up and bellowing. "Prez!"

"Krypt, wait," I yell. "H-h-h-he said that if I don't trade my life for hers, he'll kill her. I can't let him kill her; I can't."

Krypt spins around, his expression livid. "You'll not be doing any such fuckin' thing."

"She's my best friend. I can't just let her die."

"That's where you have to trust us."

"No," I scream. "He told me no cops or bikers, or he'll do horrible things to her, and I know he will, Krypt. I know he will."

He lunges forward, taking my shoulders. "You need to fuckin' trust us."

"What's goin' on?" Maddox says, appearing in the doorway.

"Howard's finally made his move. He wants Ash. He's got her best friend."

Maddox hisses a curse. "Fuck."

"Yeah," Krypt growls. "That's what I fuckin' said."

"You need to let me go, please," I beg.

Krypt shakes me just slightly. "There is no fuckin' way I'm lettin' him kill you. No fuckin' way."

"Krypt please," I say, hysteria rising.

"You're not fuckin' goin'," Maddox barks. "So quit fuckin' thinkin' it."

"We'll sort this," Krypt assures me, but I don't believe him.

"My office, now. We need to call a meeting." Maddox storms out.

Krypt stares at me, and I know he doesn't trust me. He sighs and holds my wrist, taking me down the hall. He leads me into a room, opens the drawers and pulls out—oh hell, no. I squirm against him, kicking out because it hurts too much to move my shoulder. Because of my injury, he overpowers me quickly.

He snaps the cuffs onto my wrist and locks me against the bed.

"I'm sorry, baby."

"No, Krypt," I scream as he backs out of the room. "I hate you. I fucking hate you."

He disappears, leaving me in hysterics.

Oh God, please don't let them kill her.

CHAPTER EIGHTEEN

KRYPT

"This is fuckin' bad," I bark the minute I get into Maddox's office. "I left my girl in there fuckin' screaming, and I can't trust she won't run. Howard has got us good on this one. He'll make sure we can't ambush him."

"No," Maddox mutters. "He's counting on us ambushing him."

I narrow my eyes. "What are you talkin' about?"

Tyke, Grimm, Ray and Zaid enter the room, their eyes going straight to Maddox. "Fill us in, boss," Zaid mutters.

We fill them in. Then Maddox turns back to me.

"He wants us to ambush him, Krypt. I have no fuckin' doubt about it. He will have this set up so the cops will be on our tail the minute we show. That, or he'll kill the girls and leave them there, with only us in their presence."

"Then what the fuck do we do?" I bark.

"I don't fuckin' know," Maddox growls, running his hands through his hair. "He's got cops on the inside, he's got fuckin' guards on the inside. If we get picked up, we're fucked. We can't afford to let him beat us."

"Even if we got somethin' on him, his cop buddies will make sure he doesn't get locked away," Tyke points out.

"We're royally fucked," Grimm mutters.

"There's a way. I just gotta think of it," Maddox snaps. "I won't let those fuckers hurt them girls or my fuckin' club."

"I got an idea," Tyke murmurs. "But you ain't gonna like it."

All our eyes turn to him.

"I ain't got nothin' else right now, so speak," Maddox orders.

"You send a girl in."

"No fuckin' way," I bark.

"Listen," Tyke snaps, his eyes flashing with anger. "If we rock up out the front, sayin' we wanna make a truce, then the attention will be off Claire. If there's already a girl in there she can get her out. . ."

"We ain't go no one we can send in, for a fuckin' start," Maddox growls.

"We do," Tyke murmurs, his eyes falling on Maddox.

A chair skids back as Maddox launches from it. "No fuckin' way will you be touchin' Santana."

"Howard and his men ain't ever seen her, Maddox. You've kept her quiet for a long time. She could slip in as a whore easily."

"Over my dead fuckin' body."

"You got another option?" Grimm yells. "'Coz if you don't, I think Tyke has the closest thing we have to gettin' that girl back."

"I said fuckin' no. I'll find another way."

"I don't want you to find another way."

All our heads snap around to see Santana standing at the door, her arms crossed over her chest, her eyes glaring through Maddox. He storms over to her, his fingers curling around her shoulder. "There is no way in fuckin' hell I'm lettin' you near that club. Now stop eavesdroppin' and get out."

"No," she snaps.

"So help me fuckin' God, Santana. I'll put you over my knee and—"

"First of all," she yells, getting in his face, "you're not my father, so stop acting like you are. Second of all, you don't own me, so I can make any choice I want."

"I said no," he roars.

She shoves herself further into his face. "And I said you can't stop me."

She turns and walks out. Maddox spins to us, glaring at Tyke. "This ain't fuckin' finished."

Then he storms off after Santana.

Fuck.

CHAPTER NINETEEN

ASH

My shoulder aches, but not nearly as bad as my heart. All of my friends have been hurt or are in danger because of me. That makes me sick to my stomach. I have no way to help them when I'm injured like this. The very fact that I even got shot makes fear course through my veins. It doesn't feel nice.

Not at all.

I heard the commotion a few hours ago, and Krypt filled me in on some basics. They can't find a way to get Claire back without sending someone in. That someone is Santana. Maddox isn't happy about that, and all hell broke loose. I'm not a fan of the idea, but it does make sense. Howard is relying on the fact that Krypt will never let me show up alone, and he's planning an ambush. He won't expect Santana being sent in.

"Hey."

I look up from the bed to see Krypt walking into the room. His gaze slides over me, as if checking I'm in one piece. Then he takes a seat beside me, his hand sliding up to cup the back of my neck. "Santana is goin' in."

I gasp, trembling all over.

"What if something happens to her, Krypt?"

"Santana is a smart girl, and she isn't someone they know. It won't be hard for her to get picked up as a whore. We'll make a distraction and she'll get Claire out."

"What if she gets there, and Claire isn't there?"

He squeezes my neck. "Baby, Claire will be there. Howard wouldn't leave her anywhere else. He's counting on us showing up."

"Then it's a risk."

"No, not if we don't get off our bikes and stay far enough away. It's a distraction; it isn't a war."

"If something happens to Santana because of me . . ."

"Hey," he says, giving me a hard expression. "This isn't on you. You were in the wrong place at the wrong time, but if anyone is to blame, it's those corrupt guards."

I nod, tears welling in my eyes.

"Hey," he says, his voice low and husky. "Don't you crumble on me now, eh?"

I nod, blinking back my tears.

"It'll all be okay."

"I hope so," I whisper.

And I do.

Because I don't think I can take anymore.

~*~*~*~

SANTANA

I look like a two-dollar hooker.

My boots are up to my knees, my shirt is so tight my boobs are poking out the top, and don't even get me started on this skirt. Whores would cringe at this shirt; even they would probably throw holy water over me. I try to jerk my top down, but it's no use. If I pull it down, my boobs will pop out for the world to see.

Peek-a-boo.

"You have no fuckin' idea how much I want to lock you away, especially when you look like that."

Maddox's voice fills the room behind me, and I sigh. I don't need anymore of his lectures. Maybe this will prove to him that I am old enough to take care of myself, and that he doesn't need to keep hovering. When I was a terrified teenager it was one thing, but now I'm a grown woman, and he has some serious control issues.

"There is no choice, so there's no point in going over it," I say, not looking at him.

"You'll likely get fuckin' raped, or . . ."

"Maddox," I snap. "One of the guys will be with me. I won't get raped."

"When you're in that clubhouse there will be no protection, and—"

"I'll be fine."

"—you'll likely—"

"Fine, Maddox."

"—be thrown over—"

God, the man won't stop. I spin around, glaring at him. "Shut up!"

He glares back at me, but he stops talking.

"I'm doing this. Even you know it's for the best. Now, can you please leave? I have to finish getting ready."

He tilts his head to the side, giving me a look he's given me for years now. It makes his blue eyes even more piercing, and his face seem far more intense. His lips twitch with unspoken words as his eyes narrow. "Just come back to me, do you hear?"

I stare at him, surprised. He's always got something nasty to say, some smartass remark that makes me think he doesn't care. I swallow and nod, turning before he can see my eyes misting.

"I will."

I hear him disappear, and something in my chest tugs violently.

What if I never see him again?

~*~*~*~

"Three steps behind," I hiss to Ray, who is following me.

He snorts. "We ain't even close, Santana."

"I don't care. If someone is watching you, it could blow everything."

"Hearin' ya, babe."

I roll my eyes and walk down the street, my heels clinking. As we approach the bar the Tinman's Soldiers are said to spend most of their time at, my anxiety levels rise. I can do this; I just have to be believable. They'll know right away if the guys are going to recognize me; that's why Ray will be outside, with backup ready if need be.

"You're on your own now, Tana," Ray says after another few blocks.

I turn to him. "I'll call you if I need."

He nods. "Stay safe."

I force a smile, and turn, making my way towards the club. I round a corner and see a group of bikers right away. I guess they were right. *Jackpot.* I straighten my shoulders, poke my breasts out, and strut past them to the front entrance.

Wolf whistles sound out, and my anxiety dies down just slightly as I realize they haven't figured out who I am. There's hope—small, but it's there. I reach the line at the front door, and slip in. A group of girls are snickering behind me, muttering words like "whore" and "skank".

I roll my eyes and just keep shuffling through the line. I show my I.D at the door and enter the loud, packed club. Neon blue lights shine into my eyes the moment I step inside. People are everywhere, their bodies grinding. I spot the bar and shove through the crowd, heading towards it. The best place to get noticed is right here.

I order a drink and position myself on a stool, crossing my legs so my skirt rides up my thighs. I let my eyes scan the crowd until I notice another group of bikers at the far end of the bar. At least eight of them.

I stare at them until one turns and notices me. A slow smirk appears on his lips.

Time to get your whore on, Santana.

I give him a sly smile, turning back to my drink and sliding the straw into my mouth, swallowing it down. I have no doubt he'll make his way over. I keep drinking until I feel a presence behind me. A hand grazes up my arm. I want to gag, but I force a smile on my face and turn.

The biker standing in front of me is actually quite stunning. His eyes are a crystal green, and his skin a light olive. He's got ruffled dirty-blond hair. His body is huge, and he's clearly built—I can tell by the way his muscles bunch and pull around his forearms as he takes a seat beside me.

Such a waste of sexiness.

"How you doin', gorgeous?" he purrs, his voice husky.

I bat my eyelashes at him. "I'm fine, and how are you, handsome?" I make my voice sound light and a little slurry.

"My night just got a whole lot better."

I lean in close. "Oh, honey, so did mine."

CHAPTER TWENTY

I drag my feet as I walk into the main living area, having had far too much to drink to take the edge off what's going down right now. The bikers are piled on the couches at the bar and in the kitchen. They're restless; why wouldn't they be? A storm is brewing, and they know it's going to blow up very soon. When it blows, it will cause a big mess all around, and that's not something I think they're entirely prepared for, no matter how good they are. I notice Krypt sitting back against the couch, Penny tucked in beside him.

My heart does a little flip-flop, seeing them like that, because I still don't understand the relationship between them. He keeps coming back to me, and yet he protects her. It's glaringly clear that she's not interested in being an old lady; she just doesn't have it in her.

Being an old lady scares me, too. I'll admit that. Not just because it's a lifetime commitment, bigger than any marriage would ever be, but also because it would mean my entire world would change. No only would I lose my job, I'd lose so much of my family. They'd never understand, especially considering the reason I ended up in this position. How could I honestly ask them to just accept it? They love me, of course, but no one is that willing.

Krypt lifts his eyes and they fall on me, his face quickly changing from bored to lustful in seconds. I know he wants me, he's made it clear, but I don't know if I can ever give him what he wants. Besides, Penny, regardless of her fears about being an old lady, is not backing away from him anytime soon. I can understand why, but it makes the situation just slightly more confusing.

Especially when he lets her.

Krypt uncurls his arm from Penny's shoulders and stands, walking straight past me and out the opposite door. As he passes me, he gives me a look that I'm not entirely sure I can read. It's either a look that says *I don't want you*, or a look that says *I do*. I have no idea which one it is, but I find myself turning, the alcohol consumed earlier flooding my veins as I follow him down the hall.

I find him in one of the rooms, leaning back on the couch, staring at the door. His face is tight, his eyes slightly hazed from the alcohol, and his big body seems wound up awful tight. He looks up at me when I walk in, and I stare at him for so long, I have to shake my head to break the heated glance between us.

"What are you doin'?" he asks, lifting the beer from his lap and taking a sip.

"Shit is going down, you were out there with Penny and I…I don't really have anyone to talk to."

"You made it clear you don't wanna talk to me," he points out.

"I did not," I say, my voice soft. "You hurt me, Krypt. Not the other way around."

He stares at me, his eyes burning into mine. "Yeah, I did, but you told me I wasn't what you wanted, didn't you? In saying that, what I said about Penny meanin' somethin' and you not…"

"I know," I say, my voice low. "You've done nothing but show me how much you want me, it's me who has been a little bitch. I care, Krypt. I do or it wouldn't have hurt."

His lips quirk, but he quickly swipes it away and nods. "I still shouldn't have said what I said. Penny matters, Ash. But I should have never made you think you didn't matter, too. 'Coz you do. More than you know."

My hazy mind processes his words, and my lust kicks up. I find myself taking a step closer, wanting him again, needing to remember how his mouth tasted. I don't ask him; I don't even speak. It's a risk, I know that, but I walk forward and climb over him, straddling his hips. He sucks in a breath as my mouth lowers, finding his neck and sucking the slightly salty skin there. God, he tastes so good, and when he rumbles I can feel it radiating through my body.

"You think this is a good idea?" he growls, placing his hands on my hips.

"Why not?" I murmur, sliding my tongue up his flesh. "We're both alone, and we both want it. I need you to make me feel, Krypt. Please. Everything is so bad right now. You're the only good thing I have left."

"Fuck," he mutters. "What about your shoulder?"

"My shoulder will be fine while I ride you," I whisper, nipping his earlobe. "Don't turn me away, you know I need you."

"Do I?" he growls.

"Yes," I whisper.

"Shit is complicated right now. You know that," he breathes, his big body relaxing beneath me as my mouth works his flesh.

"Because of Penny?" I whisper, moving my mouth across his cheek until I'm kissing the side of his mouth.

"Yeah, amongst other things," he groans, and I can feel his fingers tighten around my hips.

"Is she your old lady?"

He jerks my hips forward, grinding them against him. "No."

"Is she going to be your old lady?"

He hisses when my hands find his jeans, and I unbutton them. "No," he rasps.

"Then there is nothing stopping me from riding your cock right here and right now."

"Babe," he protests, but it's so weak his voice really doesn't sound like he means it.

"What do you want, Krypt? Decide, now, because I won't be the play thing between you and her," I growl, sliding my hand down into his jeans and rubbing my palm over his already throbbing cock.

"You know I want to fuck you," he hisses. "I need to feel your pussy around me, squeezing my cock like it's the last thing it'll ever do."

"Then there really is no question, is there?"

I slide his cock free, raising myself up and slipping my panties aside before lowering down and letting just the head of his thick length slide into my opening. "Do you want me to stop?" I murmur, meeting his lusty gaze.

"You know I fuckin' don't. Shit, babe, if you're goin' to torture me at least make it fuckin' worthwhile."

"Oh," I breathe, sliding down further until he's stretching me so perfectly. "I'm going to make it worthwhile."

I shove myself down hard and fast, causing an agonized groan to leave his lips. His fingers tighten around my hips and he mutters a few choice curses before he pulls out and thrusts back upwards, causing my fingers to go up and curl in his hair, tugging until his head comes forward and his lips find mine. My shoulder aches, but it's not enough to stop me. Kissing Krypt is like licking candy—he tastes so damned good, and his lips are so rugged and manly. He kisses a girl like he's never going to see her again, and she means the world to him.

He makes it count.

His tongue does things to mine that I can't even begin to describe. He brings my body to life as if he's always been the lighter to my torch. My nipples turn into hard peaks, and I lean forward, rubbing them against his chest. This earns me more curse words and a "you're fuckin' wild." His cock seems as though it continues to swell inside me, stretching me, opening me for his assault. His mouth devours mine and our bodies mold together as if we were made to fit.

"I need to come, Krypt," I whimper against his mouth as my pussy clenches tightly around his invading cock.

"Then come," he barks, his jaw tight. "I want you to come so fuckin' hard I feel it in my spine, so fuckin' do it."

At his words, my pussy convulses and I lose control. I throw my head back and cry out his name. In a rugged tone, he grates out my name, all the while slamming his hips up harder and faster until I can see it in his face that he's about to find his own release. He gets this look, this gorgeous, pleased look that has my skin prickling. His lips part just slightly, and his eyes flutter partly closed, almost as if they're too lazy to stay just slightly open.

"Baby," he rasps, his voice low and husky. "I'm goin' to fuckin' come so hard in you right now."

I whimper, watching his face, my own body still coming down from my orgasm. His eyes pin mine as he comes, and it's the best fucking moment of my life. I'll never forget the way they glaze over, like they want to roll back. His chest rumbles with his pleasure as he shoots jet after jet of his release deep inside me.

I cup his jaw, stroking my thumb over his cheek as he comes down, his body slowly untensing. He turns his face and captures one of my fingers, sucking it into his mouth, and swirling his tongue around the tip. I watch him, our eyes locked, our breathing slowly calming down. It's a powerful moment, so powerful I turn away, forcing myself to disconnect our blazing stare. I slide off him, pulling my panties aside and straightening my dress.

"You always so scared of intimacy?" he asks, causing my spine to stiffen.

"No," I say, not looking at him so he can't see the lie in my eyes.

"Babe, fuck. You just came in here and gave it to me like you actually meant it, and now you're gonna walk out?"

I turn to him, keeping my face impassive. "I wasn't…"

"You get up and walk outta here, there won't be another time. You get that?"

I swallow, lifting my elbow into my hand to release some of the strain on my shoulder. I stare at him, my eyes soft from our time together.

"You came in here and fucked me; now you're goin' to stay and tell me why the fuck you won't give me more."

"You confuse me, Krypt. You said I mean something just now, but then there's Penny and I don't know—"

"Penny matters to me, but it ain't in the way you think," he says, cutting me off.

"Then how is it?" I whisper, my head slightly hazy. "Because you pushed me away the minute she showed up. If you want me to give in, Krypt, you have to as well. I know nothing about you, yet you're asking me to just be with you."

He sighs, dropping his head in his hands. "I don't wanna let her down."

Let her down?

I walk over, sitting beside him. "How would being with me let her down?"

"Penny and I were together a fair while. I loved her but she was always so perfect. My sister adored her, and we all grew up together. When my sister," his voice grows thick, "passed, things got tense. Penny suddenly saw me as this bad man, someone she couldn't trust. When we split, it took a few months for us to find a friendship, but when we did it was good."

"I still don't understand."

"I don't want her to think I'm some fuckin' whore who disrespects women. It's not how my sister saw me, and it ain't how Penny sees me. It bothers her to see me in this lifestyle, let alone gettin' my dick wet all the time."

"She makes you feel ashamed for what you are?" I gasp.

"No," he says quickly, but I know that's how he feels. "It's just that I care about what she thinks, because of Lacey, and I don't want her bein' disappointed in me. She's the only family I have left."

It makes sense.

"Was Lacey your sister?"

He nods.

"The tattoo on your back?"

He stiffens, but gives me a jerk of his head.

"What happened to her, Krypt?"

His entire body flinches and his face grows hard. "Car accident," he rasps out.

"I'm so sorry," I whisper.

He goes on, and I let him. "Johan was a friend of my fathers, but they quickly became enemies over some pathetic fuckin' feud. Shit went down, and it went down bad. We were drivin' home one night; we'd been out with Dad. There was a car behind us, swerving and making a scene. Before we knew it, he was ramming us. A long story short, we were sent spiraling off the road. The car flipped eight times—I know, I counted them."

I swallow, reaching over and taking his hand.

"My father was dead on impact, but I wasn't. I won't give you details on how I knew his life was gone, but it was gruesome. My only concern then was Lacey. She was passed out, blood coming from her mouth. I yelled out for help, when that piece of shit appeared in the window. He smirked at me, the dirty son-of-a-bitch, then he looked at Lacey and back to me. His last words were, 'such a shame,' before he walked off and left us there."

Tears are flowing freely from my eyes now.

"Lacey died before the ambulance arrived. I was the only one to survive. When I got old enough to start lookin' for that piece of shit, I couldn't find him. I was messed up and angry."

"I'm so sorry," I breathe.

He shakes his head. "He's dead now. He's paid for what he done."

"Doesn't make it easier."

"No," he says, staring at me. "But at least he can't hurt anyone else."

Poor Krypt. I can't imagine how it would have felt for him to watch his sister's life slip away from him.

"Your mom?" I ask.

"She died when she had Lacey."

God, could it get any worse? Krypt doesn't let me say anything, because he gets to his feet. "I'm fuckin' restless. I can't sit here when shit could be goin' bad for Santana."

"Hey," I say, reaching out for him. "You're doing all you can."

"Fuckin' hate it, Ash."

"I know, honey," I murmur.

He turns, dropping to his knees in front of me. "We gotta stop this bullshit. I don't play games, Ash, and I don't have time for them. You know all of me, so now you decide if I'm good enough to hang onto."

My eyes scan his face. "Of course you're good enough to hang onto, Krypt."

"Then why the fuck are you holdin' back?"

I stare down at my hands. "I don't know how I would go being someone's property. How am I supposed to just sit around and do as I'm told?"

He snorts. "God, you've got it all fuckin' wrong. I'm not your goddamned owner. Yeah, when it comes to club shit, you do as you're told, but if you wanna work, and make a life, you fuckin' do it."

"My job?" I whisper.

He cups my cheek. "I'll make sure that job is there for you, if it's what you want."

"And my house . . ."

"If there is no danger, you can live there as long as you want."

"And Penny?"

His body flinches. "I don't love Penny, but she's goin' to be a part of my life, always. In saying that, if you're my old lady, then you're always goin' to come first."

"Even if it hurts her?"

He strokes his thumb over my bottom lip, staring at it. "Even if it hurts."

"And if I'm not your old lady?"

His eyes scan my face. "Then I gotta stop fuckin' you, 'cause baby, you're consuming me."

"I care about you, Krypt. I promise you. But…can we just . . . can we wait until Claire is safe before we do anything?"

He nods, leaning forward and brushing his lips across mine. "Yeah."

"Do you think she's going to be okay?"

He stares out the window. "I fuckin' hope so."

CHAPTER TWENTY-ONE

SANTANA

Their clubhouse is very different to ours. Gone are the friendly smiles I received back home. Instead, I'm looked at as if I'm no more than a toy they can fuck and dispose without even knowing my name. There are women everywhere, more than I've seen in one place before. They're openly giving sexual favors, not caring whose eyes are on them.

I swallow down the lump in my throat and follow the biker down the hall. He leads me to a room. It's an old, shitty room with a bed that looks as though it hasn't been cleaned for months. My skin prickles, and it takes everything inside me not to coil back and run. I think of Ash's friend, and how scared she must be. This thought alone pushes me forward.

The biker, who introduced himself as Jayger—not Jagger, but Jayger—shuts the door. I consider his name, and then him. It really is a strange, somewhat hipster nickname for a biker. I wonder if he knows how pathetic it makes him look? I force a smile on my face, batting my eyelashes as I take the room in.

Window to the left, not barred.

I've been taking in details of the clubhouse the entire time I've been here. I made sure to note where the front and back doors were, as well as where the clubhouse was located, and how easy it would be to get away. Turns out, it is in a good position. The front of the house faces the road, where the guys can come in. The back faces thick forest, where I can escape with Claire.

If Claire is here.

"So," Jayger purrs, coming up to me and placing his hands on my hips. "You ridin' me, or am I ridin' you?"

Seriously? Ugh.

"I need to pee." I smile, biting my lip in an attempt to look sexy. "Then I'm riding you."

His eyes flash and he grins. He nods to the hall. "Three doors down, to your left."

I lick my lips, before turning and rushing out. I find the bathroom easy enough—it's finding Claire that will be hard. I wash my hands, twice, and then lean my hip against the sink. How am I going to find her? The door swings open and two whores enter. They smile at me, as if I'm not new around here, which makes me wonder if they too haven't been here long.

"Hey," I say, slurring the word slightly.

"Hey," a girl with ratty blonde hair and horrible skin smiles.

"Rockin' party." I smirk.

She nods, leaning against the wall and pulling out a smoke. "They're usually better."

Maybe not new, then.

"Yeah?" I ask.

"Yeah. When Howard is here, things get hot."

Howard. The asshole behind all this. An asshole I've never seen. Her words relieve me slightly. He's not here; this is a good thing. Then my chest clenches, because if he's not here then maybe Claire isn't either. I stare at the whores; I wonder if they'll know? I risk a lot asking, but if I play it right they might not notice.

"Yeah," I murmur. "Bet he's busy with that stupid whore he brought in."

"Right?" Blondie mutters. "Stupid bitch keeps screaming. I was sucking Lion's cock, and all I could hear was her."

"Me too," I snort. "I'm about to fuck Jayger and the bitch better not start while I'm doing it."

Blondie grins at me. "Jayger, nice choice. He's got a huge cock. I've ridden him a few times. And don't worry about the little bitch. Howard locked her in his room."

His room. Where is his room? I can't ask without looking too obvious.

"Well," I say, flipping my hair over my shoulder. "Hopefully his room isn't near where I am."

Blondie nods. "I don't think it is, Howard is right at the end of the hall. Most of the rooms are up this end."

"Good," I say, turning and heading out. "Later."

"Later," they both murmur.

Shit. Shit. *Shit*.

I know where Claire is, but I need to let Maddox know. I pull out my phone, glancing down the hall quickly before punching out a text.

S – I know where Claire is. I don't know if she's cuffed, but she's in the house. Howard isn't here. I don't know where he is. The front of the house faces the road. If you can make a distraction I can get Claire out the back. I'm going to check her out now, hang in for my text.

He replies a moment later.

M – Stay safe, darlin'. I'm waitin' for your text.

I shove my phone into my pocket and glance around again, before walking down the hall. The party is in full swing at the front of the house, but the halls are mostly quiet. I reach the very last door, and pray it's Howard's. I try it, but it's locked. I look around again before knocking softly.

No answer.

Shit.

I try the other doors and they all open, which means that door is where Claire lays. The only way I'll get in is through the back window, assuming it's unlocked and actually has one. I rush down the hall and out into the lounge area. I sway my hips, leaning down to a whore and asking for a smoke. She hands me one.

I put it in my lips, making out like I'm going outside to have it. I wink at bikers as I walk past, sashaying towards the back door.

I step out and rush down the back steps. I hear the door creak open just as I am in the darkness, and I suck in a breath, pressing myself to the old, moldy walls of the house. I close my eyes.

A moment later, the door slams shut. I listen for a second longer, but no sounds come my way. Taking a deep breath, I rush to the end of the house to where I would assume the window would be in Howard's room. I find one; I can see a dull glow coming from inside. I test it, surprised when it slides up easily. My heart pounds as I find something to help me get through. I come up with an old crate.

It takes me a few minutes to silently drag it over. I climb onto it and swing my leg into the window. There's a girl on the bed, her hands cuffed to the bedhead. I stare at her, saddened. Her face is battered. She's got a fat lip, a black eye, and her blond hair is matted with blood. Her eyes dart to me and widen.

"It's okay," I whisper. "I'm here to help you."

She stares at me, one of her eyes half shut. I rush over, leaning down close. "My name is Santana, I'm a friend of Ash's. We're going to get you out of here. Do you know where the key for these cuffs are?"

She nods, wincing in pain as she rasps, "He put them in the drawer on the desk."

I turn and run over, sliding the drawer open. I notice the keys just as I hear a voice down the hall. "Yeah, not a sound from her, Prez. Bitch has been quiet."

Fuck.

My eyes shoot to Claire's, and her face scrunches with fear. I shut the drawer and run to the window, pulling it down quietly. I don't have time to climb out. I duck behind Howard's desk, which luckily for me is positioned near some curtains that I use to shield myself.

I hear the door open and heavy footfalls fill the quiet space.

"Still here, sweetheart." He chuckles. "Didn't think you'd go far. Don't worry; your friend has decided to trade her life for yours. You'll be free soon."

"A-a-a-ash?" she croaks.

He laughs. "Yeah, Ash. Goin' to have fun with her before I slit her throat."

Claire makes a strangled sound and I clench my eyes shut, praying he doesn't come too close.

"Maybe I'll have fun with you before I let you go. I'm in need of some good pussy."

Please, no.

I chant this over and over in my head.

Please don't let him rape her. There's no way I can sit through that.

"Please, don't," Claire croaks, echoing my thoughts.

"You're too pitiful for a man like me, anyway," he grunts. "I like them wild."

I want to breathe a sigh of relief, but even the idea of breathing scares me right now. I don't know how much time I have left, but I hope he leaves soon or I'm in trouble. Maddox will come back, and he'll make a scene if I don't contact him soon.

That's the last thing we need.

"Speaking of pussy," Howard says, "I might just go find some."

Thank God.

He walks over towards the door, and I catch a glimpse of him. He's a big man, with a long, dark beard and an old, wrinkled face. Faded tattoos run up his neck. He's been at it a long time. He stares at Claire again, then he steps out and slams the door. Locking it.

I finally breathe.

My heart pounds fast as I wait for a few minutes, then I slip out from behind the desk. I open the drawer, take the keys and rush over to Claire. I lean down, whispering, "I'm coming back for you. I promise."

She nods, her eyes watering.

I reach up and squeeze her hand before slipping out the window again. I pull my phone out and text Maddox.

S – I can get her out. It's time.

M – Ten minutes, baby. We'll be there.

I hate when he calls me baby; hate and love it. I shove the thought aside as I rush back inside the clubhouse. I see Howard again when I step through the back door, but he barely gives me a second glance as I shimmy down the hall. I slip into the room Jayger was in to find him already naked on the bed.

"Fuck, that took ages. What did you do in there?"

"I needed a smoke," I mutter.

He takes hold of his cock and strokes it. He's a good-looking man, sure, but I want to go over and bite that cock right off. It takes everything inside me not to gag. I force a smile, hoping Maddox hurries up and causes a distraction.

I take my time, swinging my hips and doing little spins. Jayger seems to appreciate my efforts, and it buys me some time. I slide my hands seductively over my body, grinning at him as I move. He grins back, jerking his cock harder and faster. At this rate, he'll have nothing to offer.

That's exactly how I want it.

Commotion breaks out in the lounge, and I hear someone bark, "Jokers'."

I breathe a sigh of relief. I turn my eyes to Jayger, but he's already up, pulling on some jeans. "Stay here," he barks.

He rushes out of the room, and I wait a minute before following him. I step into the lounge, and all the bikers are loading guns. Shit. *Fuck*. What if they hurt them? I slide out the back door, my heart pounding as I run around to Claire's room once more. I couldn't get her out earlier, because I needed to know Maddox was here before I ran.

I climb through the window and rush to her bed, uncuffing her. "Can you run?" I ask.

She nods.

I help her out the window, and we press ourselves up against the side of the house, and listen for a moment.

"Just here to talk, Howard."

Maddox.

"Ain't nothin' to talk to you about. You're on my land, so I'll give you five fuckin' minutes to get off before I blow your brains out."

"We got plenty to talk about," Maddox barks, ignoring the threat. "Like why you're takin' shit that ain't yours."

"No idea what you're talkin' about," Howard growls.

"Talkin' about the little present you left me."

Maddox isn't giving away that he knows Howard has Claire. Smart. There's a long silence.

"You liked that, huh?" Howard laughs.

I don't stay around to listen. I take Claire's hand and we dart forward. We come crashing into a hard form before we've even taken two steps. I cry out and stumble backwards, falling down. There's a biker, one of Howard's, looming over Claire.

"Where the fuck do you think you're goin'?"

Oh God. I leap up, charging him. His fist flies out and hits me so hard I see stars as my body falls back onto the ground. Blood, hot and thick, runs down my cheek as I try to gather my bearings. I hear Claire cry out, and I know I have to think fast. My head spins as I pat the ground around me, trying to find a weapon.

The biker lunges towards me before I have the chance to get my hands on anything useful. I roll quickly, but his boot connects with my ribs, sending a blinding pain through my body. I cry out, my voice hoarse and broken. I try to scurry forward, but he takes hold of my ankle, dragging me through the dirt.

"You ain't goin' *any-fuckin'-where*, you little slut," the biker roars, lifting me effortlessly and bringing my face to his. "Howard is going to have a fantastic time with you."

He raises his fist and hits me so hard I feel my neck crack as my head swings to the side. Agonized screams leave my throat as he drops my body to the floor and spins towards Claire, who is staring at him, her body trembling.

"R-r-r-run," I croak.

He moves towards her and my hands frantically go around again to find a weapon. There has to be something here. Through my pain and blurred vision, I find an old piece of wood. It's heavy and solid. It'll do.

I turn to see the biker dragging a struggling Claire towards the house. The idiot thinks I won't run, he's sure he has hurt me enough. *He nearly did.* I stand; not thinking twice, and I rush towards him – ignoring the agonizing pain in my body. He starts to turn as I swing the wood. I hit him so hard he goes down with a thump. Blood pours from his temple and I don't stop to see if he's alive.

"We have to run!"

My head pounds, my ribs burn and my vision blurs as we dart into the thick trees. Blood fills my mouth and soaks everything it touches. He must have split my cheek. Claire keeps up with me, even though she looks and no doubt feels, awful. When we're far enough into the darkness, I pull out my cell.

S – We're out.

I wait a minute or two, and then I hear the rumble of Harley Davidsons as the Jokers' take off. I breathe a sigh of relief. No one got hurt. My phone flashes a moment later.

M – Where r u?

S – In the trees behind the clubhouse. I think I know where the road is. Get out of sight. We will be there soon.

Just then, the sounds of shouting and gunfire erupt from the clubhouse. Doors slam, and then torchlight flashes through the trees. Shit. Shit. *Shit.*

"We have to run, fast," I say to Claire.

I know the general direction of the road, and I run hard and fast. The sound of boots crunching comes closer, and occasionally a flash of light comes too close to us. They're still far enough away that we have a good start, but close enough that I'm starting to get worried. I see car headlights and realize the road is close.

"Come on," I urge, pulling Claire harder.

We run towards the road, frantic, our bodies no doubt feeling much the same. My heart is pounding, my mind is spinning, and my legs ache like they've never ached before. Fear has lodged itself in my spine, and I know it won't leave until I'm safe.

We reach the road just as a gunshot sounds out, zooming past my head. Shit, they're close. I run out onto the gravel, knowing we're in full view and it's dangerous. As if some god listened to my prayers, I see Maddox and the club over the other side, their bikes off, silence filling the air.

The moment they see us, the bikes roar to life. I run towards Krypt, shoving Claire at him. Another gunshot sounds out, hitting the tree and ricocheting off to hit Rhyder's bike with a loud ping.

"Fuck!" Krypt barks. "We gotta move." He pulls Claire onto the back of his bike. Maddox is right beside him, his eyes trained on my face, anger evident in his expression.

I don't stop to give him time to think about my injury. I leap on the back of his bike. He's moving even before my arms are secured around his waist. The bike is tearing down the road at speeds that freak me out, considering I'm not wearing a helmet and I'm already injured.

I pray that we don't have an accident, but I also know we can't stop until we're far enough away. I reach down, fumbling for the helmet. It won't be easy to put on, but being without it is making me uneasy. I unhook it off Maddox's bike and shove it over my head, one handed. I push it down, some of my hair going over my eyes.

It'll do.

The roaring of bikes in the distance tells us that the Tinmen aren't going to just sit down and wallow over their stupidity. Maddox speeds up, sliding around corners like a speed demon. I hold onto him, my fingers straining in his jacket as he flies down the long stretch of road. The clubhouse is about twenty to thirty minutes away.

I hope we make it in time.

~*~*~*~

We slide into the clubhouse forty minutes later, after taking a detour home that the Tinmen don't know about. Maddox hustles everyone off the bikes and orders them into the clubhouse. We manage to get safely inside, and Ash gives a pained cry when she lays her eyes on her friend. She rushes over, taking her into her arms and holding onto her.

Our eyes meet and she gives me a smile I'll hold with me forever. It says more than *thank you*; it says *you saved her life*.

Loud rumbling zips past the road. For the Tinmen to reach the clubhouse, they'd have to turn off and come up the road. They're not going to risk that; even I know that. They could be walking right into an ambush, and it's too dangerous for them to act on their need to make Maddox pay.

The bikes rumbling disappears down the road, and I let a long, agonized breath out, dropping down onto the couch. The men all turn to me, their looks filled with appreciation and admiration. Maddox walks over, kneeling down in front of me. His big hand takes my chin.

"Who hit you?"

"It doesn't matter, Maddox," I whisper. "It's done."

His eyes scan my face. "So fuckin' proud of you."

I force a weak smile. "I guess we just started a war?"

He turns to Krypt, giving him a long stare. "I think we fuckin' did, but we're ready for it."

Shit, I hope they are.

CHAPTER TWENTY-TWO

ASH

I stroke Claire's hair as she sleeps, staring down at her, thanking God that she made it through this. I don't know what I would have done if anything had happened to her. Her face is messed up, and she sat in silence as I cleaned her. I know she's scared, and I can't blame her. I can't even imagine what she went through.

The door creaks, filling the silent room with a loud sound. I turn and see Krypt and Santana at the door. Santana has a dark, angry black eye, and a cut that looks like it hurts. I'm forever grateful to her; she risked her life for my friend. Krypt smiles at me, but it's strained. "How is she?" he asks.

"She's sleeping, which is good," I say quietly.

I stand and walk over to them, not wanting to wake Claire. Santana reaches out and takes my hand. We all step out of the room, closing the door. Krypt turns to us, his eyes on me. "Spend some time together. I got shit to do with Maddox."

I nod, and his hand reaches up to stroke a thumb over my bottom lip. He turns and disappears down the hall. I face Santana, smiling at her. "I can't tell you how much I want to hug you right now, Santana, but I know you hurt your ribs quite badly. What you did…you're…amazing."

She shrugs. "Eh, what can I say?"

I beam. "You're a strong girl."

She smiles, but it wobbles slightly. "I did what I had to do."

I reach out, putting my hands on her shoulders. "No, you did an amazing thing."

Her bottom lip trembles, and I pull her into my arms – screw her ribs. I knew she was hurting; God how could she not be? It would have been so hard to do what she did. I rub her back carefully, wanting to give her whatever I can.

Maddox walks out of his office and stops when he sees her, his eyes narrowing. I shake my head at him, and I can see the clear anguish in his gaze as he fights to stop himself from walking over.

He stares at her for a long minute before disappearing down the hall. Santana pulls back, wiping her eyes. "So sorry."

"Don't you be sorry," I say, chastising her softly. "You don't ever have to say sorry."

She smiles weakly. "I'm just glad she's okay, you know?"

"I know."

"I'm going to have a sleep. I need it."

We hug again before she disappears down the hall. I watch her go with a true, warm smile. Santana and I will be great friends. I just know it.

~*~*~*~

A week passes with nothing. It's eerily silent, and it's scaring everyone. I have no doubt Howard will plot his revenge, but it all comes down to when. Santana is back to her usual bubbly self, and Claire is recovering each day. Leo is out of the hospital and has gone home, but he calls Claire each day, making sure she's okay. That warms my heart.

I'm walking down the halls one day when I hear Maddox and Krypt's voices. I peer into the room they're in, about to announce myself, but their conversation has my mouth closing. Krypt is leaning against Maddox's desk, and Maddox is pacing, arms crossed.

"You need to fuckin' tell her, Maddox. If she finds out you know, and you've known all these years, she's goin' to hate you."

"I'll risk it, Krypt. I need to know more before she can ever find out. It's going to do enough damage to her to find out what I've kept from her as it is. The least I can do is get the information right so I can help her when it comes the time to tell her."

"She risked her life for this club, you *owe* it to her," Krypt says, his eyes hard.

"Don't tell me what I owe her, Krypt. I know what's good for her, and it's why I've kept it from her for five years."

"It'll crush her, break her into a thousand pieces. She cares about you, Maddox. You don't tell her this shit soon, that'll be gone forever. You willin' to risk that?"

Maddox steps closer to him. "Don't fuckin' talk to me about carin' about someone, Krypt. I'm doin' this *because* I care."

"Fuck," Krypt growls. "Fine, but you're goin' to have to face this when it comes out."

"And I fuckin' will," Maddox says, running his hands through his hair. "But that time ain't now."

"You're holdin' back on her, because you know she's goin' to hate you. You're takin' every, last moment with her before it's revealed. You selfish prick."

Maddox snarls, baring his teeth in a dominating way. "She is all I've *breathed* for five years. I'll do whatever I can to see her fuckin' smile every morning for as long as possible. I will tell her Krypt. When I'm ready."

"Fine, you fuckin' moron," Krypt grunts, turning away.

I stare, mouth opened just slightly. Maddox is hiding something big from Santana, that's clear by the heated conversation between the two of them. What it is, though, I have no clue. Obviously it's enough to destroy her, because Maddox is holding back for a reason and that reason is because he knows she'll hate him for it.

Secrets, they have a way of destroying peoples lives.

I hope Maddox knows what he's doing.

CHAPTER TWENTY-THREE

Chaos wakes me from my nap.

Sirens. A lot of them.

Then a loud booming voice. "Come out with your hands up. Bring out the hostage."

I sit up in bed, rubbing my eyes. I look over to see Krypt is no longer beside me. We fell asleep that way, but certainly didn't wake up like it, it would seem. I slip out of the bed and pull on some clothes before staring out the window. There are police cars everywhere.

My eyes widen and I spin around, running out of the room. The guys are in the living area, talking frantically. Krypt notices me and reaches out, snatching me close to him. "Don't go out there," he orders. "Under any circumstances."

"Why are they here, Krypt?"

"One fuckin' guess," Maddox barks. "Howard gave them our information; he's settin' us up. We not only have fuckin' Claire, but Ash, too. Fuck."

"What are you going to do?" I ask, my eyes darting around the room for Claire.

"We don't got a fuckin' choice," Maddox snaps. "We gotta show with the girls."

"No fuckin' way," Krypt says. "They see me, I'm goin' back to prison."

"They got this place surrounded, Krypt. Nothin' we can do."

My heart twists and panic fills me. I don't want Krypt to go back to prison. Maddox reaches forward, taking my arm. Claire appears beside us, reaching her hand out to him. He stares at her, before curling his hand around hers and pulling us to the front door.

"Fuck, Maddox, there has to be another way," Krypt barks.

"It's okay," I whisper, swallowing down my tears. "I'll tell them the truth. It's going to be fine, Krypt."

Maddox opens the door, stepping out.

"Let them go," a police officer barks.

Maddox lets us go, and puts his hands up. I put mine up too, and so does Claire.

"Come," an officer encourages us, his gun raised and pointed at Maddox.

"They aren't holding us hostage," I say, my voice wobbly.

"Just come closer and we can talk."

"I won't come closer until you listen," I say. This time, my voice is stronger. "They aren't holding us hostage."

"Miss—"

"She's right," Claire says. "The person who took me from my home and beat me was Howard. This club kept me safe."

The officer stares at her. "If you'll come to the station to make a statement—"

"No," I say defiantly. "As soon as we're gone, you'll hurt these guys behind me, and they've done nothing but keep us safe."

"Tell me how you got here, Ash?" the cop says, his eyes still trained on Maddox.

"Howard ambushed the prison transfer, killing everyone. Beau Dawson saved me, by getting me out and helping me."

"Then why didn't you turn yourselves in?"

"Because the guards are corrupt and were making death threats. We were unsafe and scared."

He narrows his eyes. "What proof do you have of this?"

I meet his eyes dead on. "I'm sure you found your proof when you checked the crime scene."

I don't dare mention that I know it wasn't Maddox's gun at the scene. It would give it away. He set Howard up, and I don't want to ruin that.

"After all," I go on. "If you thought it was this club who took Beau and I, you would have come in before this."

"We raided the house," he says, his voice gruff. "You weren't here."

"That's because we were trapped in the wilderness for days, hungry and alone."

He narrows his eyes at me. "And you expect me to believe this story?"

"There are enough witnesses, right here."

He flicks his eyes to Claire. "You say this club didn't hurt you?"

"They saved me from that monster," she whispers. "I was out jogging one morning, and he snatched me."

"And what about Beau? He's still up for murder charges. You send him forward, and I'll consider your story."

No.

My knees begin to shake as reality hits me. Krypt, back in jail. No. I turn to Maddox, my eyes welling with tears. How the hell can we get away with this? We have proof for everything else, but Krypt killing Johan cannot be faked.

"Where are your witnesses who proved Beau killed that man?"

The voice comes from the group of bikers standing to the left. An older man comes out, his long grey beard swishing. I've seen him around the club, though he hardly says a great deal. Maddox told me he's a family member of his and has cancer but he's refusing treatment, so he's just spending his last days at the club. His name is Whiskey, and he's at least seventy years old.

The officer turns and stares at him. "Until the investigation is finished we need to—"

"How many fuckin' witnesses?"

"It was a chaotic time; gunshots, people were forced down, no security . . . It hasn't been easy. We've had numerous different stories, and it's come up that some of the shots came from outside the café. We are investigating this. Enough people have come forward and said Beau was there with a gun, he made them lay on the floor—"

"Yeah, but did they fuckin' see him pull the trigger?"

"At this point we can't share any of that-"

"Bull-fuckin'-shit!"

"He was the only one in that café."

"Wrong," the old man says. "I was there too, and I was the one who pulled the trigger. If you've done your job properly you should know that. In fact, if you're a good cop at all, you would have noticed Beau didn't have a gun on him when you arrived."

The cop studies him. I smother a gasp, because it makes sense to me now why Whiskey took Beau's gun before he got arrested. Had he planned on turning himself in all along, even though he didn't commit the crime? Why wouldn't he have come forward earlier?

Whiskey continues. "He didn't have it because it was me that pulled the trigger. I came back into the café; Beau already had the people on the ground. I saw that no good son-of-a-bitch sittin' there tauntin' him, and I wrestled the gun from Beau's hand and shot him right in the head. You raided the clubhouse; you've got the gun, do you not? If you do, you'll have seen my finger prints on it."

"Yes, but-"

"Yes but nothin'. I shot Johan Reed, and I shot him because I know what he did to my boy. I know what he fuckin' did and I made him pay for it. However, he was the only one I shot. I did not kill the other members of his family, and neither did Beau…but you know that, too. Don't ya?"

I gasp, and so does Maddox from behind me.

"You understand that you're confessing to the murder of Johan Reed, and that you'll go to prison for a very long time?"

"I know what I'm sayin', pig. I'm not a fuckin' idiot. I killed Johan Reed. I wasn't there when you arrived because I was chasin' the fuckers that made the other shots."

"Why not speak up earlier?"

"Because I was cleanin' shit up—needed to make sure things would be good for my family when I got locked up. Then shit went down with Beau, and you know what happened from there . . ."

It's not much of an answer, but he's a biker. He isn't going to give much more.

The door swings open and Krypt storms out, charging down towards the man. Whiskey's hands wrap around Krypt's shoulders, stopping him. He says something that has Krypt's fists clenching. The officers pull Krypt off before taking Whiskey and cuffing him.

"You're under the arrest for the murder of Johan Reed. Anything you say or do will be used against you in the court of law."

"Yeah, fuckin' yeah," he snorts.

Tears run down my cheeks, because I know what this man is doing for Krypt. He's giving him freedom. The officer turns to Krypt.

"You're under arrest too."

"What fuckin' for?" Krypt snarls.

"At this stage, we will need evidence to back up this claim. You escaped from prison, and we need to ensure your involvement in that was nonexistent. Then, if the old man's story checks out, you will be released with conditions."

My tears get heavier as Krypt's gazes turns to me. "I'm comin' back, baby."

I nod as a hand squeezes my arm. It's Maddox.

"We'll get him outta there."

"I know," I croak as the officer pushes both men into the car. "We need to take those guards down, Maddox. We need proof they're corrupt."

"Only one way to do that, honey," he murmurs. "You're going to make a visit."

CHAPTER TWENTY-FOUR

My heart pounds as I approach Tristan's front door. I don't know if this will work, but it's worth a shot. To get evidence on Howard is next to impossible; the man is smart. But what he didn't consider in his plan was that I am close to Tristan, and all I need is a confession from him. Maddox and the guys are close, in case anything goes wrong.

This was Maddox's plan, and I'll admit it's a clever one. If it works. I have a recorder in my pocket, so tiny it's barely noticeable. Maddox didn't want wires, because he had no doubt Tristan would ask. I raise my hand and knock on the door, then I take a step back.

A moment later, the door swings open and Tristan appears. His eyes widen when he sees me. I know I have to act this out well, so I raise my hand, and I slap him across the face. "How could you?"

"Shit, Ash, what are you doing here?"

"Doing here?" I screech. "Don't pretend you don't know. How could you, Tristan? I thought we were friends."

His eyes scan the street and road, and then he mutters. "Come in."

"I don't think I trust that," I say, my voice wobbling for effect.

"I'm alone."

"You are the last person I thought would do such a horrible thing. Really, Tristan? Guards died because of you."

He narrows his eyes. "You wired?"

"What?" I gasp.

Maddox was right.

"Is this a set-up?"

"What the hell are you talking about?"

"Turn around and lift your shirt."

I roll my eyes dramatically, and I do so, lifting my shirt's front and back. I even slide my jacket off. He leans forward, patting my pockets and legs, before staring at me. *Lucky I taped the recorder in my cleavage.*

"Why the hell would I be wired?" I ask.

He glares at me. "Because your boyfriend got arrested."

"Beau?" I ask. "He's not my boyfriend."

"Can we do this inside?"

"I'm not sure I can trust you, Tristan," I say sadly. "Why would you do something like that?"

He growls and leans in close. "You have no fuckin' idea how much money we were paid to pass information out, and set that ambush up."

Shit. I just realized if Tristan talks about the ambush, he'll give away that Maddox got there before Howard. I quickly change the subject.

"I don't care about the ambush. I'm talking about lying to me, and feeding information out of the prison."

"He was giving me a lot of money; he set me up. It was just fuckin' information on one person. It was only one fuckin' job."

"It doesn't matter," I cry. "Claire and Leo got hurt because of you. I nearly got killed."

"Do you think I wanted them to shoot at you? Fuck, Ash, of course I didn't, but you knew too much; you'd seen too much. I didn't want it anymore than you did, but I had no choice."

"And Claire and Leo?" I whisper, my voice shaky. "They didn't deserve any of it."

"We needed to draw you out. You were hiding with that club, and Howard was growing impatient. We needed to scare you, to give you a reason to hand yourself over. The sooner you were killed, the sooner our plan could continue."

"You set an innocent man up," I yell.

"I didn't fuckin' do any of that. Howard set the café scene up; Howard shot the other people. He just made it look like Beau did it. The club were then in the cop's sights. Howard only came in to us when he wanted to plan that ambush. He wanted information; we gave it to him."

"Then you continued to help him, even when your friend was at risk."

He runs his hands through his hair. "Fuck, Ash, I never wanted to hurt you."

"They're going to catch up with you, Tristan. They'll figure out Beau is innocent, and you'll go away for a long time."

His face flickers with rage and he reaches forward, taking my arm. "They'll find out fuckin' nothing. No one is going to believe anyone's story of corrupt guards. Not when the focus is on Beau, and that fuckin' club. It's worked out exactly how we needed it to."

I shake my head, snatching my arm out of his. "I wish I'd never met you."

I turn and rush off down the path. He doesn't try to stop me. I have no doubt he'll go inside and ring in my location so another bullet can come flying in my direction. I have no doubt they still want me dead, so I don't spill anything. That's why it's lucky for me that Maddox is waiting in an SUV down the road.

I climb in the car and turn to him.

"You get it?" he asks.

I grin. "Oh, I got it. Let's take these fuckers down."

CHAPTER TWENTY-FIVE

The recording was enough to have Tristan, Luke, and a police officer arrested. It was also enough, with the combined evidence and Whiskey's confession, to get Krypt out of prison. A trial will still be carried out, however it looks hopeful for him.

Maddox told me Howard also got arrested, the evidence Maddox left at the ambush scene as well as Claire's, Santana's and my confessions, was enough to lock him up, however Maddox said there's a good chance he will get out. He's got good connections.

The war isn't over; it's merely being put on hold. Howard will be back for his revenge.

For now, though, we're dealing with the fact that Whiskey is in prison for something he didn't do. Krypt isn't taking it well, drinking himself into oblivion every day. So much so it's concerning. Penny returned home after everything went down, deciding that staying was just not something she wanted to do.

So that just leaves me.

It's been three days since Krypt got out of prison. He's sitting in the old shed, bottle of Jack in his lap, staring at nothing. Every time I've tried to talk to him he's refused to answer, but today I'm not giving him a choice. He will talk to me, because otherwise he'll kill himself drinking that much.

"Hey," I say, walking in and sitting beside him.

He stays silent.

"Krypt." My voice is firm. "You can't keep doing this."

He turns and glares at me, his eyes bloodshot.

"You said you wanted me to be your old lady, but if this is how you're going to react every time something goes wrong, then I'm going to go inside and pack my shit right now. I'm not going to stand here and watch you sink. You either talk to me, or I leave."

I stand and walk towards the door.

"He fuckin' took my sentence." His voice is low and scratchy.

I turn and stare at him. He's watching me, his eyes pained.

"He's going to spend time in prison, because he took on my shit."

"He made that choice, Krypt," I whisper. "He wouldn't have done it otherwise."

"I killed that son-of-a-bitch. It should be me there."

I walk over, kneeling in front of him. "Then where would I be?" I whisper

His eyes grow even more pained. "You know what he said to me? He said, 'I'm an old man, boy. I've lived my life. I'm tired and I'm sick. I ain't got nothin' left to offer. You got a girl, a life, and somethin' worth fightin' for. Don't you fight me on this.'"

My eyes water, because it's such an amazing thing that Whiskey did for him. "He did it because he loves you, Krypt."

"Now he's stuck in a fuckin' cell!" he bellows, launching the bottle across the room and smashing it on the floor. "I'm goin' to confess. Can't live with this."

He stands, knocking me backwards. He charges for the door.

"Where will that leave me?" I scream. "I love you, Beau Dawson, so where will it leave me if you go away?"

He stops, his body stiff. He turns and stares at me, his eyes wide. I push to my feet, walking over to him slowly.

"Well," I croak, "what will I do? Whiskey gave you a gift; he didn't give it to you for you to take it back and throw it in his face. Don't you understand? Even if you confess, he's in trouble now too, and both of you will pay. He gave you something because he wanted you to have it. He's sick, Krypt. He's only got months left; we both know that. You have an entire life. If you leave me now, what will I do?"

Tears are now thundering down my cheeks. Krypt stares at me, his face torn. "It hurts me, Ash. Fuckin' hurts me."

"I know, honey," I say, stepping closer, and cupping his cheeks. "But he wanted this for you. Don't shove it back in his face. Give a dying man his last wish."

He makes a strangled sound as his hands go up and curl around the back of my neck. "You fuckin' love me?"

"God yes, you stupid fool."

"And you'll be my old lady?"

"If you promise to stay with me."

He presses his forehead to mine. "I promise."

"Do I get special cuddles now?"

He barks out a laugh. "Yeah, baby."

I press myself to him, breathing him in. "Make it count, biker."

"I always fuckin' do, and baby, I always fuckin' will."

I smile, full and warm as I look up at him. I might have hesitated earlier, but that was before I understood what it is these guys really represent. Being an old lady isn't about being a possession; it's about being cherished, protected and adored. It's an honor that I couldn't see until now.

I was stupid, but I won't be again.

This biker is mine, and I won't be letting him go anytime soon.

I'm one lucky girl.

CHAPTER TWENTY-SIX

"Stop it." I giggle, rolling onto Krypt.

He grins up at me. "No fuckin' way. Watching you scream is too good for me to let you go."

I laugh and shove at his chest. "We've fought before, biker. You know how it ends."

He pulls me close. "Oh, I remember exactly how it ends."

I roll my eyes and push away from him, jumping off the bed and sashaying across the room and out the door. It's Maddox's birthday today, and all the bikers have rallied together to give him an epic party. It's great, really it is, because it means we can take a moment to forget the shit that's been going down.

I went back to work for the first time yesterday. Legally, they had to accept me back. After finding out about the corrupt guards, they were more than happy to open their arms to me. It was a good day, and overall it seemed successful. Plus, Claire is home, lapping up the attention Leo is giving her. Seriously, those two need to get in on.

"Hit me with a tequila," I say, stopping at the bar and smiling over at CJ, the bar attendant for the night.

"Lemon?"

"You know it."

He pours me a shot, slides the salt, and then passes me a lemon. I'm about to take it, when Maddox appears beside me. He grins at me, and I can't help but smile back. We've grown a certain respect between us since everything went down, I guess he figured out I wasn't going to hurt Krypt.

He takes the saltshaker and pours the salt on the little gap between his thumb and pointer finger, then he flashes me a grin. "You have to do it. It's my birthday."

I laugh and lean down, closing my mouth over his hand. He shudders as I lick the salt off his skin. Then I take the shot, throwing it back before sucking the lemon into my mouth.

"Again," he growls.

I do it again, and again, until I've downed four shots. My head swims by the time I wave my hand to stop.

"You're such a pervert," I slur, shoving his chest.

He snorts. "It's my birthday."

"So you keep telling me."

Krypt appears behind me then, wrapping his arms around my waist. "Fuck off, Maddox. Birthday or not, you're not sharin' my woman."

Maddox grins, baring his teeth in a way that seems almost feral. "You fuckin' love it as much as I do, Krypt. Don't go denying you wouldn't like to fuck her with me."

My cheeks flush. "Whoa, boys, calm down."

Maddox winks at me. "Last chance to have a try before this bastard gets too serious."

Krypt laughs. "She ain't interested, bro."

"Aren't I?" I mumble, turning to face Krypt.

His eyes widen. "Didn't think it was your thing?"

"My thing," I snort. "Krypt, was it your hand in my pussy and my palm on your cock the other week while we watched Maddox get his dick sucked?"

Krypt grins. I flash him a sultry look and disappear. Talk about making them pant for it.

~*~*~*~

I keep drinking. The night goes on, and gets louder and more boisterous with each passing hour.

"Hey!" Santana cries, dropping down beside me.

"Hey you." I grin, blinking through my drunken haze.

"Maddox throws a wild party."

"He does," I agree.

"So, I went out with Alec."

I turn to her, eyes wide. "You did?"

She flushes and nods. "It was amazing, Ash. He even kissed me at the end."

I grin, happy for her. "Are you going to tell Maddox about him?"

She shrugs. "Maddox doesn't care what I do."

"Sure about that?"

She rolls her eyes. "I'm sure. Besides, it would never work. Alec is good for me."

I beam. "How was the kiss?"

She sighs and drops back. "Soooo good!"

I laugh. "I can't wait to meet him."

"Oh, I can't wait either. You'll love him."

I grin. "Dance with me."

We get up and make a spot on the dance floor, wiggling about until our heads spin. I stumble to the bar for another drink before glancing around for Krypt. I can't find him, so I disappear down the hall. He isn't in any of the rooms that he usually occupies.

I know Krypt has a house, but he spends a whole lot of time here. More than he does at home, which is strange. I wonder when I'll see his home. I'm pondering this when I step into Maddox's office. Krypt and him are laughing about something, but stop when they see me.

"Boys," I purr.

I walk over to Krypt, taking his jacket in my hands and pulling him down for a kiss. He growls and returns it with full force. When I pull back, I'm panting. Damn, I should drink more often.

"Where's my fuckin' kiss? It's my birthday." Maddox chuckles from beside me.

"I'm not allowed to kiss you. I'm taken." I grin, turning to face him.

"But it's my fuckin' birthday."

Krypt laughs. It's clear he's under the weather too. In fact, I'd safely say we all are.

"Give him a kiss, baby. Make him see what he's fuckin' missing."

I turn to Krypt. "My kisses are all for you."

His eyes grow lusty and he stares down at me. "I know they are, but babe, I'm not goin' to lie and say it won't turn me on to see you and him kissin' . . . especially if my hand is in your pants."

My mouth drops open. "I thought you were all possessive and psycho?"

His grin widens. "Oh babe, I am, but fuck . . . there ain't nothin' more erotic than sharin' a woman once in a while."

I pout.

He leans down. "You'll always be mine, and when we make that official no one, and I mean *no one* will touch you."

"But right now we're not official, is that it?" I frown.

"Babe, when we're official you'll be on the back of my bike, my ring on your finger, and my baby in your belly."

Oh boy. "And will that be soon?"

"Fuckin' aye."

"So tonight we're just going to," I give Maddox a sideways glance, "fuck Maddox?"

He chuckles. "Only if you're up for it."

"Just once?"

"I ain't gonna be able to share you more than once, so yeah."

"You're not going to ask for the favor to be returned and make me watch you fuck another woman, are you? Because I'm telling you right now, that will never happen."

His smile widens, big and beautiful. "Makes me so fuckin' proud that you love me like that. And no, I won't ask to return the favor. I want to see you gettin' fucked by two cocks, not the other way around."

I flush. "I, ah . . ."

"Don't dance around it," Maddox growls. "You want us to fuck you, we will. If not, I'm goin' to find some pussy, because I fuckin' need it."

I stare up at Krypt. "Are you sure about this?"

He takes my shoulders, spinning me around. He pulls my hands behind my back. "Oh yeah baby, I'm fuckin' sure."

I don't question Krypt's need to see me jammed between him and another man. He's obviously secure in our relationship because he doesn't seem worried I'll fall for Maddox and run off. Personally, I don't understand how Krypt can share, but I know it's a fetish of his. Who am I to complain?

Maddox steps forward, closing the space between us. His hand goes around the back of my neck as he makes eye contact with Krypt. Something flashes between them—an understanding. They've done this before, only this time Krypt is making it known that I'm his, and it'll be him that walks away with me on his arm.

Maddox leans down, and his lips graze over my neck. I shudder; I can't help it. Fuck, just the thought of having both of their hands on me is enough to make me go wild, let alone the fact that they're going to fuck me like that. Krypt's hands slide over my breast, squeezing softly as Maddox moves his face up closer to mine.

Our eyes meet, and he gives me a sexy smile before he brings his lips down onto mine.

Shit, Maddox kisses well. His tongue moves with a firm yet gentle stroke. His body is hard against me, his hands rough on my skin as he slides them under my shirt. Krypt releases my breasts, grinding his cock against my ass as he slips his finger into my jeans.

"Oh God," I mewl, jerking my mouth away from Maddox's scorching kiss. "Krypt."

Both men make an appreciative sound as Krypt finds my clit, stroking over it with firm flicks of his finger. Maddox's fingers reach my bra, and he jerks it up, releasing my breasts. He palms them roughly, the friction causing my nipples to turn into two tiny, sensitive peaks. I whimper as his head lowers and he captures one with his mouth. My shirt still bunched up above them.

Krypt keeps up the torture on my pussy, stroking and massaging it with almost lazy intent. Suddenly, I feel overwhelmed. Two hard bodies against me, two sets of hands, and two mouths on my body; me making a massive decision to fuck two men. Will this make me a whore? My mind spins from alcohol consumption, and I fear I'm making a spur of the moment decision here.

"Stop thinkin', babe," Krypt murmurs, as if reading my thoughts. "You just stiffened."

"I just" —Maddox sucks my nipple—"oh, God. I just . . . am I a whore?"

"No fuckin' way. Plenty of couples do this, even the married ones."

Maddox sucks again.

"Oh God."

"Give in to it," Krypt growls into my ear. "Come for me."

He's pinching my clit, rolling it around in his fingers. My knees buckle and Maddox's arm goes around my waist as if he knows I'm about to fall. I come hard, crying out Krypt's name as my knees go weak. Then suddenly I'm on the bed, two hard bodies dropping down beside me.

They make light work of my clothes and theirs.

Naked. Oh my God, naked.

I stare at them in pure shock. They are so fucking beautiful. Maddox is bigger than Krypt—his body is just so huge—but Krypt has those gorgeous, defined muscles that make you want to lick him. Maddox's arms are a little scary, thick biceps of tight muscle. His abs are equally as tight.

Eeek.

Krypt shoves my body back onto the bed, not even flinching at Maddox's presence. By the way they move, it's even clearer to me that this is definitely not a first for them. I watch through lusty eyes as Krypt moves down the bed, spreading my legs and lowering his mouth into my wet, aching flesh.

Maddox rolls his big chest, pressing it against mine. He captures my lips again, kissing me into oblivion as Krypt licks my pussy like it's a delicious ice cream. I moan into Maddox's mouth, arcing and thrashing as Krypt devours me.

"Oh God," I pant. "Krypt."

"Touch my cock, baby. Show me how much you love his mouth on your pussy," Maddox growls.

I reach out, curling my fingers around his throbbing length. He's big, like, super thick and long. A little concerning. I stroke softly, wringing a groan from his lips as he kisses me again. Together like this, our bodies all joined, makes my entire world spin. Krypt has his mouth on me; I have my hand on Maddox.

"Fuck, so good," Maddox growls.

"Krypt," I whimper.

I come against Krypt's mouth, screaming out a mixture of their names as my body convulses. Then Krypt is sliding up my body, trailing wet kisses up my belly until he reaches my mouth. By this time Maddox has moved, and is standing by the bed. Doing what, I don't know. Krypt plunges his tongue into my mouth, kissing me until I can't breath, sharing my taste with me.

Then he pulls back, staring down at me, his expression warm and loving. "Changed my mind," he rasps, turning to Maddox. "You ain't fuckin' her. She can suck your dick, but her pussy is mine."

Maddox shrugs, his big hand moving over his cock.

My heart swells, joy bursting inside me. Krypt is sharing me, but he's keeping a huge part of me as his. I love that. I want this as much as Maddox and Krypt, but knowing that Krypt is showing that small possessive side, which I'm sure he's never done before, has me beaming. He smiles at me, his expression telling me something he hasn't yet. Krypt loves me. And fuck, it feels good.

"H-h-h-how are we going to do this?" I ask.

"Roll over, honey," Maddox murmurs.

I roll over and Krypt takes my hips, sliding my body back. Maddox sits on the bed, cock in hand. He grins at me, and God, he looks stunning. He curls his fingers in my hair, and murmurs, "Suck me."

"Do it, baby," Krypt growls, coming up behind me.

He lifts my hips, sliding his cock into my pussy without notice. I cry out, my mouth opening in pleasure. Maddox uses this moment to tangle his hands in my hair and bring my mouth down over his cock.

He fills me completely, stretching my lips as Krypt is stretching my pussy.

Then Krypt starts fucking me. He begins with long, slow strokes that make my entire body shudder with want. I take Maddox's cock, sucking it with everything I have, taking him deep and hard. All of our groans mingle. Maddox's hand is in my hair, Krypt is fucking me harder now, and my entire body is erupting with pleasure.

Maddox's cock swells in my mouth, and I gasp as I try to keep sucking while feeling my own orgasm building. "I'm goin' to fuckin' blow, fuck! Hurry up, Krypt," Maddox pants. I wrap my hand around the base of his cock and slowly stroke it, while sucking deeper. Krypt snarls a curse and fucks me harder.

I'm the first to come, with a gentle bite on Maddox's cock and a clench for Krypt. Maddox roars his release the moment my teeth make contact with his flesh, sending hot spurts of come into my mouth. Krypt follows behind him with his own bellow of passion.

When we can all breathe again, silence fills the room.

I release Maddox, dropping my head onto his lap. His hand goes into my hair where he strokes it softly. Krypt runs his hand down my spine sensually as he pulls out. I lay for a moment more before rolling off Maddox, taking part of the blanket with me.

Holy shit.

That was epic.

CHAPTER TWENTY-SEVEN

Another week passes, and I finally get to see Krypt's place. He's got a nice two-bedroom unit only about ten miles from the clubhouse. I'm quite surprised, having imagined he lived somewhere more . . . rundown. Now that we have an escape, we spend far more time in his house, naked, than we do at the clubhouse.

Today, though, we're having a family cookout. It's when the club opens its doors to allow all the old ladies, wives, lovers and children in for a huge feast. It's always fun, and a lot of laughs. I really love the atmosphere as I walk around, serving food and making salads.

When I'm empty, I head back to the kitchen to join Santana again. She's preparing dessert. She smiles when I enter. "Have they eaten all that already?"

I nod, grinning. "Yep, bikers are a hungry bunch."

"They are."

One of the club whores slinks into the kitchen. She isn't really meant to be here, but she managed to come in with one of the guys. They don't usually have them around on cookouts that include family. She stares at Santana and I with a cruel expression.

"Have you got a problem?" Santana snaps.

"No problem," the whore grunts. "Isn't anyone allowed to make eye contact with you? Prez's little angel."

Santana rolls her eyes. "Grow up and go find a dick to suck."

"Yeah fuck off," I bark.

"Aw, don't be jealous," the whore says to me. "It's not my fault he's put his dick in me, too."

Too. Shit.

"No idea what you're talking about," I growl. "Now leave."

The whore laughs, throws her head back and laughs. "His little princess here doesn't know, does she?"

God, shut your mouth. I want to lunge at her and stab her in the face with the fork I'm holding.

"Know what?" Santana asks.

"That Maddox likes to make an Ash sandwich with Krypt. I saw them myself. Ash was giving Maddox one hell of a dick sucking while Krypt fucked her. And she says she's not a whore."

Her loud laughter fills the room.

Fuck. Me.

"What?" Santana gasps.

Shit. *Fuck*.

"Will you fuck off?" I bark at the girl.

She laughs, but leaves the room. I turn slowly to Santana.

"Is that true, Ash?" her voice is low, fragile.

If I lie . . .fuck, I can't lie.

"Yes," I whisper. "But I didn't know you cared about him, Santana. You said you didn't, you said you were seeing Alec and . . ."

Oh God, her face. It's twisted in agony. Shit, fucking shit. She does care about him; I can see it now.

"I'm so sorry, oh God, Santana. I didn't . . . I didn't know."

"I don't fucking care. I don't fucking—"

Her voice breaks off and she turns, rushing from the room.

"Santana!" I yell.

I rush after her, but she's already disappeared. Shit. I run outside where the bikers are all sitting around a fire. I notice Maddox and hurry towards him.

"Maddox, we kind of have a problem."

His eyes widen and he stands, Krypt, who is beside him, stands too.

"What?"

"One of the whores, ah, saw us that night when we, ah . . ."

"Get on with it," he barks.

"Don't be a cunt to her, Prez. Let her speak," Krypt snaps.

"She told Santana and . . . she ran out. She was really hurt."

"Fuck!" Maddox roars. "Fuck!"

"I don't know where she went. I'm sorry Maddox, I thought . . . She said she didn't care, and I was stupid enough to believe her."

Maddox is already gone by the time I'm finished my sentence. Krypt wraps his arms around me, holding close. How could I not know Santana cared about Maddox? I should have picked it up, but she seemed so adamant that she didn't. Then she said she was into Alec . . .

"I really didn't think she cared, Krypt. Her reaction makes no sense. She sees him with women all the time and . . ."

"And to her, those women are nobodies. Just ass that's spread around; she knows they mean nothing, Ash. With you, being someone she loves and trusts, and knowing it could mean something . . ."

"God, I'm such a fool."

"It isn't your fault; part of this is on her. Her and Maddox have danced around this for years."

"It doesn't mean I don't feel like a monster."

He grunts and holds me tighter. "It'll be fine, babe. They'll sort it out."

I hope he's right.

CHAPTER TWENTY-EIGHT

Maddox disappears for hours. When he returns, he hasn't had any luck finding Santana. I know that she's probably with Alec but I'm not sure it's the right thing for me to tell him about that right now. He might be all Santana has, if I give that away, I'll never be able to fix the friendship that was forming between us.

"You check everywhere?" Krypt asks, following Maddox into his office when he returns.

He's wild, his hands are shaking and he's frantic.

"Of course I fuckin' did," he booms. "She's in danger bein' out there, do you think I just glanced around?"

"Calm down," Krypt growls. "Ain't no reason to take this shit out on me."

"If you didn't bring *that*," Maddox swings his eyes to me, "*woman* into my club, it never would have happened."

"Hey," I bark before Krypt can speak. "You made the choice to shove your cock into my mouth, Maddox. Don't you dare blame him because you fucked up."

Maddox glares at me, but then sighs and runs his hands through his hair. "I don't fuckin' know where she is. It's not safe for her out there, she could be in trouble and I can't find her."

"Maybe I should try calling her, or looking for her," I offer.

"No," Krypt says. "Not goin' to happen. You ain't safe either."

"She's out there, alone and hurt," I protest. "I'm not going to just stand here and do nothing."

"I said no," Krypt growls at me.

Stubborn biker.

"I'm goin' to round up the boys and get them onto it, too," Maddox says, his voice strained.

His phone rings in his pocket, and he pulls it out so quickly my eyes widen. He doesn't look at the number; he just presses it to his ear.

"Santana?"

He listens to whoever is on the other line, and I watch the color drain from his face. Oh god, *no*. Has Howard's club got her? Has something terrible happened? I take hold of Krypt's hand and squeeze as I watch Maddox stare like he's just seen a ghost.

"Where?"

He nods and hangs up the phone.

"Maddox?" Krypt says, his voice low.

Maddox turns to face us fully, his skin is pale and his fists are clenched. "Santana is in the hospital."

I gasp and my hand presses to my mouth. What happened? Oh god. I don't know if I can handle hearing whatever it is he's going to say next.

"What happened?" Krypt manages.

"Someone found her," Maddox says, his voice lower and more broken than I've ever heard it. "She's been shot."

~*~*~*~

MADDOX

Secrets and lies have a way of destroying people.

I hold a big secret, bigger than *her*, bigger than *me*.

Seeing her lying in that hospital bed makes me realize I can't keep it in forever.

Soon she will find out what I've kept from her.

She *will* hate me for it.

She *will* leave my life.

Maybe she'll believe I was protecting her, maybe she won't.

All I know is I can't allow anything to happen to her, without her knowing what I know. What I've known since the day I saved her life.

Her sister, who she's believed is dead for five years, now…*isn't*.

Her sister is very much alive.

The truth will come out – and it will destroy everything.

THE END

Don't stress! You can get Santana and Maddox's story here - Melancholy (Available on Amazon, Barnes and Noble, Kobo & iTunes.)

Have you liked my page? If not, you can do it here to keep updated with teasers, future works and just plain old fun ➔ Author Bella Jewel

MELANCHOLY Snippet

2014

Santana

Bright lights jerk me awake. The shrill sound of beeping monitors is the only noise that fills my aching ears. I try to blink, but my eyes feel like two heavy pieces of lead in my skull. My tongue is dry and it burns, like a scratchy piece of sandpaper in my mouth. I gasp out a breath, flicking it about to try and get some saliva to coat it.

"Santana?" A voice calls. "My name is Roberta, I'm a nurse here. Can you hear me?"

Of course I can hear you, you're yelling in my face. The words want to come out, but my stiff tongue won't move enough to let them. Tears burn under my heavy eyelids as I try hard to speak. *Where am I? What happened?*

"You're in the hospital. Squeeze my hand if you can hear me?"

A soft hand is in mine. How did I not notice that? I squeeze it, mulling over her words. *Hospital.* You're in the hospital. My hazy mind swims as I go over the memories lying dormant inside it. Why am I in the hospital? What happened? Did something go wrong? Where is Pippa?

"You were shot," the nurse goes on.

Shot? I shake my head from side to side, confused. I cry out, but it sounds like nothing more than a hoarse gasp. The sounds of creaking doors and beeping are too loud.

"Is she awake? Why the fuck wasn't I called?"

A barking voice fills the room, so familiar. My mind swims, trying to figure out whom that voice belongs to. God, why can't I remember anything? My mind aches.

"Santana? Hey, it's me. Maddox."

Maddox?

More tears run as fuzzy memories become clearer. Running from the compound. Ash, Krypt and Maddox. *Together.* Having sex. Bullets firing at me. I hiccup loudly, and begin to cry harder as my hand reaches out for the comfort I need the most. *Maddox.*

"I'm here," he says, and the bed dips as my body is pulled into solid arms. "No one can hurt you now."

The words he's told me so many times. *So many times.* I flutter my eyes open, and everything is blurry. The nurse comes into view first, her round face staring down at me. She blinks her green eyes and smiles. "Hi, would you like some water?"

I nod, and she passes me a small plastic cup with a straw poking out. I take it, and press it to my mouth. My hand shakes, and Maddox's goes up to curl around mine. He holds it steady as I take gulping sips, desperate to ease the ache in my throat. I shift, and a sharp pain radiates through my calf.

I got shot.

Someone *shot* at me.

I let the cup go, and Maddox thrusts it towards the nurse. "Leave," he demands.

"But I have only just finished checking her vitals. The doctor will want to see her, and . . ."

"I said," he barks, his voice a deadly hiss. "*Leave.*"

"I . . ."

"Now," he bellows.

She hurries out of the room, and the door closes quietly behind her. Maddox shifts, moving out from behind me and getting off the bed. He gets a chair and drags it over, sitting beside me and staring at me with blue eyes that have clearly had no sleep. He's got dark rings under them, and his jaw is tense, his muscles ticking.

I watch him, and my heart clenches. He slept with Ash. *He slept with Ash.* My heart burns, it burns like someone has shoved a match inside and lit it on fire. I have no reason for this kind of jealousy; Maddox and I have never been an item. But the way it hurt shocked me. It shocked me, because I didn't realize it would bother me.

"You slept with Ash . . ." I whisper, dropping my eyes.

"Look at me, Santana," he orders.

I shift my gaze, staring into his, hating that I love his eyes so much, but I do. I love his eyes. I love his entire, rugged, gorgeous face.

"You have never cared who I fucked before," his voice is a low rasp. "Why now?"

"I . . . she was my friend," I say, turning away again.

His voice comes out like a deadly whip. "Didn't say you could look away. Now turn your eyes back to me."

I grind my teeth, but I turn back to him. He leans in closer, his leather jacket squeaking with each movement.

"I didn't fuck her."

I blink at him. "Y-y-y-y-you didn't?"

"No."

"But you were still with her," I whisper.

His eyes scan over my face before his mouth pulls into a thin line. "Ain't goin' into details with you, but yeah, I was still with her. Didn't know it would matter to you."

"It doesn't, it's fine. I . . . I've just had a hard time. It's nothing."

"You lyin' to me?"

"No, Maddox."

"Santana."

"Don't," I growl. "I have enough to worry about. Do you hear me?"

"Who shot you?" he murmurs, dropping the subject.

I shake my head, my tears burning again. "I don't know. I left the compound and drove to your house. I got out and suddenly, out of the blue, someone was shooting at me. I had no idea where it was coming from, or who was doing it. I leapt back into my car, too scared to go inside. The bullet hit my calf as I was diving in. I drove as far as I could, but the pain was intense. I got out and went for help, but I don't remember what happened after that."

"Someone found you out cold." His voice is hard. "By the time I got notified, you were already in hospital."

"Someone shot at me, Maddox. Why?"

He shakes his head. "I'm goin' to find out."

I nod, turning away.

"Tana," he begins, but the door opens and a doctor and police officer come inside.

Maddox growls, low and throaty, and shoves out of the chair. "Why the fuck is a cop in here?"

The cop steps forward, and extends his hand. Maddox looks at it with pure disgust. "My name is Sergeant Rambo."

Maddox snorts. "That so? Your parents watch too many movies, Sergeant?"

Sergeant Rambo, clearly having lived with jokes about his name, stiffens and nods his head. "I've heard every joke about my name. Now, if you're finished, I'd like to talk to Santana while the doctor checks her over."

Maddox crosses his arms, unperturbed. "Anything you ask her, you ask her in front of me."

Rambo glares at him, but nods. He walks over towards me, and as he nears closer I see he's quite an attractive man. He's got messy brunette hair, with light grey eyes. He smiles as he sits down on the chair Maddox was on, and I give him a weak smile back.

"How are you feeling, Santana?"

"I'm fine," I croak.

"I just wanted to ask you a few questions about the shooting."

"It was a drive-by," Maddox snaps. "Are you done?"

Sergeant Rambo growls now, turning to Maddox. "I hear you've had a few problems with your club lately, Maddox. You'll appreciate that it seems strange that this young lady was shot only weeks after one of your members was locked away."

"That shit has been dealt with," Maddox snarls. "You got Howard in prison. Anything that was goin' down with the clubs, was on him. Now, are you finished?"

"I'm not," Rambo says, turning back to me. "What happened, Santana?"

"It was like he said," I say, meeting Rambo's gaze dead-on. "I was just driving, and I got out of my car. I heard shots and yelling, and I got back into my car quickly. A shot hit my calf."

"You see who did it?"

"No," I say.

"And you're sure it wasn't aimed at you?"

I keep my face expressionless. "Yes, I'm sure. I heard yelling over the road, lots of it. Cars were going past, it was hectic. The shot wasn't aimed at me."

"It seems strange a shot would come so close, if it wasn't aimed at you."

"There were shots being fired at a car, it missed, and came towards me. I don't see how that's so complicated."

He narrows his eyes. "Very well."

He asks me a few more questions, and then he leaves. The doctor watches him go, before turning to me. He's been checking my wound. I watched as he unraveled it. It's not as bad as I thought. It hurt like hell when it went in, like a hot poker through my flesh – but maybe that's the beauty of it. A neat wound.

"Your wound is looking good, Santana," the doctor says. "We were able to get the bullet out. There seems to be no nerve damage."

I nod. "Thank you."

"She ready to come home?" Maddox demands.

I turn to him. He's standing by the door, arms crossed. The doctor swallows. "I'd like to keep her another night. She's only just come out from being put under, and I want to make sure there are no side affects."

"Then I'm puttin' two guys on her door."

The doctor shakes his head. "No, I'm sorry. The patients need their rest."

"I said," Maddox snarls, "I'm puttin' a few boys on her door. She needs to feel safe, and she will."

"You said it was a drive-by," the doctor protests. "Why would she need protection if it was a drive-by?"

Maddox charges towards him, causing the doctor to take a few steps back. "Because I don't trust any fucker, and that girl on the bed, she's *my* fuckin' girl. Now, I'll be puttin' two of my guys on, and you'll fuckin' *like* it."

The doctor nods. "Very well, but they need to stay quiet . . ."

Maddox smirks. "Unless the nurses feel like gettin' a good fuckin', they'll stay quiet."

I slap my hand to my forehead. The doctor makes a disgusted sound and Maddox laughs. I peek through my fingers and watch the doctor leave.

"That was cruel," I say, dropping my hand.

"He deserved it. Who do you want on your door, darlin'?"

I shrug. "I don't care."

He narrows his eyes and walks over, lowering himself down. His fingers go up and around the back of my neck, and he pulls me forward so his mouth is only an inch or less from mine. "I said, who do you want on the door?"

"I said, I don't *care*," I snap.

"Santana."

"Maddox."

He makes a low hissing sound, and presses his forehead to mine. This has always been his way of showing me affection. It's strange, but it's his. He smells so good, and I want to wrap myself in him. The ache in my chest is getting bigger, and I feel so frightened.

"I'm sendin' Mack in, and maybe Tyke."

"Mack is back?" I whisper, pulling away.

Maddox grunts. "Yeah."

I smile; I can't help it. I adore Miakoda 'Mack' Williams. He's Maddox's adopted brother, and somewhat of a nomad. He travels around, joining in different chapters instead of sticking with one. He enjoys traveling, and being alone.

"Then yes, send him in."

"You got a thing for my brother?"

I snort. "Would it matter if I did? You have a thing for my friends."

"Santana," he warns.

"Maddox."

With a grunt, he stands. "I'm goin' to get some things for you. I'll send the guys in now."

I nod.

He walks to the door.

When he gets there, he turns back to me. "Santana?"

I stare up at him. "Yeah?"

"Don't you ever scare me like that again."

Printed in Poland
by Amazon Fulfillment
Poland Sp. z o.o., Wrocław